Advance praise

"With its enticing undertow of secrets and magic, *The H...... ...ms* will seduce readers with its reverence fo ....ts deep empathy for its characters' longings .... village to tell a story as extraordinary as th.......................... ge has managed to do just that."
— Cristi .... *Cuban*

"Macalino Rutledge's debut novel is a tale of dreams and secrets and what is hidden inside a marriage, and what cannot be denied. The writing is vivid and evocative, the world richly textured and alive. Here the duende speaks!"
— Micheline Aharonian Marcom, author of *Three Apples Fell From Heaven*

"*The Hour of Daydreams* isn't just a wonderful book—it's a lyrical and poetic journey, one that's simultaneously magical, surprising, and mesmerizing. It's a love story, fable, fairy tale, and contemporary novel woven together with seamless thread, reminiscent of Isabel Allende. A brilliant start to a beautiful literary career."
— Erin Entrada Kelly, author of *The Land of Forgotten Girls*

"A beautiful book that collapses the boundaries between reality and fairy tale, *The Hour of Daydreams* is both gritty and poetic. The atmosphere is fresh and vivid, like a broad green leaf shimmering with raindrops."
— Elena Mauli Shapiro, author of *13, Rue Thérèse*

"An honest love story is of two minds—it reveals and confounds, it wounds and redeems. *The Hour of Daydreams* is nothing short of an honest love story, and Renee Macalino Rutledge is a singular talent."
— Jamie Duclos-Yourdon, author of *Froelich's Ladder*

"Rutledge combines the fantastic with the realist. She infuses a literary story of a husband and wife with fabulist elements, and by doing so creates a reading experience that feels more like a dream than a story. At times the beauty of the sentence-level writing is enough to break your heart. Other times, it's the imagery that seems magical. But the strength of Rutledge's writing is that even at these more fantastical moments, the complexity and nuance of the characters' rich emotional lives are very real. This is a wonderful debut, and a promising new voice in the literary landscape."
— SJ Sindu, author of *Marriage of a Thousand Lies*

"Confident and imaginative storytelling. Multiple perspectives weave together and explore the secrets that lurk between lovers, friends, and family members. *The Hour of Daydreams* has stuck with me since I finished reading it . . . always a good sign that a story has dug its way into my bloodstream."
— Elise Hooper, author of *The Other Alcott*

"The prose is lyrical and descriptive, perfect for the curiously unfolding story."
—*Oakland Magazine*

"Renee Macalino Rutledge's *The Hour of Daydreams* is a stirring and haunting exploration of marriage, culture, and gender roles. You will find yourself cheering for Tala and Manolo as they stumble through fears and desires, and you will celebrate the choral narration with its multiple perspectives on love and community. This debut novel is a delicate weaving of mythology and everyday lives and it is a necessary addition to the literature of the Filipina diaspora."
—Daisy Hernández, author of *A Cup of Water Under My Bed: A Memoir*

"It may be difficult for some cultures today to reconcile the tales and superstitions of earlier generations with modern society, yet we lose something when we forget about the past. In *The Hour of Daydreams* . . . fables may help us understand and embrace certain truths about our background, family, and community, and come to terms with who we really are and what we value. Ultimately, this is a story about human connection, ambition, and dreams."
—Sandi Ward, author of *The Astonishing Thing*

"From the very first line of the book, you know you're in for something different. . . . Lovely and utterly unique, this is definitely worth a read."
—Kathleen Barber, author of *Are You Sleeping*

"This is a book you can read for the pure pleasure of a great story well told, or for a challenging and thoughtful reflection on the meaning and value of storytelling itself. . . . At every turn, something or someone is more than they appear. But though the reader wonders along with protagonists about what is real and what is true, one never feels lost or abandoned along the way. The story slowly ripens, revealing increasingly subtle and delicious flavors."
—Bob Kanegis, professional storyteller

"Reading *The Hour of Daydreams* is like waltzing with words as Renee weaves folktale with the sweet and deceptive love story of Manolo and Tala. Be prepared for the moments the story shifts to folktale. The brief detours will quickly bring you back to Manolo and Tala, so enjoy the language, savor the images, and tuck them in your pocket."
—Karen Sargent, author of *Waiting for Butterflies*

"Renee Rutledge's beautifully crafted novel examines marriage, family, and identity. Inspired by a Filipino folktale, Rutledge deftly knits fable and contemporary story to explore the power of secrets in everyday lives. This lyrical, stirring first novel invites the reader to linger and dream."
—Kate Brandes, author of *The Promise of Pierson Orchard*

The Hour of Daydreams

ISBN: 978-1-942436-27-0

Library of Congress Cataloging-in-Publication Data
Names: Macalino Rutledge, Renee, 1976- author.
Title: The hour of daydreams / Renee Macalino Rutledge.
Description: Portland, Oregon : Forest Avenue Press, 2017.
Identifiers: LCCN 2016034358| ISBN 9781942436270 (paperback) | ISBN
   9781942436294 (.mobi) | ISBN 9781942436300 (pdf)
Subjects: LCSH: Physicians--Fiction. | Brides--Fiction. | Family
   secrets--Fiction. | Identity (Psychology)--Fiction. |
   Philippines--Fiction. | Psychological fiction. | BISAC: FICTION /
   Literary. | GSAFD: Fantasy fiction.
Classification: LCC PS3613.A225 H68 2017 | DDC 813/.6--dc23
LC record available at https://lccn.loc.gov/2016034358

1 2 3 4 5 6 7 8 9

Distributed by Legato Publishers Group

Cover design: Gigi Little
Feather modified from an original image by Partha S. Sahana
https://www.flickr.com/photos/ps_sahana/14852448109
Other images: Morguefile
Author photo: Tesa Lauigan
Interior design: Laura Stanfill

Printed in the United States of America
by Forest Avenue Press LLC
Portland, Oregon

Forest Avenue Press LLC
P.O. Box 80134
Portland, OR 97280
forestavenuepress.com

The Hour
of Daydreams

a novel

Renee Macalino Rutledge

FOREST AVENUE PRESS
Portland, Oregon

For Maya and Raina

Prologue

THEY WHISPER THAT MY MOTHER was not one of us, and whatever she was disappeared beneath a pair of wings. At school, talk of my mother floats up from a restless place beneath the ground, surfacing into the soles of their feet and out of their mouths like fog, capable of taking many shapes, spreading in the form of their laughter and murmurs then thinning to nothing, waiting to shake loose from the same furtive earth.

They whisper, but never quietly, of how I will sprout wings or horns of my own, how their mothers command them to stay away from the weird Lualhati girl. But I don't believe what they do. The fog is blinding but I know too well you can walk right through it.

She was a demon evaporates and fades to the mountaintops. *She was an angel* leaks with a thousand holes. *She was a witch* echoes once, overshadowed by the sound of my own breathing. *She was a saint* sinks beneath endless footsteps walking and forgetting.

The most surprising thing is how it goes on after school, how even the wrinkly and gray-haired can act like children and believe in such ridiculous stories. The neighbors and shopkeepers, every boy and girl, aunt and uncle and their third cousin needs to be home before dark, stay away from this cursed watering hole or that haunted tree, avoid stepping on the duwendes hiding under their feet, flee the coming aswang hungry for the taste of their blood. It's like an infestation of the mind, these fairy tales, the way they've taken root in the bodies of our people. Are our lives so bland that we need this magic, this spice to fill up the holes? Are we ghosts ourselves without them? Or is it the land itself that cannot sleep, packed with lost secrets and layers of bone by the millions, scattered for centuries across seven thousand islands?

Theories can't change the way things have been or the way things already are. My mother was just an ordinary woman who could not be strong for us, who left her own daughter motherless. I grew up with a father, two grandparents, and the endless gaping of her absence.

I grew up not knowing her.

Papa never forced her memory upon me, didn't assume I needed to fill the ripped pages or continue forth a twisted legacy. I could cry with Papa, and he understood it was simply because I fell, not that my every tear was stored up just for her.

Instead, I formed a picture of her face with the help of Grandfather Andres, whose slow and raspy words held fragments of a real person, and from these I could imagine the way she might have chewed or laughed or plucked stray petals from my hair. She walked with the eagerness of a child—always quickly, with a longing for her destination imbued in her lean, her far-off gaze. She couldn't cook to save a starving monkey's life. She had long, thin fingers that could sew ordinary cloth into anything and big front teeth that added character to her smile. She enjoyed books, but only Grandfather indulged her with discussions about their complex and elaborate plots. She was an attentive wife and mother who liked to find pretty flowers and place them in my hair. She curled up with me during my naps and responded quickly to my cries, but all along hid a terrible secret.

When he talked about my mother, with love instead of taunting, inside of me a river began to flow, stirring me from wonder into longing and, ultimately, bitterness. At her absence and the way they all glorified it. That was when the stirring stopped, the river never growing strong enough to trickle out of me in the form of tears. With Grandfather gone and no recollections of her to hold, there is nothing stirring me now, no river inside; I miss even the bitterness, because at least it was the one thing that made her feel real.

Without Grandfather Andres here to light a candle in my heart, I gaze at Papa differently, curious about the stories he hides, of the real woman and not the fairy tale, seeking her there in his hidden quiet. Without the stories, I realize there is nothing left.

Part I

1. Stolen Luck

MANOLO WATCHED HIS NEW BRIDE and felt like he had stolen the luck of the gods. He sat at the breakfast table with one leg crossed over the other and a newspaper spread across his lap. He pretended to read, but in truth, Manolo hadn't absorbed one word. He was too busy noticing that even in a simple housedress and slippers, with her long hair tied back, Tala was beautiful.

Mother sat to his right, nodding and smiling eagerly when Tala offered to butter her roll or serve her another slice of fruit. Ever since Tala had moved in, Mother came to breakfast with her silver hair combed and her jewelry on. She'd coached Tala on how to thaw the breakfast meat, brew the coffee to perfection, and season the garlic rice just the way the men liked it. She was delighted to see how well her instructions were followed as her daughter-in-law took to handling everything. Father, whose habit had been to sleep through breakfast, sat with them every morning with a newfound appetite.

Manolo never anticipated this change in his parents, who seemed to have reawakened into the carriage of their bodies, into their awareness of each other and the pleasures of being catered to. It wasn't just his marrying that sparked this transformation—

it was Tala. He was sure because the burning inside began the first time he saw her, and he saw the fire's glow reflected in his parents' cheeks, a bright sheen disguised as sweat.

But Manolo could not flip himself inside out as the old ones had done, let the fire out of his skin so she could know how deeply it consumed him. He sat behind the shield of his paper, grunting or nodding when Tala refilled his coffee cup or offered him another serving of food. He didn't look up into her eyes, but lingered on the delicate slimness of her wrist.

Behind the guise of reading, he didn't miss a single sigh or syllable. He knew whose feet tapped beneath the table or scuffled across the floor, which plate was licked clean and which was still half-full. Without looking at their faces, he could even tell when one of them was smiling. He listened to their words, some running on at full speed, others peppered by interjections or emphasized with a familiar squeal, a knowing grunt, or an unexpected snort that turned into combined laughter even he could not resist partaking in. His parents relished every attention from their new daughter-in-law. Tala teased Mother and Father, calling *them* the newlyweds because of the way they sat, with their chairs touching. Like sweethearts, Tala said. Father proudly placed his arm around Mother's shoulder, and Mother giggled like a girl. Father began telling Tala a story about the early days courting his Iolana, one Manolo had never heard before.

"I waited for hours outside the market where Iolana chopped meat," Andres said.

"I thought of him as I severed chicken legs," Iolana added.

"She did not even know that I had tracked down where she worked, bribing her little brother with sweets."

"Little Roland. We still call him that, you know. Little Roland. Even though he's forty-eight years old and weighs two hundred pounds."

"When she finally came out, I thought she would be happy to see me. It was supposed to be a surprise."

"Surprise indeed." Iolana giggled into her hand.

"She looked at me and ran off in the other direction! I never imagined her skinny legs could fly that quickly, in so much haste to avoid me. I would have chased her, but the flower vendor saw the whole thing, saw me waiting for hours, saw the sting in my eyes when she ran! How he laughed at me!"

"It was my dress. It was my dress. I didn't want him to see me in my bloodstained dress, smelling of cow guts!"

Manolo smiled, enjoying his wife's unbridled laughter even more than he did Father's story. She was a wonder indeed to stimulate the old ones as she did. Surely he deserved such a wife. After all, he was a doctor and a dutiful son who would see his parents through old age. He had hired Old Luchie to do the cleaning so Tala could keep her pretty hands soft.

But still, Manolo was afraid. He was not yet thirty, but already silver strands dotted the hair at his temples. He was no longer young nor burning with ambition, and worried that Tala, ten years his junior, might look at him one day and realize that after all, he was nothing but a simple, provincial man. His world began and would end right there in Manlapaz. He was certain word of Tala's beauty had already spread to neighboring provinces. A beauty that was not of this world, they would have described her. She was happy now as his new bride. But how long would she stay content with such a life?

Manolo surprised himself with how outrageously he was behaving, letting the business of men and women, love and marriage, spiral into the dimensions of a soap opera, even if in his thoughts alone. He kept his composure behind the protective folds of the newspaper, convincing himself that he was neither obsessed nor overbearing. Any man in his position would be foolish to ignore the circumstances. Too many a husband shut down his emotions, depriving his wife of attention with the belief that she would spend a lifetime trying to please him. Manolo didn't buy into this machismo attitude. He neither showered his wife with romantic overtures nor denied her from knowing her hold on him. But who was he to preach the formula for longevity in a marriage?

Watching Tala, he forgot himself. She could not be more graceful in the kitchen, serving his portion before her own, catering to his parents like a daughter should. She had a woman's body with a child's joy. Even the house stood more erect on its beams, waking to the tickle of her footsteps.

Outside the birds erupted into choruses then twittered slowly back to silence. The sun was already high, brightening the spaces between the acacia leaves. For the first time in his life, Manolo enjoyed the simple pleasure of fresh flowers around the house. Mother had never troubled herself with such frivolities. Tala gathered wildflowers each day and placed them in a pitcher at the center of the table. Today it was jasmine and bougainvillea. Such pretty colors, pink and white. He wanted to sniff the fragrance from the white blossoms, bring his face close enough to feel the petals against his cheeks. At the impulse, Manolo checked himself and grunted, pretending he had read something particularly thought provoking in the *Manlapaz Bulletin*.

Before leaving for work, he would give Tala his ripped trousers to sew. He would give her money to shop and extra to buy whatever else she might need—fabric for a new dress, a new book, or something small and handmade, like a basket or a bell, that she tended to pick up simply for its beauty. Upon coming home, he would ask what she had managed to accomplish during the day. And then at night, at night . . . Manolo thought of the previous night, when his body was pressed tight against Tala's. When he had kissed her tenderly, inch by inch and inch by inch again, his heart beating so fiercely he feared its thunder would betray that he was anything but composed. That without Tala, his heart might stop beating altogether.

• • •

EVENINGS WERE A TIME of sharing for Tala and Manolo. Mother and Father took to having earlier dinners, which they ate in their bedroom. *So the new husband and wife can have their privacy*, they had said with secret smiles. Manolo suspected that his parents' motives for eating separately also included an aversion to Tala's cooking. They enjoyed her breakfasts well enough, but Manolo himself was alarmed at the way she altered traditional dishes. He wanted his adobo the way he had eaten it all his life, with the perfect balance of savory and tang. Tala's different versions of the dish included sweet potatoes, lemon juice, tomato sauce, bell peppers, or peas. Along the way she invented new dishes, and Manolo eventually acquired a taste for them.

As they ate, Tala recounted the walks that Manolo knew she was in the habit of taking. She described the flowers that grew along which fences, showed him the skipping stones she had found along the shallows of the riverbank, where she'd stopped to read, recounted the smells and sounds of the marketplace, the latest gossip from one of the neighborhood wives. Manolo couldn't help but wonder whose eyes stuck fast to Tala during her wanderings. He imagined where Tala's gazes lingered when he was not with her. He began to concoct ideas that his wife wasn't thorough in her storytelling, purposefully omitting what she was up to *in between* the walks to and from home. She could have been doing anything while he puttered about among the fevered and infirm. As his imagination wandered, he became distracted on his rounds. He accidentally gave Nanang Aida acne medication for her ulcers. She sent for him the next day, wondering if she should swallow the cream or rub it on her belly. He told Tatang Rubio, a vegetarian whose ailments he had treated for years, to eat plenty of red meat in order to increase his iron levels. Manolo had always been a perfectionist. But even his recent carelessness didn't bother him as much as his wife's propensity to wander.

Manolo decided to follow Tala, convincing himself it would just be this once. Pretending to leave for work one morning, he walked to the nearest sari sari store instead. He bought a pack of cigarettes and matches and returned home. Manolo was not a smoker but opened the box without thinking, as though he had done this countless times in the past, running his fingers against the circular tops before tapping out a stick. The smoke scratched harshly against his throat at first, then gradually subsided into an aching sweetness. From the windows, he could barely make out Tala's features on the other side of the glass as she brushed Mother's hair then tried on the jewelry Mother handed her, piece by piece. Later she stepped out of the house, still wearing a pair of Mother's white shell earrings.

She wore a sleeveless orange dress made from a light fabric—linen or cotton. It flowed weightlessly around her ankles, dark against her honey-toned skin, light against her long raven hair. He stayed behind at a distance, savoring each second of watching her undeterred. She was so lovely, her steps so dainty on the gravel path. Focusing on the sway of every curve, the way her hands fell at her sides, with only one arm swinging when she walked, he couldn't help but recall the night he'd found her.

He had come to the river by accident that night. His childhood friend had died, not from the diabetes that plagued him most of his life, but by drowning in Sabanal Bay, off the coast of Ogtong. News of this death had made Manolo quiet and lonely, not for his lost compadre, who was like a brother to Manolo, but for himself. Manolo was familiar with the face of death. It was his job to outsmart it, outrun it, for as long as he could, if not forever. At such a moment he realized he was just a pawn, an unworthy opponent in a game he could not win. Death, at any given moment, could sidestep him with unanticipated moves.

It was after two a.m. when he had gotten the news of Palong's drowning. The barrio, dark and sleeping, stretched long beneath the blanket of night. Familiar shapes, at that hour, assumed new identities. The contours of his roof and fence against the blackened sky seemed to defy time; he could imagine those objects of wood and concrete posing just so, centuries from that moment. Manolo did something he had never done before—he took a walk in the middle of the night, alone. He realized now that what he had been looking for was death. In the darkness, it could take him by surprise. It could jump at him from unseen corners. He had wanted to confront death. He would fight it like a man.

Just two miles away from his house, away from the barrio, a river flowed for miles, snaking down from the ripe green mountains, irrigating field upon field, and between a grove of trees not too far from where he lived, the river was said to keep its most private secrets, like the wetness of a woman no mortal man should ever know. Superstitions of vampires, demons, bruhas, and the bewitched swarmed over the shadows across that grove, and the people of the province avoided it for their lives. That night Manolo walked through rows of rice plants, in the direction of the mountains. Toward the greedy arms of the river. And not just anywhere along its voluptuous body, but to that forbidden place of magic. He thought he heard music. As he got closer, he realized that what he heard were the voices of women. And splashing. The lowest branches surrounding the river were covered with thick white coats. They emitted a glow that surrounded the river with an otherworldly light.

Two trees stood close enough together for Manolo to hide behind. He peeked through the teardrop-shaped arch between their trunks, at a distance from which he could hear and see the women on the river without being discovered. He couldn't know for certain, but he assumed that they were sisters, as if the knowledge was evident just by looking at them. Seven of them—talking all at once, it seemed, and laughing. Except for one. She dunked her head into the river and disappeared beneath it, then reemerged and floated on her back. He climbed the trunks to get a closer look. She stroked the water from every angle, kissing it with her lips, talking only to the waves her body generated.

One by one her sisters emerged from the river. Colorful nightgowns clung to their bodies, which varied from slender to round, short to tall, old to young. The youngest, about eight years old, was eager to go home. She jumped up and down, pointing to her white coat on top of a tree. Her teenage sister, who only seemed to spring into motion when someone needed her help, retrieved the coveted object and passed it to the younger girl. Soon, only the one remained in the water. *It isn't fair to make us wait,* her sisters complained. *Not again. You always think of yourself. Hurry up, Tala! We'll be back tomorrow night.* Tomorrow night. They would be back tomorrow night. That was when the one got out of the water and he saw that she was the most beautiful of them all. Tala. Then the seven sisters put on their coats, and Manolo realized they weren't coats at all, but wings. A magnificent splendor of wingspans. Then a sudden surge of air—he watched them bend, each with her own measure of elegance, pushing up from the ground, then disappearing into the stars.

Manolo returned night after night, climbing higher into the trees to watch Tala swim beneath him. Each night, Tala made her sisters wait a little longer, then a little longer still. Eventually, they stopped waiting for her at all. The first time Tala swam alone under the moonlight, Manolo's heart burned. He summoned the courage to approach her in the river, but didn't want to risk frightening her. Instead, he stole her wings and hid them away. Then Tala emerged from the river, trembling with cold with nowhere to go, and Manolo watched for hours still. When he finally revealed himself, only the river spoke its incessant babble to interrupt their silence. Tala did not feel threatened by his presence; she walked along the river's edge without questioning him, like they were two forest animals who had navigated to the water by instinct. He left the river for a day longer, gathering the nerve to speak. On the second night, Manolo and Tala went home together, invincible against the shadows, never to part again.

She was his wife now, he told himself. Once again, Manolo found himself hiding and watching, separated from Tala by a fragrant screen of earth-scented leaves. And he nearly sprang into the path, calling out to her with open arms. But he retreated, deeper into the barrier of foliage. Looking back on those nights by the river, Manolo realized he'd found what he had been searching for. And every day since, he'd grappled with a certain kind of death.

2. What Lies Within

SOMETHING ABOUT BEING IN the marketplace felt like swimming, Tala thought. Beneath the water, everything around you echoed. And here, so much sound to swim through, dozens of voices speaking at once, amplified to the point of distortion. Then there was the current, a school here and a school there. She glided between and among the other fish.

In truth, Tala preferred the river to this bustle and exchange of goods. But shopping for dinner was only an excuse for her true errands. She could just as easily have requested Luchie, the maid, to buy what she needed.

Her first impulse was always to see Baitan.

He begged on a corner where the meat and vegetable stands dwindled to a few stray carts and a row of vendors selling handicrafts spread on blankets. Where the one bus passing through Manlapaz screeched to a stop, spewing out nearby locals returning from the crowded docks and sidewalks of Tagarro Bay, Baitan stood with his basket. It would contain a few disheveled onions, a garlic bulb, a bruised orange or two—whatever he managed to steal or find among the larger stalls. Tala usually bought the entire contents of this basket, returning home with strange varieties that she always found a use for in her recipes.

Cooking, for her, had become something of an adventure. At first, she'd felt insecure about her place in the kitchen. Even during a task as simple as cooking rice, Iolana would raise her eyebrows at her, humphing underneath her breath as Tala rinsed the debris from between the grains then measured out an extra cup of water for every cup of rice. She had to watch Iolana make rice before realizing where the criticism came from. Her mother-in-law didn't use a measuring cup, sifting instead with her fingers through the rice immersed in water to "feel" the correct proportions. Only when Tala felt confident enough to use the same method did Iolana's eyebrows return to normal.

Today Baitan's basket was filled with pistachio nuts, tamarinds, and three bananas straggled in a near-empty bunch. Tala looked at the pieces of broken shell, at the lonely looking stem, and visions of stews and desserts floated in her mind. She could substitute pistachio nuts for the peanuts that one of her recipes called for; she could mash the bananas into a creamy dessert. The tamarind she would give to Father. He liked pulling the sticky fruit from its vine-like stem and spitting the seeds into his fist. Everything in Baitan's basket had the potential to become something more than what it appeared.

Baitan himself was more valuable than his bare feet, skinny brown legs, and oversized T-shirt could ever signify. The little boy's stare, direct and unrelenting, had drawn Tala toward his basket when she'd first come across him a few months before. He had looked at her then with a blaze of recognition that drew her closer.

"You left your stall," he had said.

"Oh, but I shop in all the stalls, and your basket is just as good if not better."

She had noticed that the boy's mother let him play once he

was free of the items in the basket. So she returned again the next day.

"Why did you leave your stall?" he asked again.

"I have no stall, you silly little monkey."

He smiled. "You are even prettier today."

Tala returned on the third day.

"Will you go back to your stall then, after here?" the boy asked.

Tala felt a peculiar jolt. "Yes, boy, I will. Remind me where my stall is, and I will give you a prize."

The boy had led Tala directly to the center of the market-place, to an albularyo's booth located between two others, accessible through a little inlet that was easy to miss. Indeed, she had already missed it countless times. Like a secret room in a maze. A bare wooden plank serving as a counter guarded the stall from end to end. Behind it, a patterned ivory curtain fluttered coquettishly, weightless enough to rouse at the slightest movement, but revealing nothing of the mysteries behind it. Along the wall to the right, a row of bottles stood side by side on a low shelf, in company with two small stacks of clay bowls, silverware, candles, and a few sealed tins, all of it bedecked with flowers, petals, stems, or carved stones strewn about and among them. It smelled like a combination of coconut and mint. A single wooden chair held its place against the opposite wall, and when the woman sitting on it looked up upon their arrival, Tala met her elder sister's eyes for the first time in nearly a year.

"So there are two of you!" Baitan had exclaimed, glancing wide-eyed from one to the other.

"Finally!" Dalisay had said, shooing Baitan off her counter like she would a mosquito. "You're like a dust rag or last year's party dress!" she said to Tala. "Right in front of you when you don't need it, impossible to find when you're actually looking!"

After this encounter, Tala had learned how her sisters had wandered trying to find her, climbing gradually upward from the city sprawl, working separate stalls between them to gain ground, keeping hope steady the way only sisters could. The older sisters took turns catering to customers seven days a week from behind the wooden counter, finding all there was to know about each barrio—its gossip and scandal, its newcomers. As they sifted through the stories, they detected loneliness disguised as aching joints, read the heartache manifesting as seasonal allergies. For months they had wandered, watching and waiting for signs, moving on when no traces of Tala could be found. Until the day Tala and Baitan had appeared just like that, with Baitan pointing excitedly from one to the other. And despite all her sisterly affection, Dalisay's first reaction had been uncontained annoyance, as if Tala needed scolding for all the trouble taken on her behalf. After this first meeting, Baitan had fallen into the habit of accompanying Tala to her sisters' booth whenever she came to the marketplace. And Tala had found it only natural to bring him along.

That day, she placed the pistachio nuts and bananas in her shoulder bag along with the tamarinds for Father to enjoy later. Baitan gave the empty basket back to his mother, who was weaving a flower from bamboo leaves. Tala was amazed at the way Inday translated the world out of those leaves. On a small woven blanket, she assembled crickets, fish, caribou, huts, long-stemmed flowers, men and women in mid-dance, all made from stray pieces of bamboo.

Inday smiled up from her stool, not at her son, but at Tala. Her angel of luck, Inday called her. "I cannot keep my fingers still for a moment," she said. "Since you've been visiting with Baitan, my customers have tripled! It takes a beautiful woman to invoke envy. People want what a beautiful woman has. They buy what she buys, they wear what she wears, they fall in love with her man, even if he is a worthless thug!"

Tala laughed. "If I am the beautiful woman you speak of, I suppose that would make Manolo the thug! But your formula is wrong. Can you imagine Manolo bullying the neighborhood business owners, coming to collect his cut, making threats with injections and bitter-tasting pills?"

"Pardon me, Tala. You know you're my angel of luck. The rest of the world is foolish. That's all I meant. Ha, I'm sure your husband is nothing less than a saint! Stop fidgeting so, Baitan. You can take him off my hands for as long as you please; only luck can come his way with you, I'm sure."

"What's luckier than magic? You make magic with your hands. You make stories out of grass, what others only step on. You make your own luck, Inday."

Tala and Baitan walked on, hand in hand. They took to each other like siblings. Baitan became the little brother Tala had never had. With a family of sisters, she had grown accustomed to the wild energy of girls, each demanding her own way, her own orbit to circle an insistent gravitational pull. But Baitan seemed to revolve around her, a little lost planet confusing her for a sun. She would give him whatever light she could, anticipating the day he would outgrow her to make his own brightness.

Each evening, as she recounted her adventures over dinner, Tala yearned to tell Manolo about her family beyond their walls. But she was no fool. She'd come to learn Manolo's ways, his preference for privacy, his possessiveness over their life together. Loud and crowded parties, new faces he could neither place nor trust were a nuisance to Manolo. It was endearing to know how well he treasured her, and she shared his relish for a quiet life, the thunderous way it could open one's heart to the sound of rain and the slow, rhythmical pulse of each day's existence. But she allowed herself a bigger sphere to wander than he might have wanted for himself.

Baitan would have been a delight to her husband, someone he would ask after and share her affection for. Someone who would brighten their nightly conversations all the more. Manolo would have gone overboard with generosity, purchasing shoes and sweets for the boy and placing his mother in a proper plywood stall. But still, Tala held back. Baitan knew about her sisters, with whom she shared a strict code of anonymity. They had their rules on making revelations between worlds, but each sister regarded the rules differently, every day the more so. So Tala returned to the market stall a few times a week to argue for Manolo's sake.

A different sister always waited at the stall to check in with Tala—to gossip and compete and argue and blame. Between the bickering they read herbs and petals for customers, predicting futures, prescribing medicines that were foreign to doctors, curing ailing hearts, helping couples conceive or sacrifice the unborn children whose destinies were already written in the stars.

That day, Imee fanned herself behind the counter. She had her short hair pulled back with a bright yellow handkerchief, revealing a string of hieroglyphic lines tattooed along the side of her neck. She wore loose-fitting brown pants that had once been a skirt, and over her outfit, a purple apron. Tala still remembered the day Imee welcomed her teenage years by cutting her long hair and sewing an extra seam into all of her skirts. Dresses aren't practical, she had said, and Tala had not seen her wear one since.

Behind Imee, Baitan crouched on the ground, drinking iced gelatin and rolling marbles. The curtain, tied in two knots to stay open, swung a cranky cotton fist in response to Baitan's abrupt passing. Tala drummed her fingers against the counter and watched the marbles spin and snap.

"I can't imagine settling down. Coming back here is only bearable because one day, I know I'll leave. Just like that, and this boxed-in view will change," Imee said.

Tala believed her. Dalisay had always been the one to nag, complaining to everyone else when circumstances of her own making didn't suit her. Imee was the first to leap for a different possibility, never content with discontentment.

"You don't settle down when you marry," Tala replied. "That's the big misconception. You spend your life looking for ways to reinvent yourself, and when you marry, you can look outside yourself for once. It's liberating, actually."

"And Manolo lets you have your freedom?"

"Manolo is my freedom."

"Tell me, Sister, when we lost each other, what stopped you from telling him all about yourself, about us, your sisters, who've gone to such lengths to find you, to see that you're okay with this man you disappeared with, who's taken the inventing out of your life?"

When Tala remained quiet, Imee did not insist on an answer. The sisters retreated back to a silence that was punctuated every now and then with the pleasing snap of Baitan's marbles. Tala appreciated Imee's ability to keep quiet when quiet was due. It was a trait her other sisters did not share.

Located a few yards away from the crowd, the booth emitted the comfortable aura of home. The alley leading to it was the width of a stall. The foot traffic on this alley was light, but they could see a portion of the wider sea of walkers beneath the tent of a perpendicular stall. Like an open window to the outside. When Tala glanced up at Imee, her sister had her eyes set like stone in that direction. A corner of her upper lip was curled, almost maliciously.

"What is it, what do you see in the crowd?"

"What do you see, Tala?"

Tala sighed. "Let me guess. A runaway thief just got caught, and now they're setting his pants on fire. Let me look. No, I don't see anything special. What is it?"

"Let's put Manolo to the test once and for all," Imee said in reply, still looking out toward the crowd.

Imee gave Tala a square wooden box, painted red. It had a gold latch with a key attached.

"The box!"

Imee smiled coyly and Tala laughed.

"Remember what we tell all our customers. Your lover is forbidden to open it. Keep the box where he will see it every day, with the key still attached. Let us see if Manolo deserves your trust. Now, humor me and play along. Remember Tala, for people without wings, without freedom, the box is everywhere. They walk among secrets never knowing how to unlock them. Their lives are boxes, and they steal the first opening they can find. If Manolo can keep the promise not to peek inside, I'll believe that he loves even the parts of you he can't see."

Tala walked home with the box in both hands. She knew how the box worked its temptation for the stricken lovers who came regularly to the booth, but more than this, she knew how much she believed in her husband. She was surprised to find Manolo home so early. She ran to greet him, but he seemed out of breath. His hairline was moist with perspiration, as if he had just come in from jogging. But Manolo did not exercise, though he regularly advised his patients to do so.

He looked at her with an expression she could not decipher.

"How was your walk today, Tala?"

3. A Second Look

MANOLO BELIEVED IN HIS trade, unlike other doctors inspired first by prestige, financial security, and admiring nods from the community. He liked the smell of alcohol, the powerful sting against the back of your tongue as you inhaled. This was medicine, its healing antiseptic smell. He liked the sensitivity of a stethoscope, its magnified ear that could amplify breath and heartbeat, tunneling into the very being, that field of energy fueled by imagination and love, and with just the cold touch of a flat metallic ear, without intrusion or pain, he could gauge the sound of a human spirit, healthy or ill, sprightly or flagging. He even liked the interaction, the daily exchanges with his patients—not too chummy, never too involved, but with a level of intimacy and trust he worked hard to earn. In medical school he had received top marks, studying while other students went to parties, memorizing facts about biology and anatomy and chemistry long after his peers had gone to sleep. He believed in these facts, that there could be such a thing as an absolute truth. That symptoms had a cause; that medicine provided a cure. And yet, he could never forget the code of the duwende.

Perhaps because of the mountains, wise and secretive among them, lifting them closer to the great unknown, his fellow countryfolk listened with a middle ear. They heard voices in the ground, whispered murmurings among their footsteps. They believed these sounds belonged to the duwende, grown men the size of toddlers, with the power to possess and paralyze, destroying lives with a single stare or recitation of a dreaded curse, muttered under dwarflike breaths.

Duwendes' homes were said to rise from the earth in mounds or gape open from the knotty bases of ancient trees, where they tunneled into burrows running parallel to the ordinary world. So the countryfolk were careful where they trod, paying their respects with the words "Excuse me, just passing through, sir," every time they walked passed a hiccup in the earth. Years could pass without incident, and suddenly, the woman down the street, friendly and cheerful as could be, would one day come home changed. She would lie in cold sweats, barely speaking, with her hands on her stomach and her body hunched in pain. Her family would call upon Manolo's expertise, and when he asked her where she had gone or what she had eaten, she would reply that nothing in her day had been different . . . except for one important thing. She had passed the anthill by the well, forgetting to say the words everyone knew . . . forgetting to say "Excuse me, just passing through, sir" to the duwende who might live there. Manolo could only recommend rest and gentle foods, perhaps a laxative or painkiller, but inevitably this woman would worsen by the day, her silence changing shape, elongating to strange mutterings, the corners of her mouth beginning to froth. They would no longer call him to follow up on her condition. Instead they would visit an albularyo, and in extreme cases, a babaylan, who would chant a powerful healing spell over a strand of the assaulted woman's hair, and afterward the family would return to the anthill offering steaming plates of food with their apologies to the duwende. If they were lucky, this woman would awaken the next morning in peace, returning to her routine, just as cheerful and friendly as before.

Every neighbor knew of someone like this woman, someone who had been cursed or possessed by the duwende. Someone whose luck had changed from good to bad, someone else who became a different person altogether, forgetting their friends' names, forgetting how to finish a sentence or walk in a straight line, someone who'd become a thief or a beggar overnight, their personality, their sanity, swallowed by the wrath of an offended dwarf. Sometimes, the curse could be lifted in a matter of hours; other times, the victim could live for years thus transformed. It only took one case for the villagers to understand Manolo's limitations. They would not call on him for these matters, not anymore, and he was glad. He didn't consider himself qualified for the plight of the mind, of the spirit.

Manolo had never seen a duwende, though his parents both had. They recounted these instances with bizarre clarity. He didn't know what to think of their stories. Since childhood, he'd heard the same details from the two most levelheaded people he knew, never inconsistent, never with a shade of doubt. While his mother was a shameless gossip and his father liked to pass his days reading magazines, they were no liars. Did this mean his mother had actually watched a duwende drag her school friend fifty feet by her hair, and his father had watched a good friend turn from a patient, good-natured compadre to an eccentric who stared into the emptiness and uttered bits of strange mumblings to pass his days? Manolo could not share their superstition—the duwende was not based on fact, but supposition, fear, and perhaps, deceit.

Yet, he couldn't escape the etiquette or deny the spaces in the earth he walked on. As an adult, he had tried to break from the habit's persistent grip, but the words left his mouth as if they weren't his to keep. In their backyard, a mound of earth rose up near the base of a guava tree, and when he passed it several times a week, he had to say the words:

"Excuse me, just passing through, sir."

After that first night he'd seen Tala fly from the river, the mound seemed all the more conspicuous. He regarded it with new eyes, thankful for his perseverance.

As HE FOLLOWED HER, he tried to avoid stepping on the obvious bumps along the road, sparing himself the verbal incantations.

Manolo was grateful that Tala kept a straight course, never peering over her shadow for a second look at the path she had just crossed. She walked with blind faith—that everything she needed to see was there in front of her, and whatever came before had received its due attention. In this he found her even more beautiful. She seemed to belong in the spaces where each footstep placed her; she filled in the picture along with the sun and the trees.

He was apprehensive at first. His heart hammered in his throat; he could not keep his hands still. Particularly when there was nothing nearby to hide behind, and with a single turn of her head, Tala would see him. But she continued on in a way that eased his misgivings. The farther she walked, the more confident he grew. He began to lose the reluctance that came with the guilt, nearly convincing himself that even his following her this way was natural.

There were tricky moments along the path, a few feet of sparse foliage, entire stretches of gravel without a single tree in sight. Manolo maneuvered around these obstacles by giving Tala a wider rein. He watched her walk ahead until he could no longer see her past the bend of the road or the other side of a hill. Then he waited, calculating distance and time by the ticking of her footsteps.

Once they arrived at the market square, Manolo felt more

at ease. The ringing of the church bell overpowered the drum of his heartbeat. The activity of commerce filled spaces with sound and movement, laughter and bickering, children circling their mothers, traders hauling cartloads of goods, all of it distracting him from the conspicuousness of his breathing, the dangle of his hands, the shifting lines of his silhouette. In this crowd it would be safe to light up another smoke and speed things up a notch, shortening the distance between him and his wife. Should Tala turn his way, it would be easier now to find cover—behind a colorful piece of fabric, a potted plant, a display of jewelry. He came across a row of fans and purchased one. It was made of paper, blue on one side, red on the other. He opened the fan and held it in front of him like a screen, and just as soon realized this womanly prop looked ridiculous in his hands.

"Is that you, Dr. Lualhati?" the vendor named Malakit asked aloud, looking at Manolo quizzically. Manolo quickly dropped the fan and moved on without answering.

Farther down the street he purchased a big straw hat. As he walked, he unbuttoned his shirt and slung it over his shoulder, wearing only a white undershirt. Manolo was never one to wear undershirts by themselves, or to wear hats. He kept the brim low, nearly covering his eyes. If Tala should glance over her shoulder and see him, the hat, undershirt, and cigarette would disguise him, and she would notice nothing but a blur of strangers.

But these precautions proved unnecessary. Tala was like an arrow already cast, her destination set. He began to wonder why she walked so determinedly, not stopping to compare prices or browse for the freshest vegetables. The orange folds of her dress swooshed around her ankles, in keeping with her momentum. The stalls became fewer in number, and still Tala walked. When the stalls nearly disappeared altogether, Manolo felt a jolt of displacement, as if waking suddenly from a dream. At the edge

of the outdoor market, every detail set in with perfect clarity—
the saltwater smells of fresh seafood driven in every hour, the
black railing of a fence, the uneven pavement, cluttered with
holes. Within the space of a few yards, he'd gone beyond the
border of the market that his imagination had scouted, and he
could no longer predict what he'd see next.

The village around him swelled in countless directions. A
few steps away a blind woman sat against the fence, her hands
open on her lap, asking to be lifted up and out, back into the
flow. Manolo strode toward her with uncertain purpose, only
to see she wasn't blind, but sleeping.

He scanned the road ahead and quickly found Tala again.
All along, he realized, he had anticipated witnessing a certain
notion of her predictability. He had expected to watch her shop,
to learn whether or not she haggled or paid the first sum offered.
He had wanted to feel envious of her admirers, to watch other
men stare at the woman who came home to his bed. Tala was
supposed to carry wildflowers home with her groceries, then
prepare for the evening meal, and like talismans, these images
of her would have flickered back to him during his rounds. But
now the market was nearly behind him, and Tala, up ahead,
had somewhere else to go.

A nervous premonition made his palms begin to sweat and
his heartbeat quicken. Could it be that Tala was on her way
to meet a lover? Manolo clenched his teeth at this uninvited
notion. He lingered at the last stall and purchased a walking
stick. It was just the right length for his height, with a swirling
pattern etched into the wood.

It dawned on him that Tala could have motives, other than
groceries, for going to the market square. But a lover wasn't one
of them.

Other possibilities swarmed through his imagination all at
once, making him lightheaded. His heartbeat slowed from a
sudden surge of cold. Was she seeking out her wings somehow,

or figuring out a way to replace them? He leaned involuntarily on his new cane. To calm himself or simply out of habit, Manolo tried to recollect that first image of his wife at the river, but he couldn't picture what the length of her hair had been. Had it dangled just below her shoulders, or farther down her back? Without this detail, others began to unravel. Manolo always envisioned her wearing a blue dress, but now he wasn't so certain. Had it actually been violet or turquoise? Had she worn the same shade every evening?

He watched as Tala shopped at last—from a pauper's basket, as if she had only received a few centavos earlier that morning. She sat cross-legged on the ground, conversing jovially with the woman selling what looked like leaves, twisted to strange, unnatural contortions. From what he could see at a distance, it was possible that the leaves resembled familiar objects, but Manolo assumed they were manifestations of the beggar woman's fancy. Neither possibility made them worth buying.

Manolo felt surprisingly detached trying to pinpoint the woman's association with his wife. Was she a friend of Tala's, or were they meeting for the first time? He could not tell, but decided that Tala's dress at the river had been purple.

The boy with the basket leaned too consistently in Tala's direction, standing close to her even when her attention was focused on his mother. Something about Tala and the boy made Manolo uncomfortable. He was still a child, not beyond the age of asking question after question, but old enough that the questions he asked would ring with a peculiar wisdom, one that only the very young and the very old seemed to possess. He still had the silky complexion and round eyes of a child, accompanied by a thick mop of hair and clothes that looked like they had been handed down by someone much bigger. He wore a shirt so aged that it fell around him like an old man's sagging skin, nearly covering his basketball shorts entirely. Manolo imagined that the bottom of this boy's bare feet had the same color and consistency as the street. Yet they were similar somehow, Tala and this boy, in a way he could not describe. He imagined two seeds blown into the wind, riding the same breeze.

Tala got up and took the boy's hand, leading him back into the thick of the marketplace, toward Manolo. Ducking back into the stall where he bought his walking stick, Manolo forgot just how beautiful Tala had looked after swimming, when she had been unaware of his presence behind the green. It struck him now that Tala hadn't invited the attention he expected she would during the course of this walk. The image he had had of her parting the crowd with a single step couldn't have been further from reality. She blended in, so much so that he almost lost her now. He let her outline fade until it became distorted, whether from his staring too long or the widening distance between them, he could not tell.

Manolo adjusted the rim of his hat, swatted a fly from his shoulder blade with a snap of his shirt. He leaned further into his new walking stick, watching his wife's advancement into the throng, comparing this perspective of her to the semblance of a ghost.

SEVERAL DAYS AFTER HE'D followed her, the images he'd seen and the sensations they evoked still made him sour.

Dark had set in by the time he returned home from his last appointment. Light from the windows brightened the familiar path to his front door, promising a welcome return. Instead of going in directly, he proceeded to the back of the house for a smoke under one of the many shadows offered by the yard's abundant plants and trees. For the past few days, the smallest interactions with his wife had made him edgy. Ever since he'd seen Tala in the marketplace, hand in hand with a beggar, then cavorting with a common albularyo who played at healing, he'd fought to contain a torrent of questions. Every conversation with her since that day had become an opening for confrontation. Did she know how much the albularyo's trade belittled his training? Or did she buy into the witch doctor's spells, more so than his vials and prescriptions? Did his wife have something in common with these people? Tala had come home clutching the red box in both hands. He recalled again the albularyo, the bristles of her hair barely long enough to show beneath the yellow bandanna, the intensity of her demeanor, something so familiar. . . . It frustrated him all the more that he couldn't ask Tala his questions because she'd offered nothing of her whereabouts that day, except for the usual nonsense about the birds, rocks, and something about bananas and pistachio nuts.

A dog howled in the distance, echoing loneliness, and the crickets began a scattered melody. The moon stood halfway between the earth and sky, resting on the dark silhouette of a nearby mountain. Manolo let another woman's face occupy his mind. Somehow, his patient's look had infected him, fueled whatever disappointment Tala's recent behavior provoked.

This last call had been for an unexpected delivery. The woman's husband had sent for him after combing the entire province for her midwife. When the midwife did not answer her door, the husband had wandered from neighbor to neighbor, then a bit farther, beyond neighbors to acquaintances, and farther still, beyond acquaintances to strangers.

The husband told Manolo that reports of the midwife varied: She was away, delivering a baby in Mahanao, some said. Others said she was keeping her distance to avoid an unhappy family, whose child she had delivered stillborn. Still others reported she had been kidnapped by ghosts. In the end, when her midwife could not be found, the pregnant woman refused a substitute. "Get a doctor," she had said to her husband. "Doctors treat every patient like a stranger. I'll be no different from his regulars."

The woman was almost fully dilated by the time Manolo arrived, her contractions only three minutes apart. Soon after her waters rushed forth, the baby followed, paddling with his arms and legs, still hoping to swim in the warmth that had enveloped the whole of his existence. After the birth, the woman's attitude toward Manolo changed. Holding her infant, she thanked him with unmistakable reverence in her eyes.

Manolo was accustomed to being treated well. His patients sent him home with gifts, seeing him as the intermediary between themselves and a higher power to whom they prayed nightly for strength and healing. That night, he knew he did not deserve the credit. This woman had done the work on her own, only needing him as a witness to her glory. But at the moment when their gazes met, Manolo interpreted gratitude. Long after he had forgotten her, she seemed to say with her eyes, she would remember his hands lifting her son into the world.

This brief encounter, a silent understanding between doctor and patient, was not the look that lingered in his memory now. Instead it was a second look that preoccupied him, one he had stolen just before leaving the patient's room. The woman sat up on the bed, propped up against a small stack of pillows, with the baby asleep upon her chest. Every movement of her arms and fingers, of her head and neck, was slow and deliberate. She was mindful of everything she touched. Her eyes were at once alert and completely at peace. It could have been the quiet after the pain. But Manolo realized it was much more—a transformation particular to a newly anointed mother. He realized too that the reverence he had seen in her eyes a moment before was not for him alone, not for him at all.

Just then, the back door yielded, accompanied by the shuffle of the old ones' footsteps. Manolo put his present thoughts aside. He nearly coughed out a cloud of smoke and scattered it with the flap of his hand, then extinguished what remained of his cigarette. He saw Mother's trim silhouette first, followed by Father's round gait.

"She's moody waiting for Manolo to come home. What could they be bickering about? Are they already tired of one another?" Mother asked.

"Surely, no. I'm old, not blind. Our son and his wife are in love."

"Sometimes I wonder if Tala isn't to blame. Don't look so surprised, husband of mine. A woman knows these things. She seems so young and inexperienced. I worry that underneath the innocent demeanor, she knows more than she seems to about how to manipulate men."

Manolo stiffened at his mother's words. He was irritated and confused by Tala, but not enough to hear a word of criticism against her. Particularly not from his mother, who showered Tala with unsolicited praise on a daily basis and who did not know a thing about the source of his irritation or confusion. Perhaps Old Luchie, the maid, with her arthritis and sagging chin, who avoided everyone as often as she could—perhaps she was the only honest female he knew. Manolo shook his head, denying the possibility.

He had forgotten that his parents sat in the yard to talk after dinner and hoped to be spared from eavesdropping much longer.

"I can't help but worry about him, you know, because of what happened before. He never got over what Dalaga did to him. And to think that their wedding was the next day. She didn't even come home for Palong's funeral."

Before their conversation could drag on further, Manolo stood reluctantly to announce his presence. They would probably discover him soon and pester him with questions. But Father's next suggestion forestalled the need.

"The past is the past, my love. Our son has moved on, and so shall we. But let's go back in," Father said. "Manolo should be back any second. I want to see how they get along when he gets home. Just beyond newlyweds and already bickering, such a shame. Besides, I smell smoke. I'm afraid to know what's lurking in the trees."

"You smell it too! It's a kapre for sure. I sense an evil spirit nearby."

He saw Father straighten the edge of Mother's skirt, which had wrinkled and folded over slightly when she sat. She thanked him by removing a crumb from the corner of his lip. After they had disappeared into the house, Manolo sank into a crouch and looked up at the acacias, the palms, the fruit-bearing trees scattered in the yard. On such a hot evening, there was a windless calm in the treetops, and only starlight illuminated the leaves. Still, Manolo could see the tips of each leaf quiver. He dared to imagine what his parents had, that the kapre's breath blew upon those leaves as he exhaled from his pipe, smoking from a giant's height, invisible to the eye.

Manolo climbed to the top of the highest palm tree, determined to be eye to eye with this giant, this kapre. At the top, Manolo called out to the kapre and realized he had only reached the giant's kneecap. He heard the rumble of laughter in the clouds. With the flicker of a fingertip on the tree trunk, the kapre shook the palm fronds into a frenzy. Manolo scrambled back to earth and stifled the urge to scream into the night. To run wild beneath the trees. To burst into the house, grab Tala by the shoulders, and shake her until she cried.

Instead he stared hard into the back of the house, through paint, plaster, and cement, as if he could see Tala through the walls. What he saw was the image of her wings, hidden away behind the panel in his closet, and even now, pulsating, pulsating against his skull.

There was no way those wings could be still. They never stopped beating, even in his dreams. Manolo could follow his wife in secret all their lives and never come to understand their mystery. The places from which she'd come and the places to which she might wish to return, at any given moment. He wanted the wings to be still. Manolo returned to the tranquility and glow of his patient's face. To the sense of assurance she had of existing in the world. And in that moment, he knew why her face had haunted him so. It was a look she gave that Tala had never given him. But she would. Tala would one day look at him with the same reverence, and when that day came, the reverence would be real. He had the power to instill life in her, make her round like the moon, to prove that even in his mortality, he was something of a god after all.

4. Openings

THESE WERE LAZY, SLOW-MOVING days for Luchie, when she dusted for the show of it, swept for the show of it, and showed up for the show of being a housemaid, knowing she was really just a ribbon on the doorknocker, a gesture of love for a prized wife.

But times weren't always lazy. Or slow.

There had been a long sweep of years when everything was frantic, the last of them under Manolo Lualhati's employment. She would wake up by accident on the mornings when Manolo expected her, an hour earlier than she needed to, sometimes sooner, convincing herself back to sleep, praying even, to rest just a little longer. It was always in vain. Because as soon as her eyes met the dim outline of her room, ordinary objects pushed visions of sleep into regions of the forgotten, grounding her back to life, and there was no going back to the comforting swaddle of dreams. As she shifted into alertness, she gazed at her wooden dresser and the extra clothes folded on top, the single photograph on the wall, and her red shopping cart beside the bed.

In those days, her wakeful mind was a nervous mind, particularly on the mornings she needed to get up for work. There were no fresh starts for Luchie. Even before the day had a chance to begin, she thought and worried, questioning whether or not she was meeting Manolo's expectations, mulling over the trivialities his family depended on her for.

This fever lasted throughout the day, so that her shoulders grew tense and she had to remind herself to relax her jaw. Her legs, spongy in the thighs and narrowing to spindles, felt disjointed from the rest of her body, as if they led her from place to place with a memory of their own. On the bus ride into Manlapaz, she worried she wouldn't arrive on time, wishing she could enjoy the view of the countryside at that hour, when only the birds were awake and bustling, the fruit doves and the sparrows, woodpeckers and bee-eaters. She would remember nothing of the walk from the plaza to Manolo's house, except for the sensation of her legs moving, left then right, swing step swing, brittle, stiff, with a memory of their own. Then, on the bus ride home, she went over everything she had or hadn't straightened or scrubbed and imagined who might notice.

Their house was always painfully clean.

Manolo had not given her instructions, assuming, she believed, that a maid's job was straightforward enough. He was rarely home when she was there. Or he spent hours on end holed away in his clinic at the end of the hall, emerging only to escort his patients in or out or to gulp down a quick meal. The women were too distracted with themselves to outline her duties clearly, so Luchie discovered on her own that there were places in the house where she wasn't invited. From there, she forged safer pockets of work to keep her occupied.

She soon realized, for instance, that Iolana was a jealous woman. Twice Luchie tried to take Andres's plate following his afternoon merienda, and each time Iolana intercepted, placing her hand over Luchie's, like a secret handshake, then peeling Luchie's fingers off one by one. One morning, Iolana followed Luchie into the couple's bedroom, wordlessly reclaiming the socks and briefs Luchie had picked up from the floor. That was when Luchie stopped picking up after Andres.

She assumed that Tala followed Iolana's example, dutifully cleaning up after her husband, because Manolo's life was perfectly ordered. He left no clutter or mess, no articles of clothing, not even a dent to re-fluff in the sofa cushion—not a trace of him lingered about where he wasn't supposed to. Every sign of his existence was neatly folded or tucked away, safe in drawers and closets. Luchie realized that aside from his paying her on time, she had no idea what kind of man Manolo really was, nor did she care.

Then there was Tala, always smiling-smiling. She made Luchie uncomfortable with her intensity. Luchie assumed she was a young wife, restless and bored. Restless because she was young, bored because her husband spoiled her. In the beginning it felt as if Tala, like her, was feeling out her place in the house, probing Luchie as a way to gauge her own sense of belonging. She was the type of girl who wanted to know how Luchie was doing, smiling-smiling and wanting to talk. But Luchie wasn't the smiling, talking type. She came to work and sought approval without becoming her bosses' friend. She didn't know how to relax in their home, on the job, let alone in their close company, and so avoided Tala whenever she could.

Luchie spent most of her time hand washing and hanging laundry, what little of it there was, and never underpants. In other homes, she had regularly scrubbed the menstrual blood off panties, the sex from sheets. There was nothing to hide from a maid. Luchie thought it funny and odd, even a little flattering, that the Lualhatis kept these facts of life to themselves.

She had no role in the kitchen, so she swept and dusted when she finished the laundry, always keeping busy. Always moving, working, thinking.

Then she came across it one day, a blinding hot day like every other, when everything was the same except for it—the box on the shelf, a square-shaped alteration to the previous day. A curiously red detour from a gray blur of worries, worries carried by brittle legs that hoarded memories like colors. She opened it.

The smell.

Luchie had to stop, arrested by the sensation of something so familiar, like childhood, impossible to recapture, but infinitely hers. She closed her eyes, breathing in deeply.

The smell.

Soft, creamy, velvet. Yes, the wood.

The fruity aroma of the wood—it was made from a kamagong tree, perhaps the very tree she played beneath before there was such a thing as work, or such a feeling as worry.

Luchie touched the pattern of faint lines and could almost see the natural ebony color of the bark underneath the red paint. She could taste the velvety tart of its fruit. The kamagong tree had another name—mabolo. Similar to Manolo. She thought of the way Manolo had reacted on the day she was to move in. *I cannot live here after all,* she had told him, not offering any excuses. Too much like living in an office, just a few doors from where your boss slept. She couldn't bear the idea of twenty-four-hour surveillance. She had lived alone for too long, cultivating a preference for solitude, the only thing she inherited from a family she outlived and a son who disinherited her.

Luchie breathed in and out evenly, inhaling a forest of kamagong trees.

Instead of getting angry, she recalled, Manolo had been apologetic for her change of mind. *Of course, of course,* he assured her, as if the terms they'd both agreed upon during the interview were imposing, unrealistic even. They would not need her every day, he nodded, and her coming in three days a week by bus was a perfect arrangement, a good suggestion on her part.

She'd realized then, hadn't she, what she could get away with at Manolo's house?

The way he had looked at her, reminding her of her age, a woman nearing seventy, older than his mother. He must have hired her not to work. By then she knew how to recognize this built-in reflex for guilt, even for wrongs that didn't belong to him. Yet after taking the job she toiled, afraid, minute by minute, toiling through that fear, when no one ever noticed the timid movements of her arrival, the quiet draft of her leaving. She had already spent years acting out of her own sense of guilt. Devoted to having a purpose, even if it was only to keep house, to scrub clean the menstrual stains for women who didn't recognize how significant they were to her.

How significant she wanted to be to them.

Luchie had put down the box with its smell, its distinct velvet sweetness, ripe red fruit melting in her mouth. She decided then to have a seat, and she could probably count the number of times she'd gotten up since.

By now she'd slowed down long enough to watch their show, the Lualhatis, and there, Manolo loitering on the other side of the glass, looking in, not at work after all. That quickly, and the show had begun. Slow and lazy, her bones thanked her, brittle legs recalled a hint of warmth, sending colors back up her spine in a shiver. *Aaaahhh.* She still remembered how to smile, and felt at that moment, she was doing the job she was hired for.

It only takes a moment, she reflected now. To take a seat. Or get up and join the show, act it out at your own pace. Then one moment to the next, changing the course of a life from frantic to lazy.

Luchie had chosen then, or the moment had chosen her. To embark upon a slower era, when she dusted for the show of it, swept for the show of it, showed up for the show of being a housemaid, knowing she was really just a ribbon on the doorknocker, a gesture of love for a prized wife.

• • •

THERE ARE DREAMS THAT you dream, knowing you are asleep. Knowing you are dreaming. You are adventurous then. You fly, walk through walls, make love, move mountains. If you are brave, you don't hold back; you make memories like secrets, not for the waking world to know.

Iolana was having just that kind of dream. In this dream, one object, a small red box, sat on the living room shelf, the key attached like a finger curling, inviting her in. Iolana hated the box, wanting it for herself, only for herself, jealous of whatever it contained. She felt the grip of nightmare and ecstasy, both. She rushed to the box, opening the lid with a shaking hand, a quiver between her legs. A rush of light enveloped her.

She was young again. Naked beside Andres. She wrapped her arms around him and he tightened his embrace, both of them fighting to be closer. Then, nothing but the need existed, each kiss fueling the need for more kisses, their tongues searching for the source of that need, stoking it, again and again, until she disappeared into the flames, neither dreaming nor waking, everywhere and nowhere at once.

She lived with him there for years, dreaming an endless dream, never losing the need for his skin, his smell, his taste. But all along she remembered someone else, Manolo, her son. She could not stay in the dream without him. And so the love-making changed, fueled by a different kind of need: to conceive her son and give birth to him again. Become the mother of her dreams.

No conception followed. She remained barren. She grew older, forgetting to wake up. Worrying that she would lose Manolo forever. He became a memory, a secret, not for her dreaming world to know. Her son was someone she had dreamed in another life, buried and almost forgotten. Sometimes she couldn't distinguish his having lived from history or myth, dream or reality.

One day, Iolana considered that perhaps she wasn't barren

after all. Perhaps Andres was the defective one. Iolana considered this possibility and the lengths she was willing to take to make Manolo real. She called upon the gods, night after night, begging for a son. She cut her hair, which had grown to the length of a blanket, sweeping against her feet. She sent the strands up into the wind as an offering to the gods.

In her dream she dreamed of a beautiful winged man, youthful and rippling, with shiny, raven feathers. He came for her at the window when Andres was sleeping. She climbed upon his back and flew with him to the doors of heaven, into the rooms within.

When she awoke from the dream within her dream, there was a single black feather on her pillow. She quickly looked at Andres, afraid he would see the feather, learn her betrayal. She placed the feather on her tongue and swallowed it. Afterward she began to grow, in roundness and in happiness, knowing that her son, Manolo, was finally on the way. She vowed to guard her secret, the secret of Manolo's true father, through every layer of life. She would keep Andres's trust intact, their love whole.

Iolana's birthing pains were so powerful that they woke her from the dream. She sat up in bed, drenched in sweat, still aching within the depths of her abdomen. She touched it—a loose pouch, not the bursting belly of her sleep. She looked at Andres, sleeping peacefully, then searched above and beneath her pillow. No feather.

Iolana got up from bed and walked to the living room, certain to find nothing but what had been there the day before, a shelf with Tala's silly stones, dried flowers, bamboo-leaf figurines, candles on rickety little stands. What she saw was impossible, the box of her dreams, sitting on the shelf, small and red, its key attached like a finger curling, inviting her in.

She felt the heat rise along with her desire, an ecstatic nightmare, reminiscent of winged men and heaven's rooms.

Iolana could not tell if she was awake or dreaming. Only the secret was real. It had followed her in life, in dreams, in the sleep of dreams, in their waking confusion. She would guard her secret through every layer, each as real as the last.

SINCE HE WAS A boy, Andres had enjoyed women, not just their looks and smell, but their things. Like this new red box, so pretty.

He remembered trying on his mother's high-heeled shoes, her lipstick, and her clothes, all the while feeling closer to her laugh, holding her softness against him like fabric.

After he married Iolana, he liked opening a drawer and seeing her barrettes and brushes arranged side by side with his comb and razor blades. He relished the sight of beaded necklaces hanging from the opening of her jewelry box, the makeup scattered on the counter. He found it comforting to live in the company of a woman, to be surrounded by the essence of her femininity.

While Tala was out and Iolana was napping, while Luchie was in the yard scrubbing clothes, he lingered before the living room shelf, finding traces each had left behind—three butterflies shedding wispy cocoons. Andres thought of Manolo. His son had always been a serious boy, never one to stop and observe the little things around him. So caught up in his thoughts. Andres himself had never been a man of conflict. Perhaps this difference between the two of them was the reason they had never gotten close—unlike father and son, more like acquaintances living under the same roof.

Life was simple, he wanted to tell Manolo now. Meant to be enjoyed. Women were meant to be enjoyed. Women were, by nature, complicated beings, but this alone was no reason to complicate a marriage.

He put the box down and picked up the shell Iolana had

kept on the shelf for years, taking pleasure from the shape and weight, the spiky edges that warded off intruders, the beautiful coral and white colors that attracted admirers. Part of a vast, impenetrable ocean. He could only listen to its echo from the opening, catch a hint of its mystery. This, to him, was enough. Manolo, he thought, always wanted more. Would not be satisfied until he had plunged headlong into the deep, captured the source of that mystery for himself.

Perhaps that was why his son had chosen to become a doctor.

Andres liked the cleanliness of the shelf, Luchie's work. No more dust building on memories. Tala brought new things to the shelf, miniature bouquets of flowers that she had dried, delicate enough for fairies. Bamboo leaf patterns he turned over and over in his hands. Candles. So pretty. He sniffed each one. They smelled good. And the red box with a key. He held it again, turning it over in his hands. Lovely craftsmanship, made for an angel—a woman.

Andres wanted to tell Manolo to take the time to look at it, the box, for instance, look at the things inside his house. The workings of his woman.

Marriage was, after all, like the shelf in the living room: You let a woman in and then you share it. Reorganize, reshuffle, leave room for the barrettes and the jewelry, the makeup and the pretty red boxes.

Andres had always enjoyed his Iolana, how soft she was to the touch, how easily she laughed. How obviously she loved him. Even the way she fought with him or among the other women, because of him.

Manolo needed to let go of his hang-ups, loosen up when it came to Tala. She was just a girl. She would grow old, and so would her beauty.

Andres enjoyed touching the surface of the box. He didn't bother opening it, imagining and then believing in the image of its hollowness. Objects were simply objects, men were men, women were women. It was all so simple and for now—for the simple here and now—so divine.

5. Ghosts

TALA PLACED HER SECRETS in the box. In dreams, the box would open, spilling her secrets into the world.

They began—the secrets, the dreams like mist and muddy water. They began with a man in the water.

When she'd swum at the river with her sisters all those nights before, as her lover watched, she had seen him looking up from the river's depths—a man in the water. At first, she thought he was a reflection from above. She had looked up, seeing nothing but trees, their limbs reaching down for a taste of the river, and beyond them, a patchwork of stars. Then her younger sister Ligaya began splashing along the river's edge, inviting wave after wave, and the man faded into a billowy mass. She dove beneath the surface, expecting to find him there, holding his breath and waiting to share a secret with her. She re-emerged, unsatisfied.

Afterward she stayed in the water night after night, long past her sisters, hoping to see the river deity's face looking up at her from the bottom half of the world. Each night, her wish was fulfilled.

She looked into his eyes, certain he looked back at her. He returned her smiles. Every now and then a leaf fell from the trees up above, landing on his countenance and disfiguring it with a succession of spirals. When the water settled, his face returned, constant as the moon. He never spoke.

Tala spent her days waiting for the flight to the river. She spent her time at the river guarding his image, knowing he revealed himself only to her. Her sisters never saw her man in the water, and Tala's love grew with the knowledge that the fates danced just for the two of them.

One night she vowed never to leave him. She would languish for an eternity by the riverbank, faithful to her one true love. That same night, her sisters flew away without her. It would teach her a lesson, they had said, and she'd learn what it felt like to be left alone, with only herself for company.

Only Ligaya's wingtips had drooped; she was reluctant to leave Tala behind. Tala comforted her with her biggest smile. In response, Ligaya's wingtips perked up slightly. Her smile was not a real smile, but a summons to be brave for Tala. At her younger sister's concern, Tala had considered giving in and flying home. She watched Ligaya's small frame soar into the night till she could no longer distinguish her from the stars.

After her sisters left, Tala felt the sting of their disapproval. But she wandered barefoot on the damp earth and enjoyed the feeling that ensued—as if the minutes and seconds belonged to her. She walked with her arms crossed on her chest, embracing herself. When she discovered that her wings were gone, Tala was not surprised. She had willed it so.

She searched for the man in the water and waited, trusting in his arrival. As she searched every corner of the glassy surface, she heard footsteps approach and turned to see the river deity himself. No longer a deity, but a man. She greeted him with a calm suffused with joy, believing she had willed him to life, thankful that her lover was no longer cursed, no longer imprisoned by his own likeness.

• • •

WELL BEFORE HER MOTHER-IN-LAW fried milkfish and garlic rice for breakfast, filling the rooms with salt and smoke, Tala loved morning and its distinct smell. It was an earthy smell, of skin that had breathed into linen over the course of a night. She learned her own smell through the morning sheets, now tinted with the musky hints of tobacco smoke that Manolo carried into bed with him every night.

She was lying in bed with her eyes closed, pretending to be asleep. Breathing in the morning, but without her habitual pleasure. Manolo was not so distant now, no longer leaving for work without bothering to wake her as he'd done all the previous week. But the presentiment stayed with her, the worry he would relapse into a dismissive withdrawal without her knowing why.

She listened now as he rustled around the room. A drawer slid open then shut, followed by the light flap of clothing, the heavier thud of shoes. For a moment the sounds disappeared. She felt his soft lips press against her cheek and opened her eyes. She reached for his hand and squeezed, and he kissed her once more before leaving.

She had wanted to show him the box much earlier, at her first opportunity. But the day she brought it with her, he'd gotten home from work especially early. Tala had been thrilled to see him, showing him the things she bought from the market, one by one. He had not indulged her as he normally did, but looked at her purchases with something like disdain. She thought the box might shake the unusual cloud dampening his spirits, but she'd chosen to wait for just the right moment to present it.

It was a perfect square, a shade of red comparable to lava. The sides were engraved with alibata script, the strokes resembling pictures rather than words—here a bird, there a hand in gesture, expressing a song or state of being. A key extended formidably from the lock, brass-colored, not burnished like gold, but distinguished and ornate. It seemed like a key that had outlived the centuries, one that could have opened the first door ever built.

She'd found her opportunity nearly a week later. Andres and Iolana were out visiting Iolana's brother, Little Roland, two barrios north, and Luchie was napping in the living room. Tala's husband had been in a reflective mood, unoccupied and sitting in one corner of their bed with the *Manlapaz Bulletin*. He'd enjoyed an early break from work to sip iced tea and relax in shorts and bare feet. Up until then she'd been skirting around his temper, a quiet collaborator to their invisible quarrel. She knew better than to get defensive; prodding him with complaints, simply to get his attention, would only make him more sour. With his guard down, it was a good time to charm him into a better mood. She approached him nonchalantly with the box in one hand.

"Promise not to open it," she had said. "There's a surprise in here for you, but it's not ready yet. Promise you won't spoil the surprise?"

Manolo acquiesced easily. He glanced at the box without interest and seemed to forget it in the next instant.

"Don't bother me with surprises. I prefer to know what's coming."

"In any case, I'll put the box on the living room shelf. No peeking. I'll know if you do."

Manolo linked his hands together and placed them behind his head. He leaned back against the pillows and looked at her. While his body seemed worn by exhaustion, every sign of fatigue had left his eyes.

"When I get you presents, I let you pick them out yourself," he said. "Then I know for sure you'll like them. I never understood surprises."

"This one you'll like." She joked with him. "Like a good wife, I know what you like even more than you do."

"If you say so." He moved to where she sat on the edge of the bed, speaking the words near her, as if he wanted her to hear them with her lips rather than her ear, words so close to her mouth she could've spoken them herself. She thrilled at the warmth of his breath against her face, realizing how many days it had been since they'd last made love. Her body tensed with anticipation as he began to kiss her neck, slowly unhinging her with his lips, tuning her like an instrument to the exquisite sensation of his hands. He cupped her breasts and cradled the nape of her neck, guiding her onto the mattress as she abandoned her body's weight. At the gentle probing of his tongue, any possibility of resistance melted away. She pulled him in, with every part of herself seeking every part of him—seeking, needing, loving—forgetting all else.

And each day since, she'd watched him walk past the box. It might as well have been the wall on which the shelf was propped, something he took for granted, not needing to look at twice because he already knew it was there, supporting the foundation of the house. She wasn't sure this was the reaction she had hoped for. If he had wanted to know what was inside, if he had been the least bit curious, he would have shown stronger proof of his resolve in agreeing to keep whatever hid beneath the lid a mystery.

He was not the man in the water, but a stranger. By now, the man in the water knew her well enough to meet her eye to eye. He would have approached her directly. Her first instinct toward the stranger was suspicion. Then she saw that he averted his eyes in embarrassment. If he intended to speak, the words couldn't get past his quivering chin. Even his hands shook.

He had the type of face that seemed younger than his years, betrayed by a few strands of gray beneath his ears. He was slender, with contours that signified a man's strength. Sadness showed in his eyes, but not a defeated sadness. She sensed that his timidity wasn't merely cowardice—that he was a man full of feeling.

She decided to let the stranger be. She knew he wasn't going to harm her. They were together by chance, two anonymous callers paying homage to the river.

She continued searching for the man in the water. He'd kept her waiting all night, so she was surprised at how calm she felt. She waded knee-deep, navigating the periphery of the river with her head and shoulders bent, looking in. Here the river swelled to the width of a narrow pool. Only at the very center was it deep enough to tread water in. The path from the fields led to one bank; the other bank ended at the edge of a tall slope leading to a thicker grove of trees that gathered at the foothills. It slowed to a trickle where there was nothing but pebbles and stones, then swelled again farther along its path. On the other end the water disappeared beneath a mass of reeds.

She swam toward the center, diving in and up again. Her dress clung to her like scales. It bunched between her knees, dripping water over her bare legs when she waded the shallows.

The stranger had found a flat boulder to sit on. Ligaya had used the same boulder as a stove, bed, or operating table, depending on the game she was playing.

As she searched she realized the stranger's presence never left her. She was surprised at this. He was quiet and kept to himself. She'd expected to forget he was even there. Instead she sensed him in every motion of her body, imagining his sad, engulfing eyes watching her every move. It was a strange feeling, but more and more she realized she liked having him near. She felt comfortable in his presence. That sense of comfort around another person, a stranger, was a new feeling, a nice feeling. Her curiosity began to flutter like dragonflies in her belly, their wings gaining momentum and speed.

She couldn't help but glance his way. She saw that his chin

quivered a little less and his gaze had begun to settle away from the shadows and treetops. It was as if he were in his own room with the lights off, and his eyes had finally adjusted to the darkness.

Now he sat with his legs propped up and an arm resting on each knee. His hands dangled from his wrists like sleeping fish. The sight of his hands relaxed, no longer shaking, made her happy.

But she came back to herself with the impression she had forgotten something. The man in the water, still missing, distracted her. She thought of the stranger on the rocks as she circled the edges of the water, from deep to shallow and back again. She was conscious of his posture, the particular sounds that caught his attention—a stone tumbling, a lizard slipping across the weeds.

He caught her watching him and she saw that this time, he did not look away. His eyes were full of life. She felt a million points of contact on her skin from his eyes alone. Her throat felt stuck, as if the air could no longer reach her lungs.

Then she only pretended to search, but the man in the water had become a billowy mass, elusive and fickle.

TALA STAYED IN BED, thinking with her eyes open. The box could not be a test of honesty and resolve if her husband did not feel tempted to open it. She reflected upon his aloofness following the day she brought it home. She delved into possible reasons for his displeasure, allowing the tiniest prick of guilt to stab her conscience. She kept much from Manolo—this she knew. The long afternoons with her sisters at the stall, when they traded news and gossip, sending Baitan to buy them snacks while they fanned their feet and waited for customers. The growing interest she'd taken to healing herbs, oils, and flowers and her budding hopes to join her sisters' work. And, of course, the knowledge of those sumptuous nights long before, when the river buzzed with fireflies and her body's undeniable static.

She recalled trying to talk to him at dinner one night that week, but he'd brushed her questions aside.

"Sometimes, when you're around sick people all day, you just want to rest your mind. I don't feel like talking all the time," Manolo had said.

So they had eaten in silence. It hadn't been a comfortable silence, the kind two people share when they're close enough to know each other's ways without the constant need for words. This kind of silence heightened small sounds, making the quiet even louder. At first, she thought he might've disliked the meal—a new interpretation of lugaw made with the palpable addition of cilantro—but then his spoon scraped the bottom of the bowl and she sensed her husband's agitation in those sharp clinks.

Tala was even more hurt when, the following night, Manolo's parents had joined them for dinner. With Andres and Iolana in their company, it was easy for Manolo to avoid her. She wondered if Manolo had persuaded his parents out of the private dinners they shared in their bedroom. Andres and Iolana usually set up trays on a small table in front of the television. They sat together on the bed, yelling out answers to the game show they watched every night at that hour.

By now the smell of salt and smoke crept into her bedroom, wafting in from the crack underneath the door. Soon, even the bedspread wrinkled up against her cheek would contain her mother-in-law's cooking. But the prospect of sitting with Iolana cheered her. Tala placed her fingers on her cheek, remembering the press of her husband's recent kiss. Since his moodiness had passed, she could safely predict the sentiments that would accompany his homecoming: hunger, fatigue, an undeniable brightness in his eyes when he found her again. Though her husband was selective about the amount of affection he showed, she knew his love, his hunger and his need, knew it because she shared it, helped feed it, and fed from it in turn.

She got up to begin her day.

ON THE SECOND NIGHT, the stranger spoke.

He'd left the night before without breathing a single word. After he had gone, she'd slept at the bottom of the riverbed, strangled by dreams. She dreamed it was her wedding night, that the riverbed was her marital bed with the man in the water. They needed no clothing, no blankets to keep warm. The water covered them completely, like a layer of skin or sleep, a shared womb. She turned to embrace her man in the water but he had no face. Before she could gasp in horror, the faceless man became the stranger, his eyes full of life. The impact of the stranger's eyes sent her body shooting to the surface, where the cold air shocked her into waking.

After waking, Tala had felt restless. She'd never been to the river during the day. In the light, it felt like a different world. The trees had color. Everything had color. And a brighter set of sounds replaced the night sounds. An endless chirping emanated from the trees' boughs, where the lightest of feet made a constant commotion.

But Tala was alone. She wondered if her sisters would return when the sky grew dark. She waited for the light and shadows to change, searched for the man in the water in every gleam of light bouncing from the wet canvas. She thought of her many nights with the man in the water, and his sudden disappearance fell on her like a stone.

That night, Tala looked up at the sky, searching the stars, missing Ligaya's laugh. Her sisters did not come. She felt sure her man in the water would return with the moonlight. After her frantic splashing that day, she walked the bank in the evening feeling more subdued.

Hours later, the man in the water eluded her still and disappointment stung her chest. She wondered why the man in the water had abandoned her just when she'd given up everything she knew to be with him. Tala felt as if nothing could console her.

In the fullness of night, the stranger returned. She was surprised at the way her heart lightened at the sight of him. Like her, he was drawn to the river and carried himself with the weight of something pressing against his heart. He seemed to know her sorrow, to share it, and somehow, he lifted part of it away. She felt as if together, their sorrows could be unloaded, passed into the river's arms for another place and time.

Joined by the stranger, Tala kept her head down, grazing the surface of the water with her eyes. Then he spoke.

"Did you lose something?" he asked.

HER FATHER-IN-LAW WAS ALREADY seated at the table, eating a plateful of garlic rice, eggs, and fried fish. He invited Tala to sit by pointing at the table with his chin.

"Good morning, Daughter," Iolana said. She sang the words, the notes getting higher with each syllable. Tala met the same enthusiastic greeting from her mother-in-law every morning. Unlike her son's, Iolana's moods were consistent and predictable, and Tala was grateful.

"Good morning."

"Eat now," Andres said.

"It looks good. Such a good cook, Ma." Tala was grateful that her mother-in-law was always quick to man the stove when she felt like sleeping in.

"Why do you think I'm so fat?" Andres clutched the generous rolls of his belly. "I didn't look like this when I first met her. Now, I spend all my time adjusting my belt—tight in the morning and a notch looser after every meal."

"You're still a movie star." Iolana touched his arm and looked at Tala. The shine in her eyes concealed a wink.

"I tell you she did this to me on purpose. So the other women would stop fighting for me."

"Ha, you stuff your mouth and blame me."

Every one of Iolana's words was equivalent to a smile. She reminded Tala of the pleasure of morning. There were the smells and the feeling of good things. Her mother-in-law was always cheerful, always dressed up. Today she wore a gold necklace with a flat jade pendant shaped like a rose. She wore earrings to match—smaller jade roses that dangled just beneath her lobes on delicate gold stems. Her blouse had short sleeves and buttons, a scoop collar. It was tucked in neatly beneath her skirt. Her face was rather plain, Tala thought, but still, Iolana was pretty. And yet, it would've been a homely face on a woman without Iolana's poise.

"When I met her, I was as skinny as Manolo."

"I feed you to keep you happy."

"You feed me to keep me fat."

They bantered this way, but Tala did not sense bitterness in their words. Instead it always seemed as if Manolo's parents were having fun. Tala realized that the food in her mouth made her stomach turn. She felt hungry, but the idea of swallowing made her throat revolt. She quickly washed the first bite down with water, wanting to empty her taste buds of the strong flavors. The water made her want to gag. Out of politeness to Iolana, she swallowed her own sour bile.

"What's the matter, aren't you hungry?"

"It's all so good, Ma. Maybe it's just too early for me to eat."

"Aren't you feeling okay?"

"I'm fine. The two of you are too much. You spoil me with attention. I'll have breakfast in a little while."

But as soon as she got up the nausea swirled. She ran to the sink to vomit.

Iolana pampered her for the rest of the morning. She brought a pillow to the sofa so Tala could rest there. She made hot ampalaya tea and left her alone to recover, checking in on her every once in a while to see if her appetite had returned.

Luchie was already stationed in the living room, fanning herself on the rocking chair. Tala had noticed the maid sitting in the same spot the past several days.

"I think it's about time," Luchie said. "How long have you been married now? I've been with you for almost a year."

"What do you mean?" It wasn't typical of Luchie to initiate conversation. And now that she had, Tala thought, her words were like a puzzle.

"And your menses? Have they stopped?"

At Luchie's question, Tala realized why Iolana seemed more excited than worried about the sickness that came over her at the breakfast table. The hope had not crossed Tala's mind until that moment. It came suddenly, and everything around her transformed, taking on the shape of her joy. Her senseless bickering with Manolo seemed so trivial then, and she felt silly for giving it so much weight. Her husband was entitled to fluctuations in mood. Indeed, it would be senseless for him to behave otherwise, like some automaton who experienced each day just as the last. She wanted to laugh out loud. She adored the light that filled the room, the cozy spaces it enveloped, the sounds of familiar voices she had grown to love, and even Luchie, whose silver and black hair grew from the mole on her chin. The hair moved whenever the maid talked.

"In any case, we'll soon find out." Luchie was the picture of contentment. She propped her feet on the edge of the coffee table, pushing against it with the balls of her heels. The slightest effort on Luchie's part initiated a steady rhythm of rocking.

Tala got the urge to get up and embrace the maid like a long-lost aunt. She wanted to ask her all the questions she had never been brave enough to ask her, like, did she have any children of her own, or, where was her extended family? Luchie seemed different now, different from Luchie, as if she might be more receptive to Tala's questions.

Before Tala could act on the impulse, Iolana returned.

"Oh good, getting up already!" Iolana said. "Let's go next door to Camcam's."

THE LIE CAME QUICKLY. "Yes, I've lost a necklace."

"Let me help you."

The stranger took off his shoes and rolled the bottom of his pants up to his knees. He began walking along the lip of the water, where it saturated the sand with kisses. His feet got wet first, then his ankles. Spots of water darkened the color of his pants.

They searched different areas, crisscrossing here and there. She held her breath during the moments they were side by side.

"What does it look like?"

"It's a . . . gold, with a heart-shaped pendant."

He walked closer and closer to the center of the water. By now his pants were drenched and the water covered him waist-high. Neither of them spoke. She circled the edges of the river in the opposite direction. At one point she felt as if they were walking a labyrinth, reaching closer to the center then out again, passing one another at different points along the journey.

There was something deliberate about the way he moved. She enjoyed watching him kneel or reach, watching the slow extensions of his body. He was careful with his hands, attentive with his fingers.

The stranger seemed intent, focused, as though finding the necklace was something important. He made her feel important, too. She wanted to know what motivated him to help her, and if any part of his motivation was a desire to please her.

He stooped down, picking up an amber-colored stone then tossing it away.

She realized she had him searching for a necklace she hadn't lost, one that didn't even exist. Suddenly his concentration was absurd, silly. He squinted his eyes and wrinkled his brow while he searched.

A loud splash broke as the stranger reached down, dropping his hand into the water like a spear, as if he'd found something promising that might swim away at a moment's hesitation. But he'd merely speared another pebble. Tala couldn't suppress a chuckle. The sound made him look up, and his inquisitive expression made her laugh all the more. And then she couldn't stop laughing.

He did not laugh but watched her, smiling. She had never seen anything as beautiful as his smiling face.

They stopped searching and sat together on the long, flat stone.

SHUT AWAY IN CAMCAM's bedroom, without their husbands or children, Iolana, Camcam, and Lourdes became girls again, each of them bursting with words. They talked rapidly and their conversation was like a dance; as one took the lead, the others were eager to follow. It was a meandering dance, circling from place to place, even across time. Iolana took the others back into the morning and her conversation with Andres, how he blamed her for how well he ate, too well. How he complained about the girth of his stomach while swallowing another bite of rice.

The others went back further, into girlhood and back again, revisiting schoolgirl crushes and chaperoned dates. They danced in the cities, in their bedrooms, in dreams of being overseas, always returning to the moment. The music was in their voices—rising intonations, low, serious tones, always punctuated by laughter. Laughter in shrieks, wails, tears, barks, bells. Their music was loud. They danced, celebrating life.

Among them Tala felt forgotten, perhaps because her mind

wandered away from the circle of women, and part of her felt she wasn't there at all. She felt lost in her own bubble, and she floated above the women's heads, watching them talk and gesticulate. Then she was flying again.

In her mind, she flew farther and farther away. She felt her back against the ceiling and lingered there before hovering over the rooftop, over many rooftops, over trees, then high enough to see the landscape, the rice fields, the banana fields, the river winding like a snake, the mountains in rows and ringlets, up, up, into the sky.

She was in two places at once. She feared the strain might tear a hole in the sky, send her pummeling across space to a void where she'd cease to exist. Tala placed her hand upon her womb and knew she needed to make a choice.

She listened for the murmurs, the women's voices in the wind, like a code at first, indistinguishable from the buzz of insects, then louder—fleshy, warm, alive. The women carried her back. She rode the vibrations of their laughter, floating down upon their wave of sound.

For an instant, she wasn't sure if she had really returned. The way they chattered on, as if she weren't in the room. Then she saw the boy.

She remembered him, Camcam's grandson. He did this every time she came to visit, appearing suddenly from behind the folds of a curtain, the other side of the sofa, even between the protective stalks that were his grandmother's legs. Camcam had explained the reason why he hid from her.

"Datu has a crush on you. He can already spot a pretty girl."

But Tala was not so sure. The boy peeked at her now from the hallway. She couldn't see his eyes, but recognized the outline of his hair and cheek. She knew he watched her and couldn't imagine if rapture, fear, or something else altogether provoked his fascination.

She reflected that no one in the barrio questioned her about her background. They had learned her story through Manolo and his mother. How she had run away from home, escaping the tyranny of an abusive brother, the indifference of her mother. How finally, she ran to save her life when they wanted to give her away, sell her body to strangers, foreigners whose intentions weren't clear or trustworthy.

Tala did not know this girl, this runaway.

The boy was right. He avoided her as if she were a ghost, something deceptive and fearful, stranded between two realities, neither a part of one nor the other. She wanted to earn her place among the circle of women, lift her child into the brilliant sway of their dance. For her, the steps always led to Manolo. The steps could traverse distance and time, and surrendering to the rhythm, she would fly all the while.

"I THOUGHT YOU WERE A GHOST."

They'd been talking for nearly an hour, like two old friends, when he confessed this first impression of her. His eyes were still sad, she thought, but calm.

"Do I look that bad?"

"It's not the way you look. It's the river. No one comes here. They say it's haunted."

They sat close without touching.

"I'm not superstitious," Tala replied.

"You're the only one in the countryside who isn't, then."

"Are you? Superstitious?"

"I guess I am."

"Then why did you come to the river?"

"To find a ghost. Or the devil."

Tala thought she understood. That he wasn't merely having fun with words. Earlier in their conversation she learned that he'd just found out about a compadre. That Palong had been a good swimmer, and how ironic it was that he died in the water.

It made him angry, he had told her, as if the devil were taunting him, laughing at his weakness.

So she wasn't surprised at his motive for coming to the river. She already felt she was getting to know him. She celebrated that trickle of knowledge and the sensation that she would soon be saturated, saturated with Manolo and everything there was to know about him.

"I think in a way all of us are ghosts," she replied. She thought of the solitude when her sisters had left, when she walked the bank alone. "No one can ever really know another person. Not completely." As she said this, she realized how the words conflicted with the hope she'd just had to know everything about this man in front of her.

She didn't know just how close two people could be. But sitting with him that second night, she wanted more than anything to find out. Tala wanted to convince Manolo to stay with her beside the river forever. She knew it was an outrageous idea, one she could not say to him out loud. Once again, she felt alone, only with Manolo right beside her, it was a loneliness that went beyond any she had ever felt.

In her despondency, she caught his stare. He watched her without reservation, in a way she had never seen him do before. It was as though he'd already memorized her features and needed something more, deeper than the eyes or lips. His face was before hers, as close as her own reflection. Only there was no mirror, no glare to blind her, no waves to rob her of looking.

She recognized him.

The look in Manolo's eyes sent her shooting into the river's depths, into the bliss of her marital bed, where the warm water soothed her into an endless dream.

SHE EXCUSED HERSELF FROM the women's company, saying she could use a little fresh air. She felt their stares on her back, burrowing into her as she walked away, perhaps seeing right through her. This wouldn't be the case for long.

She knew it was possible to be in two places at once. That the living could escape into dreams while their bodies kept burning sugar and excreting it away, their eyelids twitching in the dark, or, if their eyes were open, they'd remain blinking all the while, never seeing a thing. And it could also happen the other way around, when the phantoms stored in a living consciousness grew so vivid, they took on a life of their own. They walked the earth side by side with those they haunted.

But she was neither a sleepwalker nor an apparition and would accept no such life.

He didn't know that she'd found him, watching over her in the trees, waiting. And that when they'd finally sat laughing together on the stone, eyes buried in leaves spoke to her in ancient truths as old as the river. She knew then she'd done the right thing abandoning her wings, risking everything on the hope he would end her own endless waiting.

There was no reason for him to know. With their baby on the way, she would be in one place and one only, as real to Manolo as he was to her, even if it meant giving up her past for good.

6. The Veins of a City

So TALA BUILT A city. The way a traveler piles the earth with footsteps, the heavier ones walls and ceilings, the lighter ones open doorways, and if you connected the footsteps with lines through all the places the traveler has been, you would see the framework of skyscrapers and trees, entire forests of people with their many seeing eyes. Tala piled her own city with bricks, each with the weight of this traveler leaving home once more and for good; she left a comfortable protected life, and herself within that life, to a new city with slanting rooflines she had not looked upon every day for years. All of it was alien and therefore merciful; starting over from nothing, hers was a fortress made from love and love alone.

She built a city the way the mother builds a world within her womb, becoming both woman and house, both mortal and god. The cells of her body divide and multiply, and within her own borders there is only potential, a chamber of limitless will and the love that makes it possible. Tala found this city within and built it from the inside out.

It was a city in progress, always in construction and reconstruction, her mind the builder, her eyes the lens from which it sprang, and for her it was a matter of placement, situating herself at once and forever among the bricks and sand and walls, the particles that surround the dwelling of a husband, the matter for a wife to embrace and raise her child in. She would relocate to this city, find herself in that maze of winding streets, and the woman she found would no longer be her, then, but the ever-changing her, the growing-older her, the tired her and the her with regrets, the loved and the damned and the loving her, the mortal and aging her, but like every being in this new city, still divine, still making and building, choice by choice, tearing down walls along the way, in this city or that, watching the silhouette change and grow and sometimes decay.

She found her house alongside the labyrinth of streets, marked with a number that would take the place of her name, for this symbol belonged not only to her but to him, and she lived with him in that number on that house in that parallel city, and she did not look back.

A SINGLE NAIL GAVE rise to the foundation of a house. From the window of that house she watched the city rise, and out of that city, inhabitants sprang to life, filling the empty rooms and courtyards. Like her, these new inhabitants had no past. But Tala's city gave them each a face. Matter cannot exist without space, and given a sphere in which to live, the people claimed the validity of their own existences.

Within the perimeter of the city, the people came together in groups, forming networks in which to gather and work. Families arose. Friendships were made and broken. The city was large enough that each person only interacted with a small number of the population each day. The majority were strangers to one another. Anonymous faces in an endless sea of faces.

But every single inhabitant was connected, tied one to the other because the city itself touched them all. The soles of their feet scraped against the same floors, even if only once in their entire lives. Sometimes, two people never passed shoulder to shoulder but looked upon the same street post each day. The walls and city gates absorbed a multitude of fingerprints, and these fingerprints were ingrained in the wooden fibers, an oily residue solidified into cement, stuck in plaster, painted on the metal, forever tracing the city's multitudinous identity.

THE BODIES IN HER city began as shells. At first, she didn't know how to fill them. For inspiration, she looked to the streets of Manlapaz, where men, women, and children were so full of life it spilled from their mouths. The children burst with laughter and shrieks. The woman at the vegetable stand could not stop with her commands. *Fill this, get that, help me, stop, go, no, forget it, hurry up, again.* She learned to translate this woman's words: *Listen to me, listen to me, I am here, I exist.* The old man by the fishing docks at the edge of the island could not let anyone forget that he used to be young. Anyone who bought his bait left with more than worms; they came away with another perspective of the old man: as a little boy who was good at math, as a teenager helping his mother in the kamote fields, as an athletic boxer who would've gone pro if it weren't for a bad knee.

Then there were those who seemed like shells—a beggar outside the same restaurant every afternoon, waiting vacantly, too tired to ask for food. With no words to feed the city. The schoolgirl on her way home from school, reluctant because her father did not treat her like his little girl, and so her eyes escaped to another place, leaving her body behind so that she couldn't walk in a straight line. But they weren't shells after all. Each of them had a story, many stories, stories that filled them, lifting them out of themselves, or weighed them, dragging them closer to the ground, some stories fighting, one against the other, helping them move forward, lulling them to rest, each minute presenting an option, pulling them in so many directions. They intersected, the people with their stories, exchanging fragments of their lives, invented fragments or obvious facts, memories, personal truths, secrets, deceit— and with each intersection, they altered the stories of others, confirmed what others already knew, extended their plotlines, raised questions, sparked the synapse that would spark more synapses in the cauldron of infinite lives. She knew how to wake the bodies in her city.

She would fill them with stories of their own.

She did not know quite how to do this. She weighed different possibilities. One, that there were no new stories, that each person relived a different version of the same story, and this pattern repeated with every individual, continuing endlessly in time. Another was that there was a handful of stories, and each person was designated one, and every individual lived a different version of these five stories, sometimes joining two stories together to create something new. And then there was the possibility that no two stories were alike and each was spontaneous, a matter of choice, and because the choices were endless, the possibilities for a life story were also endless. She forged ahead without the answers.

HER CITY BEGAN WITH a face; she read the lines like lines on a map, the eyes the lakes, the nose the mountain at the center of the land. She had grown into the habit of taking day trips with her husband, if only to find a face in which to recognize the geography and the life living there, so familiar she could claim it. She'd seen many faces on these trips, and watching the maps on each face was travel itself. The skin told of distant continents, the thickness of hair of untasted foods and their undiscovered textures. The sounds from the lips curled around the edges, hinting at far-off currents. And in every voice and pimple, glossy tear, or lift of the eyebrow, she saw part of a story, made from one day or a sequence of days, seen through the eyes of a face on the map of some unformed city.

"Look, Manolo," she'd said one day at Tagarro Bay. "There are people from every part of the world and every background here in one place. If you could be part of someone's story, whose would it be?"

"Yours," he'd replied. "I'd be part of yours." He'd said the words without pausing to think, looked at her with eyes that were not lakes but familiar rivers, and they were gleaming because he was flirting, touching her without touching her, and that quickly she was swimming again, flying in air that was water that was Manolo's eyes. And she told him what he already knew, that he was the main character, a starring role.

Then without his knowledge she continued her search, for a city, for a past, so that afterward (in time) she could call the faces of her daughter and husband her original homeland, built from the inside out.

She even gave him a peek at the gates, evaluating the faces and their stories out loud like it was a game. How she would not choose the sailor with the brisk lift of the arm, the loosening belly out of which echoed the extension of every laugh, confident and protective of wife and family. She would not choose the fisherman, bustling, busy from line to stall, filled with the duties of work and responsibility, sleeping well and dreaming little. Nor would she choose the expert saleswoman, who knew when to charm and when to bully and how to disguise a bloated price tag as a bargain. When she found him, she knew. He was a lanky figure in plain, dark street clothes, smoking a cigarette in the middle of the plaza, watching the crowd as she was watching the crowd; he met her gaze through the middle of it all, a body bent into the narrow curves of a question mark.

"I'd be in his story," she said. "Because it wouldn't be fair if everyone chose the fairy tales."

And when she had her own personal map, she followed it. Yet there was so much more to do.

SHE WAS NOT CREATIVE. She had to start with what she knew. She began with her mother. Because everyone, including her, knows a story about a woman and her letters to a lost love.

THIS WOMAN IS A prostitute. She lives by the naval base in Tagarro Bay. Getting clients is easy; she averages ten appointments a day. She does not take the men home. They do it in cars, in the park, in the alley, in the warehouse of a shipyard, in an empty bunker, in a dirty bathroom. It's faster this way.

She falls in love with the man who pays her to talk. The one who doesn't touch her. She sees him every day; he pays her for three appointments. If he had more money, he tells her, he would buy all ten, so she could talk to him all night. So the other men wouldn't have to touch her.

She brings this man home. She stops taking his money. On their first night in her cramped room, surrounded by hampers full of dirty laundry, abandoned toys, and other clutter, they do nothing but kiss and talk. With this man, she discovers her desire. She wants to make love. She wants to stop taking money from the others. She envisions a different kind of life. He tells her he will take her away, out of her poverty, to his world across the ocean. Where the streets are clean. Where the life she envisions is everywhere, growing on trees, ready for her to pluck like an apple.

He confesses. He was like the others all along. If he could have, he would have had her on the first night, he tells her. He would have gotten what he paid for. But he is sick. Dying. He does not want to make her sick. Her stories made him forget. Her poor, sad world filled with mango trees made the sickness taste a little sweeter. He does not love her, he says. He leaves.

But the sickness, she learns, has already spread. She is

infected with this man. Dying. She continues talking to him every day, in letters. She cannot take clients. She is famished. She buys stamps and envelopes before food. She writes on napkins, on the backs of soda labels that she finds in the streets. She sends a letter a day. He never writes back, even when she tells him that she has had his child. She goes on with her life, dictating its passing in words. She imagines her scraps of paper pushed into the points of branches, growing like leaves on the trees overseas. Collecting into a life as it's meant to be lived.

She believes he is dead. Then she isn't sure. She knows he is alive. She wonders if he was ever truly sick. She makes appointments with clients because her children are hungry. She talks only in her letters, only to him. Writing becomes a matter of habit, then purpose, cultivating the tree she can grow because of him. The infection never spreads and never completely heals. It stings underneath her skin, but most of the time, she forgets all about it.

THEN THERE IS THE story of a man in despair. Teetering on the brink—any moment poised to land in the way of salvation or fall into utter hopelessness. On the brink, he feels safe. But he is merely lost. He is her brother.

He goes to the same bar every night. It stays open long past the others, until the sun is out. It's possible they make an exception for him, because in the morning he wakes up, aching all over, his chin against the hard table, moist with drool or alcohol or both. Once again, he is the only one there, except for the crazy witch behind the bar. She is always around and always alert. He wonders if she ever sleeps; he wonders if she is even human.

He doesn't know he's an alcoholic. There is no such thing in his world, no AA meetings where lonely bachelors and sorry husbands confess their problems. His problems start at home, then multiply. Since his ma started taking the sailor home, he has no place to stay. He is embarrassed to tell his friends. He doesn't go to school. He can't remember the last time he ate. Or what he did yesterday.

The crazy witch lets him drink as much as he wants. The burning liquid warms him and makes him forget. Forget the memory at five years old, when his pa took him to the cockfight. The way one rooster made the other bleed to death then afterward collapsed, the way it twitched to its own death while its owner tried to sew its neck together. He wanted to cry or throw up until his pa patted his head, laughing, telling him, *What a fight, nothing better than a good fight*. And he tried to like it too. Then his pa was gone, and for a long time that fight was the only thing he could remember about him.

Until he turned twelve and his ma forgot his birthday then ignored him for a week straight. He set out to find his father then. Tracked him down to a plush home, with maids and a beautiful wife who looked like the light-skinned women on billboards. His father pretended that he didn't know him. Or maybe he wasn't pretending.

But that was two years ago. And the crazy witch is saying something.

"Pay up. I said pay up."

"I don't have any money."

"You think this is a free house? You think I'm your grandma?"

"I'll wash your dishes."

She laughs and the creases on her face multiply. She looks fearful, like a monster, her eyelashes thick like spider legs.

"Dishes! You'll wash dishes? Pay for the alcohol. And all the nights you used this bar as a boarding house, rent-free for you."

He explains again that he is broke. She signals with her head and he follows her through the dividing doors between the bar and a back room, where crates of beer are stacked among piles of newspapers and dry goods. A metal rack is pushed to one side, where a jacket and two dresses dangle alongside a row of empty hangers. He follows her through a hallway, then another. They walk through a room filled with boxes, where a woman sits at a computer in the corner, looking up as they pass, then returning her attention to a piece of paper she is holding. She files it. They walk on, through a little outdoor courtyard separating one building from another. His footsteps crunch on a landscape of pebbles. It is a strange hidden world behind the bar. From the front, all you see is a cozy little hut, something you might find in a tropical paradise. He never imagined it could extend this far. It feels never-ending. He wonders if he's dreaming.

Finally they arrive in a room crowded with girls. The younger ones glance up curiously from their game of jacks. Two others do not stir from their napping, and the pretty one staring him down is not much older than him.

"You'll stay with them."

"No way. What is this place?"

"No? Then you work for me. Come back this time tomorrow, after you've washed your face. Consider this place your office, boy."

The woman laughs, creases multiplying upon creases. He doesn't know why, but he thinks only of the rooster, its neck being sewn to keep it alive, killing it.

So TALA GROWS UP without a father. His absence takes many shapes. Mostly it is in the ebb and flow. In the women at the makeup counter, craning their necks closer, enchanted by her fair skin. Others do the same—the teacher, before Mama pulled her out of school, again. The landlord coming to collect the rent, the tourists finding their way to nearby restaurants—bodies leaning in, erasing space. Then at home, a retreat. Outside, her mother is proud; once inside the door, only distance will do. Tala reminds her of him. Sometimes, after writing one of her letters, Mama will grasp Tala's face in her hands and stare at her fiercely, patting her cheeks and forehead, clutching her arms.

When she turns eighteen, her brother tells her she will marry a man who looks like her father. She will go across the ocean, where Mama always wanted to go. Maybe Tala will even meet her father there, run into him in the street. She will be happy. She will send them money every month. She will make their mama well, do her part to take the burden off of him.

Her brother comes from a world with different smells. He disturbs their quiet with raucous visits, banging his way from room to room and always talking loudly, as if he needed to raise his voice above a place filled with racket. But there is always just the three of them. Tala comes to associate his world, the world of night, the world of noise and smoke and sour beer bottle smells, with a place along the coast where different worlds meet. The place he would send her to must reek of his smell.

Her eighteenth birthday is in two days. She wants to do what Mama wants. She looks to her mother for assurance, wanting her to see that she is able, wanting her to make a choice for her knowing that she is able. She cannot explain her faith, her certainty that something in this life is hers and waiting, like an unborn child tucked safely in some hidden dimension.

Mama only stares, the same as always. Then Tala sees she is telling her to look. *Look, look.* Mama is pointing at something outside. Tala sees nothing but a tree. It is skinny and weak, with just a few triumphant leaves reaching for the sun. *It's beautiful,* Mama says, *so beautiful.*

She reaches for a pouch beneath her pillow, removing a gold chain with a heart-shaped pendant. She places it in Tala's palm then closes her hand into a fist. There are no clouds in Mama's eyes when she looks at her, only clear skies. *Now go,* she says, *run.*

7. The Inner Sanctum

LEANING INTO HIS NEW walking stick, Manolo had watched the outline of his wife and the boy lose dimension. They did not look his way when they passed him in the market square, and before they were swallowed within the ever-changing shape of the throng, he resumed pursuit.

After leaving the woman who twisted leaves on her dirty mat, his wife and the boy walked back toward the center of the square. They passed the busy courtyard and turned into a small alley, where Tala entered an albularyo's booth. The albularyo looked about the same age if not younger than Tala, and he couldn't take his eyes off them. The boy seemed to have disappeared, but Manolo realized that he had merely sunken to the ground against the heat, his belly relieved, no doubt, by the coolness of the earth. He imagined the knobby points of the boy's dry elbows burrowing into the sand, his senses knowing only the perfect smoothness of marbles rolling and crackling one against the other like tiny, incompatible worlds.

His wife leaned against the counter, not imagining for a moment that he was nearby with his dress shirt slung over his shoulder, his eyes shaded by the brim of his hat, and a silly new cane in his hand. He noticed the way she slumped into the heat, into the laziness of her own flesh as unguardedly as if she were in her own bedroom. Even Tala's tongue seemed to roll untethered, without the restrictions of social formalities. He could only imagine what she could be saying. He envisioned her words floating just outside the curve of her mouth, languishing in the still air, the syllables breaking apart then losing themselves amid the commotion of other syllables before they could traverse the distance to his burning ear. His eyes burrowed into all the potions, the strange concoctions and bottled dreams, fearing that Tala sought some way of returning to the place where her lost wings no longer carried her.

He untethered his fixation on Tala, only to meet the other woman's eyes. This albularyo had seen him, for how long he couldn't tell; but she watched him in a way that suggested she had always known him to be there.

Her stare was direct and unapologetic, catching him unawares. She stood of medium height and generous build. She wore her short hair up with a yellow handkerchief wrapped around it, the ends of the knot brushing against her neck. He compared her pantsuit to a sack because it was shapeless, dingy brown, and looked coarse to the touch. Over it she wore a purple apron that redeemed for him all the softness and femininity the pantsuit was lacking. And then there were her eyes, strangely familiar, seeking him out and latching on for seconds at a time. These intermittent clutches made him nervous enough to consider leaving. But instead of alerting Tala of his presence, she extracted an object from the pocket of her apron, watching him as she did so, watching him even as she handed the object to his wife, a flash of red that defined itself before his eyes, changing from a quick blur to a box with precise edges and pointed corners. Such a peculiar feeling seized him then.

He'd been observing the scene from a sidelong angle, through a narrow pocket of space that existed between the pole holding up the awning of a stall on the main path and a tub of live crabs propped on a table behind this same stall. It was the only angle from which he could spy the inner sanctum where Tala and the boy had gone. A single step to the left and he would only see the crab stall in front of him; a single step to the right and the women disappeared into the alley. Every now and then a crab leg extended into the air, its claw pinching, covering a portion of the scene he'd come to watch. At one point, it looked as if a crab had Tala's face in its claw.

The gravity accompanying the box coincided somehow with the woman's stare. He'd sensed its pull from that initial shock of red, like the sound of an alarm that makes everything around it fall into the background. He could almost feel the weight of it, light enough to hold because all it contained was breath, yet requiring strength, because surely it was the breath of the world passing between the women's hands. And then there was the woman's look—the look that moments afterward produced the box, the look that latched on to him as she held it, as she offered it to his wife with knowing whispers. He knew that the look, the box, and its transfer concerned him. It concerned him and yet he was only in the background, an obscure piece of something larger and possibly infinite. He thought of two mirrors facing each other, the way an object between them multiplies endlessly in their reflections. He likened the pocket of space between pole and tub to a shard of glass reflecting back to the box, one among countless pockets of space, overlapping pockets that were really just shards. Mirrors facing mirrors reflecting infinite replicas of every person and thing, of the red box in between.

"Crab legs, mister?" the man behind the stall asked. He offered a large crab, holding it by the belly with his silver tongs, its eight legs spreading, its claws snapping open and shut.

Manolo refused. He felt like he was sleepwalking. It was the only way to explain the surreal shift the afternoon's walk had taken. Even the sun's rays felt different. He felt it then, the life of it burning in his blood. But the heat was commonplace enough. Manolo looked around and could've sworn he could see the sun, too. Everywhere. Illuminating faces, fruit, clothing, the white belly of a crab, silver tongs, eyes, looks, shards.

His knees almost buckled, ready to collapse under the weight of time accumulating into a single moment in a single afternoon. But Tala changed its direction, kissing the woman at the stall and collecting herself to leave. She was heading home. He needed to get there first, to make believe he'd never followed her. Dropping the cane in his hand, he mustered the energy to run, escape the trickle of sand made of fine crushed glass that threatened to consume him.

AFTERWARD, HE PRETENDED NOT to notice the red box currently propped up on Tala's dresser. He walked past it a few times each day, feeling the geometry of his motion across the room, made up of straight lines that connected him to the box at different angles. As he crossed the room he recalled the woman's face at the market and the look she gave him when she handed the box to his wife. He imagined the wail of an alarm, a register so low you could see it more than hear it, the entire horizon shifting slightly to the left, perceptible only when the fragment of earth you stood on caught up in alignment.

Before falling asleep at night he calculated possibilities. One night he pondered the hidden virtues or vices a box—any box—could contain. The most innocent facade, one decorated with flowers or smiling faces, could stow the vile remnants of a crime—the fine powder of a victim's bones, a rich widow's stolen jewelry. The possibilities only multiplied. He pictured something easily overlooked—a box made of cardboard, its edges thin with age or use, the corners torn. The kind of box you find in the trash bin, or one stored underneath the bed, containing forgotten greeting cards that will be thrown out in another year. But the same box could just as easily be the one preserving a lifetime of savings or harboring the letters from a friend no one knows about, the friend most cherished. Appearances, he realized, give no indication of what's contained within.

Because how could one tell from the outside, he pondered the next night, so absorbed in his questions he barely moved, and because his eyes were closed Tala probably thought he'd fallen asleep long before she did. Whatever their shape or size, boxes shared one thing: a perfectly enclosed space, protected on all sides and shielded from view. The perfect place to keep a secret. He remembered his own secret, continually returned to that dark corner behind the closet wall. Tala's wings removed, leaving the skin behind her shoulder blades bare and smooth. As she slept he touched her there, lightly so as not to wake her. He did not feel any scars or broken skin, just her softness and the bones beneath, fragile, like his own.

A few nights later he remembered a client with an asthmatic son. Her home overlooked the ocean and smelled of sea mist and boiled lobster. She stood out in his memory then because of the boxes she collected. The smallest were pillboxes that adorned her shelves along with her books and vases. These varied from the size of a thumbnail to no bigger than the center of a woman's palm. They were beautifully detailed, designed to give the illusion that swallowing medicine was enjoyable, even luxurious. Larger boxes were neatly arranged on top of the piano and above the fireplace, where they were stacked in twos and threes. On her bathroom counter, she had arranged straw boxes, each of them hand painted. On the coffee table, a box shaped like a treasure chest sat beside a glass tray filled with smooth white rocks. Beside the treasure chest was a wooden fish, its eyes, scales, and fin carved by hand. He didn't know that the fish was also a box until his third or fourth visit, when he picked it up to examine it, inhaling its odor of salty wood. He'd found that the tail and the head separated upon contact, unlocking two different compartments.

He tried to remember what the fish box contained. Most likely nothing, and the box itself captivated his memory because of the deception that was at once its virtue. He'd always enjoyed visiting the asthmatic boy because all the boxes under one roof lent the same effect as visiting a museum. He liked the variety in their craftsmanship. But in the aftermath of looks and alarms, the allure of that home overlooking the ocean began to expand. The boxes became like stars out of which he could form constellations. He'd always believed they were empty. Now he conjectured every one contained something unique. Or perhaps the full and the empty rotated, and the contents changed according to the day or week. How did the box collector keep track of the system? He attempted to categorize the organization of the boxes, first by size, then by the material with which they were made, but wood and silver, ceramic and glass mingled.

As he twisted about, rumpling the sheets, he attempted to permeate this mystery, relying on a diaphanous film of memory. The home overlooking the sea grew more and more abstract. Like the wooden fish, everything in it was a container in disguise, one with multiple uses. He imagined the books on the shelf as locked cases, the pictures on the wall as openings to safes, the cushions on the sofa as soft, zippered purses. A countertop could open up to a hidden storage bin, perhaps to a staircase leading to an unseen chamber. The house itself, with its walls, roof, and floors, was one big box, its interior blocked by curtains or shutters, by a layer of paint, peeling to reveal a different color underneath, by the sprawling limbs of a tree, intentionally planted to guard the front lawn, all of it designed to keep the structure intact, preserving something essential, akin to sleep or sustenance, the necessity to breathe unseen, dream unseen, exist within the unguarded sphere of oneself, unseen. The fruit of this interior was inaccessible to a simple observer—it required breaking into.

During the day, Manolo sulked in these long, reflective silences, and like a man with a grudge, he didn't clue Tala in on his thoughts. He chose quiet over her company, and because his mood was contagious, she brooded along with him. He did not mean to punish her. He simply felt the distance between them and could not determine which one of them had put it there. He was no longer following her on the path, but somehow, he still felt like he was several paces behind her, struggling to catch up. Somehow, all of it was tied up in the business of the box.

He pondered over it further the next night, until he could not stop tossing beneath the covers and squinting across the dark for some unknown beacon. He saw only shadows, and in his fatigue the darkness was soothing, becoming the beacon he sought, a blanket covering the world so he could finally rest. Since Tala had brought the box home less than a week before, his mind had been filled with static, bewitched with the idea that he'd grasped some alternate vision, and in the dark he likened himself to a blind insect walking through the world with antennae pressed to the ground, listening. He could not see in the dark or hear vibrations in the elements, but he imagined he saw lines and reflections jutting from every surface, connecting everything to everything else.

By day, nothing within his sight appeared in isolation. Even the stones in the path were projections, moved by ordinary forces in constant interaction. They were kicked or picked up, thrown, and dropped, and each day the path looked different because of their movement. He got a peculiar notion that if he imagined their journey, the journey of the stones, he'd find answers to Tala's secrets. Tala, who he'd spied with her sisters along the riverbed, who had friends on the outskirts of the barrio: a boy who held her hand as if she belonged to him, a tomboy albularyo in a market stall who gave away looks and boxes. And she hadn't shared any of it with him. What more was she hiding? He prided himself in being a simple man, believed it should be in these details, the simplest of details, that a husband and wife could say with confidence, "I know all about it." Manolo could not say that about Tala, not even close, and without that ability, he felt slighted as a husband, married to a foreign object. Were those nights at the river even real?

Tala came forward on an afternoon when he felt too tired to work a full day, his mind preoccupied with a sense of defeat. The defeat took the form of a hole, of shapeless space, a threatening distance between him and Tala from which anything could spring to tear them apart. The chasm seemed to have grown over a distance of months, but in reality his slump had only lasted a matter of days.

When he got home that afternoon, all he wanted to do was get undressed and drink something cold. His parents were still out for the day, visiting Little Roland, who lived in a province nearby. The first person he saw was Old Luchie, who lay slumped into the sofa, drooling in her sleep. He wondered if the maid had lifted a finger all day. He headed to the kitchen, poured himself some iced tea, and went straight into the bedroom to read the paper. That was when Tala approached him with the box.

"Promise not to open it," she said.

It was the red of an organ, so close he could sense it pumping against her skin. Ancient symbols were carved around the perimeter, a patterned code, perhaps the very one he'd sensed, barely grazing with his fingertips along some outer edge, but never penetrating.

"There's a surprise in here for you," she continued. "But it's not ready yet. Promise you won't spoil the surprise?"

His attention jumped from the box to his wife. Her skin, so smooth it was luminous. Her hair, parted in the middle and dangling in soft waves over her cheeks. Then, the darks of her eyes; he saw in them two swirling pools where everything sank and disappeared—except for him. Two of him: identical twins outlined in light. He felt comforted by her physical closeness, and something in him lightened. Tala was perfection itself. She did not go to the albularyo for herbs and hokey medicine; she had no flaws that needed fixing. He knew somehow, the box was filled with some other magic. Something related to her wings and what he had seen at the river. She was finally including him in the mystery, unlocking some door to which the box was certainly a key. A part of him always believed she would, though it was a part of himself he regularly doubted.

"Don't bother me with surprises. I prefer to know what's coming." It was a gruff reply, he knew, though he said it jokingly. The alternative would have been to touch her, place his hand on the slimness of her wrist, pull her body toward his, kiss the corners of her lips before tasting their ripeness in full.

He could not deny the joy at seeing his wife brighten at their exchange. She knew him well enough to understand he was caving, that they had landed at the opening to reconciliation. Then came an unwelcome feeling, springing from a forgotten corner as if to intercept the onset of joy and propel it in another direction. He imagined her wings wilting behind the wall of the house, the feathers falling off in a heap, the slumped form like that of some dead carcass.

"In any case, I'll put the box on the living room shelf. No peeking. I'll know if you do," Tala said, seeming confident that the ice between them was broken.

"When I get you presents, I let you pick them out yourself. Then I know for sure you'll like them. I never understood surprises," he said. In spite of the guilt he wanted to smile, rebel against the gravity of his own concealed crime.

"This one you'll like. Like a good wife, I know what you like even more than you do." She seemed ready to go on talking about anything. He would not have been surprised if she'd

begun a conversation about sewing, dancing, or the pictur-
esque landscape of farms that enclosed their home. But he was
not in the mood for talking. Not yet. He drew her to him by the
small of her back.

"If you say so."

He wanted to confess. But first, he would try to make her
understand without words.

8. Road to a Landslide

FROM THE HIGHWAYS THAT joined at the base of the Ogtong Mountains, the road was born, a wide tongue of cement strong enough to carry the moving parts of cities. The highways would continue to faster, more crowded places, leaving the road to rise with the mountain's elevation, narrowing with the land's shrinking passageways, widening again through fertile valleys, and along the cliff's edges, leaving just enough space for the coming and the going to meet side by side.

The road passed busy strips of scattered towns, where stoplights slowed down traffic and neighborhoods sprawled in the backdrop of restaurants, shops, and churches. In between towns, the fields that fed them twinkled with sunlight and auspicious bursts of green, proving that the mountains were a living, bountiful force. Higher up, temperatures dropped significantly, and for long stretches of the road the driver would be alone with those voluptuous spirals, fearing their treachery or moved by their silence to reflect on the twists of fate.

After passing two small communities, miles of uncultivated land, several narrow turns overlooking rocky cliffs, with the bigger towns below visible in the far-off reaches, the road arrived at Manlapaz. It was not the final barrio on the route—

from there the road would continue on to the other side of the range, reaching remotely inhabited lands that would eventually swallow it whole.

It had survived countless storms, successive seasons of dry heat, lacerations from sharp rocks and heavy debris, the weight of a million vehicles, the heavier burden of loneliness, the chaos of music and voices arriving in a blur and just as quickly evaporating, the wearing grind of wind by night, the ceaseless beating of the sun by day. It had learned to outgrow the excitement of all things new and with time acquired the virtue of patience.

With the devastating earthquake of nearly a decade past (after which a tsunami had licked a mile of Ogtong's western coast bare), the road had also learned of ruin and the brighter consequences that unexpectedly follow. Six miles from Manlapaz, the mountain shook off a patch of its own dead skin, and the resulting landslide covered one of the road's narrowest passages—blocking in the inhabitants with an impenetrable wall that was the height and width of a small fortress.

After the quake, men and women busied themselves repairing torn roofs, sweeping up broken plates, and visiting from home to home to assess the damage and trade impressions about the tremor's strength and timing and the deep, unnerving roar that had preceded it. Several days passed before anyone noticed that the mail was late and the seafood trucks had failed yet again to arrive and someone thought to leave Manlapaz, only to learn that the mountain had closed upon itself.

Manolo and Dalaga's love had begun with the build-up of cars that appeared in a row behind the landslide, with the tents that rose to shelter the villagers driven to begin shoveling from the first sign of daylight. For such an undertaking, everyone came together, working carefully in the areas just beyond the active landslide's reach—women and children filled empty rice sacks with rocks the size of their fists, men teamed up in threes and fours to lift tenaciously clinging boulders. The farmers

brought their kalabaw from the fields to help pull and relocate heavy loads of soil. Even the teachers postponed regular
lessons to involve their classrooms in the character-building
activity of disaster relief. The barrio they'd temporarily left
behind began to resemble a ghost town as all other work came
to a halt. Shopkeepers brought their wares to the roadside—
hats and handkerchiefs for the sweaty brows, cold beers for
long breaks in between shoveling. Food vendors set up hot
frying pans over coals built into primitive stone pits at the side
of the road. Others carried slings filled with bags of roasted
peanuts, dried fruits, candies, pastries, and dried meats that
they hawked among the crowds that either worked, watched
the work, or entertained the workers and the watchers with
circus tricks, comedic acts, or one-man shows. So the road, a
transporter of temporary things, inspired a temporary city to
come to its rescue.

Manolo was one of the few who stayed behind during the
clearing, along with the elderly, new mothers and their sleeping
babes, shopkeepers who slept behind their counters because
their customers were off to clear the landslide, and others busy
preparing supplies or reinforcements for the workers who
returned dirty, hungry, and tired each evening. Home from
medical school and preparing for an exam, Manolo studied for
hours after Mother and Father left in the mornings with a car
full of neighbors to dislodge their city from isolation.

In the quiet of the daylight and the emptiness, his mind free
from the distractions of a complicated personal life, he was pro-
ductive, a veritable memorizing machine—until the patients
began to arrive. First it was a swollen foot, then a sprained ankle,
then a case of severe dehydration. They arrived by way of Pogi,
the town baker, who'd converted his van (normally used to
transport pan de sal, chocolate rolls, and mango cakes) into the
designated ambulance during the disaster effort. The first time
Pogi arrived on his doorstep, pushing a man doubled over in

pain in a rickety wheelchair, Manolo reminded him that he was not yet a doctor, but Pogi insisted that the barrio's only other doctor was busy with emergencies, and therefore, Manolo had been unanimously voted as the next one in line.

He began what he'd thereafter consider his first residency, learning with every cut he disinfected and every finger he bandaged how to enact the lessons his books had only illustrated in diagrams. Though Pogi only brought him the least severe cases, the interaction with these familiar locals taught him how to think and respond like a doctor. Many of these patients, whom he'd known since he was a boy and who felt like distant relatives, revealed a more vulnerable part of themselves once they were alone, so the simple tasks of wrapping gauze or taping a bandage felt intimate, and he performed them with the importance commanded and the concentration and finesse they expected. In return they updated him with news of the road and the work he did not get a chance to see firsthand. He learned that after weeks of effort, the road showed signs of clearing but the bulk of the landslide itself could hardly be chipped at, like a second mountain that would not be moved.

The men and women continued to bend their spines and maneuver their already-aching arms and legs in the heat, but when days passed and their efforts showed little promise, the work days became shorter and the nightly carousing with drink and dance among a dozen bonfires grew lengthier. As the barrio's supply of gauze and rubbing alcohol slowly disappeared, Manolo worried about their lack of self-sufficiency. The people of Manlapaz had been stranded in every sense of the word, with no choice but to clear their own rubble, rebuild their own houses, care for their injured, and little by little, shovel mounds of dirt from the one road that linked them to a tapestry of cities and towns leading to the capital's money, bulldozers, and stockpile of rice and medical supplies reserved for such emergencies. Would the government's bulldozers eat into the landslide and meet them halfway? More likely, they were too small to be bothered with, as good as forgotten and left to fend for themselves.

He worried about supplies, villagers succumbing to heat exhaustion in alarming numbers, and Manlapaz falling to pieces—until Dalaga came to him on a stretcher with her head held high, and the worry was replaced by a different emotion.

Palong's sister had never entered his mind outside the occasions he saw her. He had known her since childhood. While he and Palong had been busy trapping fighting spiders in jars and tying string around lizards' necks like leashes, she had been another little girl among dozens who filled the playgrounds and classrooms with the annoying wheedle that only a female voice could achieve. During the few years he'd been away in medical school, she had changed from the pesky little girl who tattled on her brother and expected her parents to spoil her. She was a woman now, in body as well as demeanor, with a chip on her shoulder to prove she was indeed all grown up and initiated into the better sex.

The men assisting Pogi set Dalaga down while she was still sitting up on her stretcher. By this time, the living room of the Lualhati home had been converted into a makeshift receiving room for patients, with plastic laminate over the sofa and a small table of regularly used medical supplies at the ready. Manolo had exchanged Mother's cloth-covered lamps for basic fluorescents and her colorful, hand-woven rugs for cheap mats, moving the decorative bowls and sofa cushions elsewhere. Rather than getting upset at her pretty living room turning into a drab hospital wing, Mother had been proud that her son was already performing the work of a respectable doctor. The men told Manolo he could find them right outside when he was finished with Dalaga's exam.

He said hello warmly, still addressing her as he would a school girl to mask his curiosity, but her greeting was cold—a dismissive smile from a face that said nothing, so instead of asking after Palong and her parents as he'd intended to do, he began to examine her arm, gently pressing between her shoulder and elbow, then between her elbow and wrist.

"How did you know it was my arm?" she asked, in so accusing a tone that for an instant, he thought he might've been mistaken.

"I'm a doctor. I can tell just by looking at you."

"That's a convenient excuse. You're not a doctor yet."

She went on to question his character—practicing medicine without a license, doing the patients he worked with more harm than good, and finally, his lack of presence at the worksite, "holing himself up with his books and his pillows while everyone else toiled in the heat." She seemed to believe he felt superior, and that the superiority was rooted years back when he first left the barrio to study medicine.

"You know only books and nothing of real life," she said, "Unlike my brother. I would consider him the nobler man between you."

At first he was offended, but at her vehemence his reaction changed from confusion to flattery at how strongly he moved her, and at how far back that partiality seemed to reach. He wanted to ask how she could convince three men to carry her on a stretcher for a dislocated elbow, but decided not to aggravate her all the more. Underneath the new and perfect breasts, she was still that pesky child—immature, hungry for approval, and too quick to judge. Besides, he was distracted—uncertain whether he could accurately perform the simple maneuver her situation required. He touched, fingers peeking through skin, at the displaced radius touching ulna, anterior band, and ligament, at muscle and tendon beside the connecting humerus. She was in evident discomfort and likely in immense pain, but made certain that her expression conveyed her disapproval.

He'd encountered somewhat difficult patients in recent

weeks—those whose smell filled him with disgust. A few overly modest personalities who made looking beneath the clothing feel dirty. Or the taciturn types who dragged the room down and made him feel disconnected from the world. Dalaga was the first who argued, from her first word—*how*—to the moment he snapped her elbow back into place and the loud crack of bone silenced them both. She remained quiet even as she panicked, as he crossed the lines of etiquette into the blurry cloud of childhood familiarity, where he held her close, shushed her, rocked her, cradled her head in his arms against the perfume of her sweat. Her breathing changed from quick gasps to slow breaths as she realized she felt no pain, and when the weight of fear left her body he reluctantly let go. She touched her elbow delicately and he moved her arm softly up, then down, feeling the layers beneath the skin with his fingers and announcing she was good as new. "You won't even need a sling," he said, his face an inch from hers. When she opened her mouth there were no more words, and Manolo fetched the men outside to retrieve her upon her stretcher.

The following day, Manolo set up his own tent at the work site—four canvas sheets held up by clotheslines, another on top, its corners woven around poles—altogether enclosing two small cots, a table with three chairs, a giant cooler, and two cardboard boxes heavy with supplies. He called himself an EMT. His immersion into the worksite was instant and fluid; like a drop of medicine, the welcome novelty of his presence spread outward, energizing the familiar faces around him with renewed hope. He saw that the barrio had been transplanted. Pogi's trusty van was set up beside a stand of freshly baked goods. Mother and Father's card table waited beneath an awning for their midday game. And everywhere people and animals moved about, the smells of food, earth, and sweat intermingled between rows that had formed between stands, and foot traffic moved steadily on the streets that separated their worksite into sections. The landslide itself was messier than it was impressive. It was a hectic first day, as every day afterward would be. He had many conversations, several with Palong, who did the work of five men and still found time to designate tasks, direct idle hands, and pep-talk complainers into action.

The two had been opposites from the start. Manolo had been the quieter, more serious one who obeyed the rules and sailed through pop quizzes. He'd never been a fast runner, but he was quick-thinking and could match wits when tested. Palong, who was as fast as he was coordinated, was always the first to be chosen on a team. With a strong, muscular physique and a baby face, he was an obvious favorite with the girls. He barely passed his classes, not from lack of intelligence but because of an uncontainable need to stay moving, jumping from one activity to the next, one idea to the next. In spite of his poor grades, Manolo had considered Palong an intellectual equal, and Palong was always coming up with ingenious adventures to prove him right.

With Manolo back at home, the two had planned to go back to their old hijinks, but the disaster site was the first where they'd gotten the opportunity to reunite. Palong checked in on him every few hours to trade jokes and false insults, and Manolo could hardly believe his disappointment in the company of his dearest compadre, when he could not stop wishing that Palong were someone else, with curvier legs, supple breasts, and a sexy pout permanently fixed to her lips. He suppressed the suffocating urge to ask Palong his sister's whereabouts. Toward sundown, as he packed up the boxes and folded the cots, she came finally, pouting even as she smiled. From that moment of relief and joy until the morning before a wedding that never took place, Dalaga and Manolo were inseparable. It would take him months to move on from the how to the why, to see that the road had always threatened to come between them. For her, it had been a way out, departure endlessly beckoning; for him, the road was a way back. As his peers from university left the islands one by one for better prospects of practicing medicine abroad, he'd kept his sights faithful and steady, always on the road and its promise of home.

9. Stowaway

THEY DECIDED TO TAKE a trip. Just the two of them, without Luchie snorting at Manolo's attempts to tell a joke or Andres's fussing after Tala as if she were a little child, still learning how to tie the sash on her dress. Without Iolana around to watch them from the corner of her eye, wordlessly critiquing their actions, letting the occasional long sigh or coy smile speak for her. Because it was tradition to share their home with family and hired help, the lovers did not feel resentful of their lack of privacy or seek to have it any other way. They only rebelled with the occasional trip. Lately, with their long hours behind locked doors, rambunctious tickle fights, and carefree teasing in all corners of the house, it was a good time to go.

The last time they had escaped was months before, on a day trip to a pineapple plantation a few hours north, with stops along the way to browse a small flea market and to lunch in a family restaurant on a farm, where the proprietors' kids provided entertainment with songs they had memorized from the radio. Manolo and Tala had sat on a sun-bleached picnic bench in the yard, the restaurant's sole customers, sharing a whole milkfish that they picked at with their fingers. The tomatoes mixed with onions and lightly doused in fish sauce were the juiciest they had tasted, and even the steamed rice seemed fluffier. As they ate, a row of clothes from a washline hung a few feet away, still heavy with dampness, with no wind to flutter them, and a couple of chickens bobbed about, occasionally weaving a crooked path between their legs. Water bags were propped to the tops of poles on either side of them, repelling the mosquitoes, and a row of ants crept along the ground in single file near one of the table legs. The green mountains appeared more distant on the horizon but ever-present, separated by miles and a misty vibration that was in fact the heat, causing Manolo to occasionally wipe the sweat from his brow with the bottom of his T-shirt.

The couple enjoyed their meal, eating slowly, chatting about the pleasant scenery, the little projects they'd left behind at home, and hopes for the future, which included visions of future children returning with them to this farm, climbing upon the table bench with their short, stubby legs, tugging at their shirt sleeves, or skipping joyfully to the adjacent field. They sat side by side, and every now and then, Tala leaned against Manolo's shoulder and he rested his cheek lightly against the side of her head. After finishing a little more than half of their meal, they saw that the children who'd been peeking in on them separately or in pairs emerged altogether in a group of five. Standing near to the clothesline, they began to sing. It was completely unexpected, comical, and sweet. How the two eldest sisters assembled the three younger siblings, how the youngest, a boy, kept wandering away, only to be herded back in line, and how in spite of the fidgeting among the younger siblings and the patient orchestrations of the two eldest girls, their combined voices ultimately found cohesion. Manolo gave Tala a wink as the performance began. She listened to the children's melody and nothing interfered with the purity of her joy.

Memories of such excursions were unscathed in Tala's mind as Manolo placed their bags in the car in preparation for a new adventure. Tala studied the familiar couple next door, who saw them off with a wave. "Don't get lost!" they joked from their porch.

"We'll try our hardest," Manolo replied from the driver's seat.

They seemed happy enough—Lasam with a beer in one hand and a beer belly to match, Lamata cooling herself with a green fan, her mouth slightly open in a half-smile. They had settled into middle age, bodies with a bit more sag, carried with an air of complacency.

"Will we be them in ten years?" she asked Manolo as they backed up into the gravel road.

"Our neighbors are like these mountains. They've always been here and they don't change. Ours is an active volcano. It won't go dormant for centuries."

Words like this from her husband's mouth pleased her. She agreed. In a sleepy country province, she would not choose the most ready story. Even for the child in her belly, still the size of her thumb, she hoped for more excitement. She almost revealed her pregnancy to Manolo then and there, but willed herself to wait. The time would have to be right. First she would fill the empty shelves of her past, shelves bolstering walls that defined houses that cut into streets of an expanding and voracious city. And they would be a real family, without secrets, simple as the neighbors on their porches, with fire to fuel their active volcanoes.

They stocked up on snacks at the sari sari store. The shopkeeper was in his early fifties, with a booming voice that could have made the canned goods on the shelves vibrate. He had crooked teeth and a wide smile to showcase them. His confident, personable demeanor went well with a strong build and upright posture, made all the more noticeable because of his leathery brown skin, hardened under the pressures of work, sun, and time. This was a man who provided for his family and earned the trust and respect of his customers. Tala liked this man, and yet, she would not choose to be the shopkeeper's daughter, someone who stocked shelves and filled out inventory slips, someone who went about her business without complication until she glimpsed the unassuming doctor from behind a row of cereal boxes. From that moment on, she would have sought the doctor's face every day she worked, looking up from her dry goods whenever a customer entered the store. And one day, she would catch Manolo's eye in return, but not before he had captured her whole heart.

"We could open up a clinic," she proposed after they'd returned to the car with armfuls of goodies. "While you treat the common cold and diagnose hyperthyroid cases on one side, I'll treat the broken heart and the plagued spirit on the other. Together we'll cure the whole person."

He could have asked her more then, about the woman at the albularyo stand, about her visits there. Had she been striving to help the barefoot kid at her side with the albularyo's medicines, which his struggling mother could not afford to buy? Did she herself nurse a "plagued spirit"? He remembered her at the riverbank—storms had come and gone inside of him before he'd summoned the nerve to speak to her.

They drove for hours, passing fields broken only by sky, watching the mountains scatter as they wound down to flatter ground, the road beneath them changing from narrow and pockmarked to wide and even. Houses multiplied in number; intersections emerged with potential detours. Eventually, the country road became a city street, which became a highway, and across the bay before them, tall buildings reached for the same sky the mountains of their Manlapaz had already kissed.

"Ma's palm wine used to get the whole province drunk," Manolo recalled. "If you're interested in nursing broken hearts or plagued spirits, it might be worth researching the tricks of the bottle."

A silly thought crossed her mind—of selling Iolana's palm wine from her sisters' booth, in shot-sized bottles, labeled as the remedy for shyness or reticence.

They drove into a thicker swarm of cars at the port of Tagarro Bay. With its big ships on the dock, islands in and of themselves, and its wide boardwalk dotted with shops and outdoor vendors, Tagarro Bay was a gathering place for stow-aways. She saw faces, bicycles with their baskets full, shoppers satisfied with their candies and parcels, seabirds perched on metal railings, the outline of ships, the twinkle of water, dirty napkins tossed alongside empty soda cans and Styrofoam trays, crowded benches, palm trees, a thousand pairs of moving legs from a thousand different places, low hedges and skinny trees, beggars with signs and near-empty cups, a puppet show dis-played from a cardboard theater, seabirds eating discarded food, and the smells of every object came together in a muggy stew that engulfed them immediately, swallowing their aroma of mountain and earth to season the stew all the more. With this view from her passenger window she decided she would not be the politician's daughter, suited up and keeping pace with her escort in high heels to meet a ship's captain or a high-ranking general. She would not be the young movie actress, driving by in a chauffeured car with tinted windows. She would not be the woman on stilts, face painted and head lost in a higher elevation. These were the fairy tales of others. She thought of who she wanted to be most, wife to Manolo and mother to their child, and she realized that every battle, even the most brutal, was fought for the simplest of freedoms.

"Look, Manolo," she said. "There are people from every part of the world and every background here in one place. If you could be part of someone's story, whose would it be?"

"Yours," he replied. "I'd be part of yours." He had parked

the car and they remained seated while he dangled the hand with his cigarette out the window, neither of them rushing to join the noise and madness of the crowds. His stare drank her in, the kind of look a man gives a woman when he anticipates making love to her, and receiving that look she smiled, the fine hairs on her arms standing on end as she recalled the last time he'd looked at her that way, the pleasures it had led to. She told him he was definitely the main character, a starring role in her story. She returned to window watching, and whenever she noticed a particular character, from the busy fisherman to the overzealous preacher, she pointed them out to Manolo, imagining their stories out loud as he listened.

Then she found him, a stick-figure type, elegantly thin, with an edginess that defied his body's elegance. Striking in his aloneness, he smoked in the middle of the plaza, watching the crowd as she watched the crowd. He seemed to meet her eyes through the blur of nameless faces in constant motion.

Manolo followed the direction of her stare to find a typical boardwalk scene unfolding, one with too many people on their disparate missions, none of them connected except for the fact that they had all shown up at the same place on the same day; but suddenly a pathway cleared and a silhouette emerged within it—another crowd-watcher at the other end of their gazes. For no more than a few seconds that slipped discreetly past him, they watched each other instead of the crowd, three observers with the universe bubbling in between them.

She was hungry and told Manolo so, so they disembarked toward the seafood stands for the shrimp fry that she craved. As he ventured toward a suitable vendor, she pointed to the benches where she would go to find him and went to meet her phantom. To learn his story, and hers. Before her eyes the city began to rise up—not downtown Tagarro Bay, with its looming skyscrapers and discreet alleys zigzagging behind the big ships, but the one she had built in its shadow.

10. Out of the Lonely Sky

FATHER HAD DEVELOPED A strange, new habit of patting him on the back. As they met in the hallway, Manolo on the way to the washroom with a fresh towel over his shoulder, Father leaving the washroom with minty breath—pat, pat, pat, pat. As they met in the kitchen, Manolo coming in to brew a pot of coffee, Father searching the refrigerator for the remainder of the condensed milk—pat, pat, pat, pat. As they met in the yard, Manolo to do the watering and Father getting up from his favorite shady nook—pat, pat, pat, pat, pat. Sometimes, the pats would sneak up on him after a casual conversation. Like yesterday, when they had stood together in the yard after merienda, and Father wished out loud for a comfortable spot on which to nap outside. After chatting for some time about the possibilities of a hammock—what type they might purchase and where they would hang it—Manolo had momentarily forgotten Father's recent affection, until he turned back toward the house and—pat, pat, and pat.

"What's the meaning of all this?" he'd asked then and there.

But Father mistook his question and walked away feeling a bit offended.

"If you're not a fan of hammocks, you should've just said so in the first place."

This wasn't the only suspicious behavior sprouting about the place. The other day, Manolo had found Mother and Luchie talking animatedly in the hallway, only to stop their chatter once he entered their sight. "Carry on," he'd invited them, but this only incited silence and expressions of exaggerated innocence, which caused him to think the two women ridiculous, if only because he wasn't in on their little secret.

Tala, too, was off somewhat. She had returned with him from their trip to Tagarro Bay, only to settle into a more reticent mood—reticent as well as distracted, staring for long moments at the contents of her closet when she was getting dressed, stirring her tea into a cup-sized whirlpool, and spending much more time in the bath, as evidenced by the wrinkles on her fingers and toes when she emerged.

So at the end of the week, when he came out of his office with his last patient for the day, bidding her a good weekend and accepting her gift (a bag of ripe figs from her fruit tree) as he walked her to the front door, he was relieved to find his parents setting up the card tables. They opened two portable tables and placed them side by side on the outdoor patio next to the sliding door that separated their dining area from the backyard. Whenever they had the family or neighbors over for mah-jongg or cards, something they'd done since he was a boy, Manolo felt comfortably fixed in the routines of home, as if all things were as they should be. And a bit of normalcy was just what he needed.

Around those parts, they said gambling was in the blood— you either navigated toward the weekly circle of card addicts who frequented living rooms and back patios, placed your bets at the raucous cockfighting arenas, or waited hopefully for your numbers to be called at the church-sponsored Bingo nights; or you turned your face away, believing gambling to be a complete waste of time and money, something reserved for the idlers and miscreants.

As a young boy, Manolo had always enjoyed the nights that uncles, aunts, or neighbors came over to gamble with their coins and bills stacked impressively on the table. He would sit on Father's lap, listening to his elders talk, and they often forgot he was there. They spoke of frightening but magical creatures—half-human, half-demon beings who came out after dark, preying on passengers in the lone pickup truck rumbling down the country road or the foolish wanderers exploring moon-drenched nooks. He found out about the family friend who'd become possessed by the duwende, the pregnant neighbor who'd lost a baby to the aswang, the landowner who'd become rich because the diwata favored him, reading his dreams as he slept beneath the shade of her tree.

This eavesdropping was also the way he learned of infidelity and its dirty trail of temptation and humiliation. He learned of cheating neighbors and scandalized husbands. When they thought him too young to remember or understand, the drunken neighbors had turned to him and insisted he find a nice, simple girl when he grew up—the less attractive, the better. *Not a whore, Manolo. Oh, but you can never tell! Please, you can always tell, even the quiet whores say how much they want it with their eyes.*

The gamblers often spoke of their children, who had won what prize in school or had narrowly escaped a coma falling off a coconut tree. But mostly, it was about how deep the hurt could be when a child was left disappointed, or when a child did the disappointing. The elders had consistent dreams for their kids' futures—visions of movie stars, doctors, nurses, ambassadors, and scientists circled the table. They had no aspirations for their children in local government; the system would swallow even their giant, unspoiled hearts, wringing out the compassion for anyone beyond a numbered few. They had seen this happen far too many times to believe it could turn out differently.

Manolo had ascertained early on that his parents' moods brightened on these nights as did his own spirits, and for a long time they believed he was one of those born gamblers, addicted from the start. But the game itself did not appeal to him. He'd meandered to his Father's lap because he enjoyed watching the concentration on the players' faces and hearing their jovial conversation, peppered with hopes, sorrows, disappointments, and desires—feelings his parents didn't speak of with him when they were by themselves.

On this night, four couples—Camcam and Hildo, Lourdes and Jing-Jing, Lasam and Lamata, and Mother and Father— came together on the patio, filling their yard with laughter and regular sprinkles of cigarette ash. By this time the sky was a deep and mysterious blue, with hints of stars already winking mischievously. Nearby, other neighbors had assembled outdoors as well, taking advantage of the night air to sing drunken and euphoric songs accompanied by a clumsy guitar melody. Camcam and Hildo's dog had followed them over and was busy sniffing the tree trunks in their yard and spraying them with whatever drops he could muster from his aged bladder. Every now and then, Hildo would lose a promising hand and drop his cards onto the table with a loud exclamation—"Pu tang!"—and the dog would react to his master's voice, jaunting over at a slow but determined speed to sit beside Hildo's legs until he felt assured that all was once again right. Like her husband, Camcam was a competitive player, though more quietly so, muttering sly warnings each time she picked up a new card. "Ah! I've got this one now. . . ." Lourdes and Jing-Jing took turns playing, watching, scolding, and rooting the other on when they weren't in charge of a hand. They laughed at the same time or shook their heads simultaneously, depending on the numbers, shapes, and colors they conspired with. Their hosts, Mother and Father, kept the mood easy and welcoming, with coffee brewed and palm wine at the ready should their tastes change to something a bit looser. They sat with their chairs touching, Father chuckling happily at regular intervals and Mother getting up to fetch snacks from the kitchen when their bowls needed refilling.

Far beyond the age of sitting on his father's lap, Manolo sat with his wife in the garden encircled by flowering shrubs and bordered by tall trees, where their blanket was within earshot of Hildo's curse words and the high pitch of Mother's occasional laughter. Every now and then, the visiting dog would amble into their enclosure, sniff their feet, and be off once more.

Reclined with her on the blanket and watching the sky's hue deepen, Manolo thought back to his childhood and its night sounds, the gambling voices and the crickets, coins tinkling into a pile at the center of a table and oil popping on the frying pan. It was a comfortable and carefree time, but he remembered those nights he had gone to bed with a tight feeling in his chest. He would shut his eyes harder then, as if this might make the feeling pass, and the darkness would engulf him all around, an infinite gaping mouth into which he would endlessly fall alone. Sometimes, for comfort, he would escape to his parents' bed, safe with their protective bodies breathing warm beside him. And the tightness would either return or go away, making way for sleep. As he got older, he found the tightness never failed to come back, sometimes after a very long interval, sometimes sooner, and he came to know this feeling had a name—sadness. Being an only child meant having the occasional, inevitable loneliness, but even when he spent time with Palong, who was like a brother to him, or went off to university, surrounded by the distracting habits of peers his own age, including those he liked and respected, the feeling still returned habitually, like the smell of that gaping endless mouth in the dark. He waited for a remedy, and like most young men he believed it would come in the shape of a beautiful woman.

That beautiful woman had come, only to bring him more sorrow, that which had a source and a motive, unlike the sadness of his childhood, which was the color of space, of innocence waiting to be filled. In spite of his hurt, he'd appreciated learning the difference at last, between the waiting and the knowing, and when he became a doctor he understood even more that such emotions couldn't be left in the hands of medicine and that even the least pleasant ones, those thrusting hearts into darkness, should not be numbed but entered into, with the body as well as the mind, sprawling in that stifling endless space, so as to find a way through the dark that always comes and goes.

He watched the night sky, knowing its coming and going. This fluctuation was life. Those enormous colors, truth. Tala, beside him, was still. She was not the first beautiful woman in his life, but she was the first to make it here, into the sounds of his childhood, beside the boy completely at home among the gamblers' stories and heartbreak. Together they had their own quiet circle of comfort in the dark. She was family to him now, closer to him than anyone and more beloved, and yet, it was still possible to lie side by side and feel the ghostly scratch of loneliness, like an animal trapped in the depths of the earth. The sky was dark now and infinite, and he knew this would never change, that every one of us contains a depth that could never be seen or reached by another person.

"Even the beauty of the stars can't compare to family," Tala said, still gazing heavenward. As though she were reading his mind, or perhaps because the vastness of the cosmos inspired similar thoughts, Tala told him she had been thinking of the dark and lonely places from which she had come. "You've brought me into your home, and now your family is mine." Her words and tone were full of gratitude, and love. She placed his hand on her belly. "And now, we're starting a family of our own. Manolo, I'm pregnant."

Manolo felt tall enough to leap into the kapre's tree, for the first time past the giant's kneecap, above his waist and shoulders, the sinuous veins of his neck, and the malodorous stench of his breath. He stood on the giant's nose, eye to eye, sharing a whiff of the kapre's ever-present cigar. His view of the stars was endless. This infinity took his words, demanding quiet and reverence, then glory. He lifted Tala up and whisked her gleefully through the air. They would have a party, he exclaimed, invite the whole barrio, summon Little Roland two days in advance to roast the finest pig, busy five women in the kitchen to cook an endless feast. He led Tala by the hand to the circle of gamblers—the four couples, including Mother and Father, with their expectant faces, shiny under the moon and all their hopes for the future.

When he made the announcement, there was general applause, followed by the distant clapping of some neighbors, who joined in the applause for the sake of congratulating, without knowing who or what they were congratulating. There was a yelping and whooping through the night, and everyone knew that something good was alive in the Lualhati home. Mother beamed and Camcam bounced giddily in her chair, a different woman from the serious gambler determined to win. News of a baby brought people together. Father stood up in his chair and placed a hand on Manolo's arm. With the other hand—pat, pat, pat, pat—a gentle warmth and signification of pride. Manolo laughed heartily, finally understanding the meaning of that gesture—his father and the women had discovered the news before he had.

Later, in bed, they were too excited to sleep. During their ramblings, Tala spoke of Inday, a woman who wove miraculous figures out of banana leaves, and her son, Baitan, a boy with a heart of gold, who had nothing. It was the first time she'd mentioned either of their names.

Following this confidence, he decided to ask Tala about the albularyo, recalling his wife's relaxed body language in the albularyo's stall as they exchanged conversation and a little red box.

"Speaking of the market," he said casually, "it's easy to get wind of what people are saying, even when you're not sticking your ears out. Have you been visiting regularly with an albularyo?"

"Why would I? I don't believe in such witchcraft," she lied.

11. Possessor of Fortunes

"Do you see him?" Iolana asked her husband. She held the curtain to one side and hid herself behind it, standing sideways like a curious, peeking bird. Andres walked directly to the window and looked out.

"He's gone. But what's the worry? He's as thin as a reed. If he shows up again in his Captain Suave sunglasses, Luchie will blow him over to the other side of town with a few waves of her fan, and that'll be that."

Luchie rocked evenly on the chair, fanning herself and yawning. She picked at the little hairs protruding from the mole on her chin. She had not seen the mysterious thin-man lurking around the neighborhood. She certainly had a bad feeling about it all, but the most she did was wrinkle her brow, frown, and pick at her mole hairs. And besides, no one had asked for her opinion.

"Should we tell Manolo?" Iolana asked. She'd released the curtain and now pushed it open again just a crack, peering through it with one eye.

"Why worry him? Knowing him, he'll stop working to keep a lookout here, and then we'll all starve," retorted Andres.

Luchie suspected that something strange and unnatural was afloat. Prior to the pregnancy, there had been the gossip. Intrigued by its scent, Luchie followed it to its source: a bitter old man with a loose and biting tongue, who'd somehow come to resemble the candles that he made for a living.

The nosy candlemaker was the type who enjoyed suffering, as long as it wasn't his. She herself had wriggled in discomfort under this man's scrutiny. He watched every customer who visited the albularyo's booth across the way, as if that were his business and the candles were a side job. Then he'd yammer on with the basketweaver in the booth next door about the way their faces changed, from tragic to hopeful, depending on whether they were coming or going. The regulars would be his favorite, those whose faces were nearly always tragic, whose remedies were sought and taken in vain. He dedicated most of his time to them, to their sorry fortunes and wayward lives, connecting them in some way to everything wrong in the world. Sometimes, these same customers visited his booth for candles or incense, and surely then, he'd try to find out more. About where they lived and with whom, and he'd change his theories to match.

Now the basketweaver also loved gossip, but only after announcing himself as the kind of man who minded his own business. He kept his head immersed in work like an honest man, he'd say, even when the customers were scarce. Even so, he relished the candlemaker's nosy speculations more than he admitted. Luchie knew this because he'd tell his wife every detail of it that same night. *The candlemaker said this and the candlemaker said that, and what a character that candlemaker is, but you know, he's got a point about so-and-so.* Then he'd add his own theories, even about the pretty girl who came by the market a few times a week. He didn't agree with the candlemaker that she was married to a seaside toad, he told his wife. It must be some kind of prince that she went to all that trouble for.

The basketweaver's wife was Lourdes's sister. *My husband is a man who minds his own business,* she'd say first, to either Lourdes or to her cousin, who was also Camcam's husband. With this tribute to the basketweaver's good name she passed the gossip on to the neighbors who lived on Manolo's street.

So it didn't take long for news from that not-so-anonymous market corner to reach Luchie's willing ears, then for the speculations to begin traveling both ways, until theories, then conclusions formed in the shape of Tala. She was in fact the pretty girl who went to the marketplace to visit regularly with the unpopular albularyo. No one trusted an albularyo who spoke so little, who got to the point without so much as a prelude, not like others of her kind with nothing but talk for as long as you had the money to listen. And with this woman, they were seldom the words one came to hear.

More than that, Tala's visits with her were rumored to be long, so long the neighbors joked Manolo would go bankrupt while his wife tried to fix whatever was wrong with him.

But Luchie was not silly enough to accept the sour end of gossip, when curiosity changed to malice. She did the math, and in the end agreed with Iolana. Iolana, too, ignored this line of gossip and dared not let Andres's pride be wounded by hearing condescending rumors about their son. Tala was not unlucky in love; she and Manolo adored each other in equal measure. She did not have prematurely thinning hair or pimples. Neither had she been bitten by a manananggal disguising itself, and its thirst for pregnant women, in an unsuspecting human form. She never displayed the ill health or excessive paleness of the bitten, and she was too level-headed to have been possessed by a duwende. But there was another reason why a young lady might visit an albularyo. Tala had simply been unlucky for too long, and she had been ready to conceive by whatever means necessary.

Luchie was convinced that no good could come from meddling with one's destiny. After working its powers, planting a seed in Tala's womb, the magic would waste no time demanding its due; it would take from Tala's life whatever was necessary to earn back the luck it had forged, or worse, make a profit, with Tala as the losing gambler.

After her last honeymoon with her husband, the girl spent much of her time nesting indoors, and Luchie compared the pregnant Tala to the smiling-smiling girl of a year before. She was a mother-to-be now, long past the stage of seeking her place in the home. Recently, while playing a game of Scrabble, she'd asked about Luchie's mother. Luchie could not tell her much. She'd been younger than Tala when her mother died. She could no longer tell which memories were real and which imagined. But she never did forget the feeling, that of losing everything joyful in the world. Like the seas draining, suddenly and frightfully, leaving an emptiness behind that would never be right.

"Losing a mother," Tala had replied, "is probably the saddest thing in the world."

"Not as sad as losing a child," Luchie said, wishing she did not have the misfortune of knowing this was true. Luchie's son was not dead—she had long been dead to him, a far worse predicament than the grave itself. Like many in his generation, he'd gone to school and immediately left the country for better opportunities abroad. With her son sending money like clockwork, she considered herself retired. She had lived and worked long enough, slaving away in other people's mess so her son could have a future. Her dedication to his schooling—ensuring he always had new clothes to wear to class, spending her bonus checks on his latest whims to keep him motivated—all of it had finally paid off. Then her son sent her a letter—he had found himself a woman and they were starting a family. She gasped at the idea of a grandchild. Any day, she expected a letter from her son proclaiming that her petition had gone through and that her plane ticket would be next to arrive. Instead, she never heard from him again.

Old enough to be Tala's grandmother, Luchie had enough experience to recognize that the mistress of the Lualhati household, in spite of her grown-up role, was still just a girl, bright but impulsive, well-intentioned but careless. She could not know that the decisions she made now would impact all her life, set the stage for every minute ahead of her. Meddling with dark forces she had no business meddling with, she would eventually have to contend with the consequences.

There was another reason Luchie was so convinced. It started when Tala, in her ravenous state, began stalking the kitchen to munch on dessert rolls or leftovers from the night before. When the rolls disappeared and the leftovers ran out, Tala would make an omelet with the last of the eggs, then search the refrigerator for tapioca pudding. She repeated this pattern throughout the day. In the process, she neglected the market for a week at a time, all the while consuming all the food in the house, mopping up the chicken salad with a loaf of bread, cutting up an avocado to ice in milk, or stir-frying vegetables between meals. She opened and closed cupboards and stared into the refrigerator for minutes at a time. Finally, when it seemed Tala might eat the refrigerator itself, Luchie grabbed her red cart and some money from the envelope Manolo kept for her in the drawer. She had long ago memorized the list of foods the couple kept in the house.

"If you happen to come across any tarot cake, I would adore that, my dear Luchie," Tala managed to yell out as Luchie rattled her old bones in preparation to leave.

Like most men, Manolo loved his meat, the pork bellies and beef tongues and slippery tripe. There were the habitual fruits and vegetables and canned goods Tala had grown into the habit of using. And then, Luchie liked to throw in little treats here and there to mix things up: plantains to fry, raw mangoes with salted shrimp, bagged pork skins to dip in vinegar.

Pulling her red cart behind her, Luchie moved at a steady, even pace, which others might have considered painfully slow. She was not young, and hurrying, she was sure, would only bring her closer to whatever unpleasantries awaited at the end of all the hurrying.

She could not remember why the curiosity hit her. The albularyo's booth was at the end of that short alley that she normally avoided. For years, she'd made it a point to keep her distance from the perverted candlemaker. Particularly after an incident, when his meddling had gone too far, far enough to ask her if she'd ever been touched by a man. Afterward she could only bear to come as close to his booth as the intersection, whenever she had the inkling to buy fresh crab.

That day, though, she'd given herself an excuse out loud, for her own benefit to hear: *I'll rub my nose into the nosy candlemaker's business for a change.* But her true intention was to satisfy a curiosity to see the notorious albularyo for herself. She already knew what to ask for: a moisturizing salve that could fill in her old lady wrinkles.

The air had been dry and seemed even drier as soon as she passed her feet across the threshold of that inconspicuous alley. An eerie wind rustled, sending the debris afloat from one dusty corner to the next. She greeted the basketweaver upon passing, heard the raspy sound of her own voice melt quickly into absence. He nodded in return like a statue version of himself. He did not know her, could not know that with the help of his chatty wife, she was acquainted with a handful of his bedside habits, none of them flattering.

The candlemaker was not around. But his booth was open, the candles lined up dutifully: tall, short, thin, fat, all of them lifeless. A plain young woman read a magazine behind the counter, looking up without a trace of enthusiasm in her bang-swept eyes. Luchie looked toward the albularyo's booth and saw she was there: alone, her face down, her long hair falling over her cheeks, obscuring her. Luchie walked closer. And the woman behind the counter looked up, waiting, then expectant, her posture straightening.

Luchie continued walking until the two of them were face to face, and then she gasped.

Tala herself was the albularyo.

Luchie muttered something about losing her way and walked off without waiting for a response.

From then on, the vision of Tala behind the albularyo's booth tugged like a distant, bad dream. Surely an omen for her to look ahead toward her next move, to whatever means the world might allow to keep her body fed and her feet warm. She weighed her options, considering which of her alternatives would be most merciful on an aging old woman. But then she shrugged it all off and sat back down on the rocking chair. What else was there to do? Like many things that seemed so convincing at first, the certainty of it began to fade. Luchie's own life was a metaphor for this fact, and she didn't need her fortune told to admit it. She never thought she'd end up alone. Now her solitary routine suited her like a comfortable pair of socks on a cold floor.

She would watch the household drama until it was time to go home or refill the cupboards. Today, that drama consisted of Iolana, Andres, and the question of the strange reappearing thin-man.

"It's odd," Iolana said. "Tala doesn't go out these days, gallivanting for flowers or what-not, and suddenly, this man starts coming around."

"And what does one have to do with the other?" Andres replied.

"There's always a connection, my dear husband. One just has to make sense of the dots."

"Well, our daughter-in-law is quite engaged with expecting our first grandchild. That's all I know. It's good she's settling down for a change."

"Wait, it's him. He's back, Andres, he's back!"

Luchie perked up in her chair and craned her neck to see, but Manolo's parents blocked the window.

"Well," she asked. "What is he doing? What does the thin-man want?"

When they didn't answer, Luchie stood up and wedged herself between them.

"But that's no man. That's just a boy," she said.

"Stranger number two, Luchie. Another dot to connect."

The boy had knobby knees, oversized clothing, and long, unwashed hair sweeping across a sun-brown forehead. He leaned toward the Lualhatis' front entrance, all of his energy devoted to the direction in which he leaned, though his feet were firmly planted. He saw them peering at him through the window, but seemed too timid to approach the front door.

"Susmaryjosep," Andres said. "This could last all day."

Andres went out front, with Iolana following close behind. Luchie kept her place at the window, where she could see and hear everything without having to look over a pair of meddlesome heads.

"Hoy, you there. Come here, child. Yes, closer, go on. Are you lost? Is everything okay?"

"I am Baitan, from the market. Is Tala here?"

"She's napping, son," Iolana said. "What is it?"

"Can you please tell her. A man has come to our mat, and to all the market stalls?"

"A man, son?"

"Yes, a man. He's looking for her. He says he's her brother. And can you tell her. The albularyos—they're all gone."

"All? Well, just how many of them were there?"

"They've disappeared and the stall is empty."

12. Shapes in the Water

THE BOATMAN ARRIVES BY the third sunrise, collecting lost souls stranded between worlds, shepherding them to the Land of the Dead. When she was not there to meet him, her sisters set up the market stall to watch over her in this new life. To us, this narrow market stall is in fact as wide as an ocean.

Tala herself closed the door to that infinite sea. She did not know that Dalisay, Imee, Ligaya, and her other sisters had been shut off with her, banding together against the fate she'd dealt them.

I did not wait long before she arrived with her husband, as I knew she would after the boy had delivered his warning. I invited them to the interior of the booth, sniffing the back of her neck and touching the hem of her skirt without their noticing. When they were seated, I sealed the back of the booth from view with a fresh white sheet substituting for a curtain.

Who am I? No one but a simple albularyo. One who can read this pregnant woman and her husband. A voice escaping a box, a voice escaping a dream. To many, I am no one.

I placed a bowl between them, with a rim as wide as a plate, filled with water and sprinkled with leaves. The wood-paneled walls around us were bare and aged, the spaces between the panels having widened over time, letting in the outdoor air. To me, there was no such thing as place in that moment, only distance and the illusion of time. In the back of the booth, the trinkets and bottles weren't visible, but their smells were everywhere. She had settled on bubble gum, he on mint, and I smelled the aroma of ten different flowers, all of them associated with the occasions in my life I've had the misfortune to grieve.

I did not speak. I sensed his anger growing in the bristling of his eyes, his resistance to wait in silence like a fool. But soon his eyes left my face and settled on the water swirling through the bowl. Its movement mesmerized him. It took shape, many shapes, a scalloped edge here and a thumb-sized dent there. Its variations were limitless. Reflections in the water began as specks of light, then came to resemble the hot sun in a pair of eyes, staring at him. He saw Imee's eyes, watching him. He sensed lobster claws snapping. He remembered Tala visiting with Imee, her relaxed gestures in the albularyo's company, the boy playing with marbles at her feet.

He had hoped to find answers by coming here with her today. But instead, he'd found me, with these wild, unbrushed curls framing my murky eyes, seeing him as if from a great distance. He saw that they are old eyes, and frightening, older than the face in which they are embedded. He questioned who Imee was, who I was. Would Tala ever tell him of her otherworldly life, the life he believes he stole? She was opening up to him about her past, filling in the details, but they included no wings, no sisters, no stars. He pondered how she could have a brother, an entire past in the slums of Tagarro Bay. He felt pain and fear, for her, and for himself. The thought of their child in her womb flickered in the water, cheering him. He squeezed Tala's hand.

Tala was lost in clouds that swirled throughout the interior of the bowl, in a familiar, soothing weightlessness. The clouds moved, parting for her underwater visions. A dream of colorful nightgowns and women splashing. A beautiful tree with no leaves. A mama who is not me, pointing at the branches, telling her to *look*, telling her to *run*. Manolo's face in the water. She felt the urge to dive in but was fastened to the ground.

And he saw the feathers falling from the sky like snow, his father pointing at the feathers, telling him to open his heart and *look*. He saw the maid sweeping away the feathers, his mother stroking the last from the ground with the tip of a finger. He understood the feathers were from Tala's wings, that Tala was gone.

She saw the little girl standing, so beautiful, so immensely beautiful, rooted to the ground, getting smaller and smaller, swallowed by a whirlpool she had no strength to control. She saw the little girl disappear, and her universe with her.

I passed a hand over the bowl to stop their meanderings. Others who knew only water asked those like me to look in for them, so that I could catch traces, mere reflections of their own eyes gazing. My daughter and her husband saw for themselves, without recognizing their own capacity. They'd already dismissed what they'd seen, looking to me for more.

Their visions had shown me more than I could ever show them. I mourned the waves already in motion against them. At the current they fought and the momentum it had gained. At the direction they'd chosen to swim. This losing struggle hurt me more, much more than her blindness to me.

I told her she was with child. My knowledge of this revelation pleased her, though a stranger could have guessed at the melon-sized bulge at her middle. I wished I could place my ear against her stomach, hear the drumbeat, listen to the spirit's rhythm. She wanted to know more. Her visions had shown me that the child would be a girl; I told her what I'd seen. She nodded eagerly, saying she'd known it all along. Her eyes grew larger as she touched her belly with affection. I reached into my pocket to give her a present—a barrette in the shape of a star. I told her it was for her daughter to wear, that it belonged to my daughter Ligaya, who would've wanted her to have it. She was content.

I turned to him. You thought you'd know me, I said, but you don't. She does not think she knows me, but she does. I turned to her and winked. He did not enjoy the game. I thought up clichés: accept things as they are, nothing's perfect, love conquers all. She smiled at each. I was proud of her, after all.

He stared. I stared back. He needed another. Forgiveness, I said, must start with one's self. His stare slackened.

It would have to be enough, for another fork in the water's path beckoned. Perhaps they, too, can help me, I said. I promised a free session in return for their indulgence. I described a jewelry box. In sum, it was one-of-a-kind, blood red in hue, an antique, with a key to lock its hidden treasures. A tragic loss. Did they happen to know of a good place to find one like it? He looked down. I chatted about our own personal possessions, the way they felt so very important, that this thing I'd lost contained the impossible to replace. But that I had to try. I asked them to forgive my dramatics, adding that if my own box fell into the wrong hands, it would feel like all mayhem breaking loose. I gazed at him intently, forcing him to look up, meet my eyes, and know this was no frivolity. The box could have the answer to many things, I added.

She told me she would give me one of her jewelry boxes to help me feel better. He had nothing to add. I thanked her for the gesture, insisting that she need not bother and offering her another trinket in return for her kindness. It was a gold-colored chain, with a heart-shaped pendant dangling from the links. I let my hands linger upon hers as I transferred the possession. I told her one day, she would remember who it came from. She would never forget, she said, she would never forget. But even the best of dreams can be forgotten like mist. The best of reality forsaken. And the most simple albularyo mistaken for a madwoman.

No room existed for us there, not anymore.

Part II

13. Playing at Life

WITHIN TWENTY-FOUR HOURS, NEWS of her brother's arrival had traveled from storefronts to kitchen tables to the steps of the square, and finally to the Lualhati home. He had asked after Tala at the fish market, the convenience store, the bus stop, the fabric stall—a tallish, lanky man who chain-smoked and reeked of stale beer, though he was never seen holding a bottle in his hand. The store owners, bus driver, shoppers, and afternoon amblers wondered aloud about this suspicious stranger, gossiping among one another after he had sauntered off, and once at home, they told their wives, husbands, sisters, or neighbors of the out-of-towner who looked something like the vampires portrayed on television, sickly and somber, but also intriguing, in a sinister sort of way.

They weren't afraid of him. What they felt was more like a morbid curiosity. Gossiping led to worry about the stranger's appearance, like that of someone up to no good, lurking around with no effort toward camaraderie, and sometimes, it circled back to his relationship to Tala, a reminder or a signal that she, too, was something of a mystery to them all, with a shady background that was finally catching up to her.

After their return from Tagarro Bay, Tala had felt aloof from the charms of the country, with its protective mountains, suspicious of lofty dreams, and the simple people with nothing to hide but always on the alert for another's secrets. It had taken her longer than usual to settle in to a routine, with most of her preoccupations revolving around the pregnancy, and once Manolo had learned of her condition, they dreamed of the baby together, imagining the weight of that bundle in their arms, brainstorming potential names, and already thinking of stocking shelves with diapers, angel-scented lotions, and neatly folded rows of clothing the size of a doll.

From this place of wonder and possessiveness of the future, news of her brother was a jolt from complacency, unwelcome, but necessary. She had been expecting him to come all along, and the dread of waiting was finally over. Up until recently she had never spoken her brother's name, nor of the dark apartment beside the alleys where she'd guarded her nose against the stench of days-old garbage and fresh urine. Since the instant she'd heard news of Charo, the walls rose up before her, a labyrinth of streets filled with people walking in every direction, all of them on a journey toward the center, where the meaning of all those intersections promised revelation, but more often than not, its realization was lost on some detour—a congested highway, with foot peddlers weaving through traffic; a stuffy bar, where another drink sufficed for the answer to the riddle; a fifteen-hour job, through which the journey was forgotten, a little more each day.

She revisited the dilapidated apartment within those rising walls, where her mother lay in the dark, immersed in the past, more and more forgetful of her health and her children each day. Her brother was the one who'd come home with the smell of cigarettes on his clothes and breath like gasoline fumes, who brought her to the bars to teach her lessons in life, of kitchen spills to clean and vomit to smear off the hallway floor, then, in the locked-up room with the six other girls, of carnal secrets, how to please or be crushed by another's pleasure, all the while remaining a virgin, with the highest price on her unspoiled sex.

Manolo had always believed Tala kept her silence about the past out of necessity, that she couldn't admit to being anything but ordinary, just as he was ordinary and their life together equally so. She crumpled her silhouette to fit the shape of a provincial wife with nothing spectacular gleaming from a distant time. Father had always warned him, "Be prepared to accept accountability for your past. It is bound to catch up with you." As a boy, he equated this with telling lies. If he lied about doing well on a test, finishing his dinner, or the places he visited with Palong, the lie would always catch up with him. So he learned to choose truth—or silence. He'd seen Tala, plastered his eyes to her like a child seeing color for the first time. Tala, with her six sisters, returning to the river night after night, departing in flights to the stars that had made him shrink with wonder. He'd chosen silence in regard to those visions, respecting in turn her silence about an existence before she called Manlapaz home. Could this existence have included a brother?

It took him days to summon enough courage—to drag aside the dusty overstuffed boxes in the closet, untouched for over a year, and reopen the hole in the back of the clinic wall. One night he'd had a dream, when he'd gone to that closet and torn it open once and for all. But fighting to reach the closet, he could hardly walk; each step demanded all his strength and will, yet the effort and sweat took him nowhere. He grabbed the walls for support along the way, pulling, dragging himself forward. At times, his legs felt numb, frozen, so that every movement seemed in vain. At other times, he could manage a shuffle, but even that required a flurry of movement that rewarded him with mere inches. By some strength of resolve, he brought himself into the clinic, not by walking, but by willing the distance to disappear. He whipped the closet door open, only to be blinded by an overpowering flash of light, flooding the room with too much brightness. The light burned through his eyes and set his cells on fire—he stumbled about in darkness and pain, reaching with helpless hands and knocking down his bookshelf and medical tray. He sought escape, freedom, relief, fumbling from the room through gaping space, more hopelessly than before.

When Manolo woke from this dream, his vision did not return. He blinked in darkness and screamed. By the time his mother came rushing to his side, where a groggy Tala sat up, attempting to soothe him, his eyesight had come back. Manolo got up immediately then, heading straight to his clinic and locking the door behind him, knowing his mother would be listening through it. After loosening some old nails and wrenching half of a stubborn board free, he looked but saw nothing but darkness through the crack. He reached in with one arm and moved his hand in the spaces behind the closet wall. The air within was cold and drafty, the surfaces he touched rough and uneven—until his fingers collided with a weightless, silky mass. Feathers, surely. A wing here . . . yes, and another beneath. And as yet, their softness! They existed there—still—and if light had a smell, that was the magic that escaped toward him then, without form, but with essence so bright it defied walls. He covered up the wall with the cracked board, knowing his work was messy and impatient. From there, brother or no brother, he would not doubt.

This brother hadn't shown up around the house since their return from Tagarro Bay. The old ones would know if he had, so faithful was their vigilance at the front window. Manolo wondered if perhaps he had decided to disappear for good, but Tala was sure he'd return, and then all their questions would be answered.

After dinner one evening, the darkness outside began to gather, and his parents retreated to the comfort of their bedroom. Luchie had left for home some hours before, taking along her red shopping cart stuffed with bags and her happy disdain. Tala and Manolo relaxed in the living room alone, their bellies full and their minds preoccupied. Around them, the house was orderly, too much so, with books stacked by a lamp on a corner table, the cushion on the rocking chair fluffed and faintly stained, the counters dusted and the slippers by the door lined up in a row.

He asked her why she no longer placed fresh flowers in pitchers around the house. Why she'd stopped walking the nearby paths or going to the market to shop and visit with the boy, Baitan, whom she'd recently spoken of in more detail. She had been occupying the majority of her days indoors, sewing blankets, bibs, and dresses for the baby. All of it was detailed with flowers, butterflies, or feminine colors. In Tagarro Bay, she'd been titillated by the bright cloth and exotic patterns from India, central Asia, and South America. Her latest creation was a basic dress with matching kerchief, patterned with pink elephants and diamonds against a deep, emerald green, inlaid with barely-visible flowers sewn in the same color as the background of the fabric. All that time and effort would be wasted, he'd told her, if they were to have a boy. But she insisted that she could feel the brush of long lashes against her womb, the tickle of soft hair, already grown thick, and the press of full, pink lips that could only belong to a girl.

She suggested walking that moment, when the sun had just retreated but the weather would still be hot enough to make them sweat. So they wandered, out of the house to wherever their footsteps led them. She wore the same dress she'd had on all day, with her slippers on over slightly dusty feet and her hair tied back to reveal a delicate pair of seashell earrings that had cost next to nothing. He observed her plainness in aspect, thinking her in league with the flower or the pearl, itself a thing of beauty that adornment with makeup or expensive clothing would only change, but not improve. And then her walk, the slightest bit hunched, only one arm swinging, somewhat awkward and off balance but ever youthful.

They contemplated walking in the direction of town to a little bar on the outskirts of the farmhouses, where they could order specialty cocktails, loosen up to some music, and share friendly conversation with familiar locals, but both preferred the opposite route, to mountain and trees and solitude, even if just for an hour before bed.

They found the river, its conspiratorial babble low to the ground, excitable and eerie, rising up in vapors that filled the overgrown nook where they'd met with the smell of dampness. At first they sat on the stone that resembled a bench with no legs, remembering how they'd done so not so many years before. "Did you lose something?" he asked with a sly smile on his face, and reposing this question, the first he'd ever asked her, led to a new way of remembering their earliest days. It was an avenue back to a beginning, even a beginning of their own invention. So they began to invent.

First they played exile, becoming two escapees from a former homeland that had cast them away as rebels. They pretended that the shore of pebbles by the river was their new beginning, an attempt to redefine home, with only each other to envision what that place might be. In jest, he stood on the rock and begged her forgiveness for stripping her of everything she once knew, and she pushed him from that platform, claiming herself as the mastermind, and him as the follower, until they wrestled into the water, tangled in embrace, wet and fully dressed, laughing at their silly game.

They played pioneer. The first explorers in a new land, drawn together to possibility. He reached down to inspect the virgin sand, feeling its texture and potential, trying not to laugh as he invented the names of the vegetables they would grow. At this, she brought him foliage from the trees with exaggerated seriousness, and they sniffed the leaves to guess the type of fruit it would later bear. Definitions along this shore did not exist, and they would not create them, the very thing they'd come to escape. The way of living here would simply come to pass each day, like a polite introduction, so that in another era, these ways could just as easily excuse themselves to make room for others. As they played pioneers turned philosophers, they used the long, flat stone as a pillow and looked up at the stars. Then he touched her round belly and she remembered what she never forgot. She felt happy to be out of the house, here by this river, anywhere, with her husband beside her, the same husband with whom she laughed and played and fought. The layers of complexity around them, the shadows and shapes and their meanings that stripped simplicity of itself—all of this fell away as they dreamed of the wide-open world their daughter would grow up in.

Then the onset of weariness threatened, and they agreed to play just one more game. They would be ghosts. They could've gone anywhere with the idea, they agreed it was the perfect blank slate and the silliest notion yet and they couldn't remember which of them thought of it first. And maybe it was because the depth of quiet had slowly trickled in to engulf them or the thought of being out so late made them lonely for home, but before they even started to pretend, his stomach felt uneasy, and she knew it wasn't the cool fabric of a still-wet dress against her skin that made her begin to shiver. They recalled simultaneously how that part of the river was believed to be haunted—the superstition had been deeply ingrained in the region for decades—so powerfully that no one ever dared to wander there. Except for them. Perhaps they were just appari-tions, clinging one to the other, playing at life.

"Manolo, let's go home."

Glimpsing up at the treetops, he envisioned himself propped up on those branches without her knowing. He felt the guilt pulse through him for a brief undulation of time, but the joy of walking home with her far outweighed the threat of past actions and their repercussions. Besides, they had bigger problems now, as vast as the city of Tagarro Bay and all its untold stories.

"Let's go."

As they walked they heard a rustle, then another—footsteps not their own. Something approached, whistling lightly and weaving through the thickness of trees. They froze together as it took form, their heartbeats clamoring in their throats—he couldn't believe all the wives' tales could be true. But some skeletal figure, then a face and dark, deep-set eyes manifested before them—an actual ghost, no, a bal-bal and eater of the dead.

His wife unthawed beside him.

"Charo," she said, taking no step forward or back.

14. They Disappear

ALL RITUALS ARE BROKEN, even those of the ages. Continents change their shape; the moon inspires peace, then bloodshed, then love beneath its glow. A people with many gods, like Malakas of strength, Maganda of beauty, and Bathala above them both, forgets their idols, depleting them of strength, raising up crosses to a new divinity. A husband and a wife turn away from their vows, abandoning their marital bed, each losing the taste for the other's body. Even animals will stray from centuries of instinct, leading to the end of their species or the evolution of a new breed.

When these rituals disappear, like water from a spent river, their markings are left on the sand bank, evidence of their passing through the thickness of time. Those who remember make stories from the river's impressions, and the stories give the rituals fresh life, born anew with each retelling—another kiss from a forsaken lover, another bow to the god of strength or the goddess of beauty, another howl for revenge beneath a high full moon. The stories themselves change shape, passing through many mouths, forming alternate impressions. Some become children, born into life, a cultural gene and ritual offspring; others become fairy tales—the exotic and wistful yearning of those who no longer remember and never believed, except in some distant realm of the imagination.

Before the seven sisters seeped into this abstract world of the what-ifs and the never-were, they made a series of distinct impressions, years of silhouettes cemented into countless moist-eyed witnesses who stumbled upon humid nocturnal visions. There was the married farmer, rushing to the field to harvest the generous fruits of his lover. She was not a young and innocent, wide-eyed beauty—she was older than his tender-aged wife. Widowed and experienced in bed, her body pliable and responsive to his touch, she showed him the strength of his body's vibrations when matched with her own unhindered release. On his way to meet her, the eager farmer saw the sisters for the first time—first a light from a shooting star, colossal as a falling planet. Followed by another, then another, remarkable enough to stop the lustful visions that had possessed him since dawn. By the fourth star, time had slowed, enough for him to see a woman's shape diving into a cluster of darkness beyond the open field, enough for him to wonder if the fall of women would go on to eternity, if it had in fact, been raining this way for all time.

There was the woman living alone at the edge of a long brown fence that bordered one side of her entire neighborhood, the woman they'd labeled an "old maid," all day sewing dresses for her long visit to death's house, when she would be the most polite visitor of all, pleasantly at home, never once complaining about the draft or the dirty spoon. She had never been bitter or beautiful, was rarely happy or unsatisfied—she'd walked always on a straight line in one direction, expecting no more or less than to be, and one night she decided to walk out of bed and out her front door in house slippers, slippers that soon grew wet, then soggy, then muddy as she stepped across night slugs in the dark alleys and animal feces in the fertile grasses, realizing after a time that she had made it finally to the other side of that long brown fence, feeling night air on her skin, hearing hooves and tapping, bats screeching and distant monkeys squealing, strange melodies of the night, more cacophonous than she had imagined. Her hair fell out of its neat pins, reaching down to her waist, and her nightdress felt like a shimmer of silk against her bare body. She reached the edge of a small forest, where she found the sisters and watched them bathe, then undressed herself to join them. Years of physical neglect peeled away with her gown, and her body felt young again; enveloped by their swimming subtle forms, she wished never to emerge. But as she drifted to sleep in the whirlpool, they left her for the stars, two then two then two then one with a backward glance, and after they disappeared completely, she decided she would not stay. Once she decided, the fear overtook her, the darkness grimaced with demons, and her return to the other side of the fence was racked with threats from malevolent ghosts.

There was the boy posse, young hotshots who clashed with their parents and left home with curses regularly, only to return like hungry little lambs. These boys banded together during unsheltered nights, still delicate and growing in body, but hearty as stallions in spirit, especially with the company of other foolish members of their kind. They smashed windows and stole food, climbed trees and hid from landowners, bullied cows with sharp rocks and slept in the shops they broke into. One night it was a game of daring, to cross the countryside and the mountains, to walk until their shoes tore, until the world finally changed around them. Beyond the distant farms the river started as a trickle, and they followed it to quench their thirst. They listened for the deeper water, sensing its sound through the brambles and thorns and the sharp edges of leaves, into a glowing circle of nude women, unbelievable women—all curves and skin and hair and eyes. Without thinking they entered the pool, four erections leading the way for their wild beating hearts as seven women watched, each in a different mood and with a different power to inflict; the luckiest boy reached the most willing and adventurous sister, the unluckiest reached the least tolerant, with a lesson to teach—each boy left the thicket at a different hour, with his own scars and story and only vague notions of his compadres' fates.

By the time the seven sisters disappeared, first six then one, the era of their river spent, these impressions had been carved and cemented, filling the space of absence and time, of flesh and years, the stories passed on and taking the sisters' place altogether, the river itself left alone, unremarkable as the words or the myth's magic—something too fantastic to be believed, too wonderful to neglect. The seven sisters transcended into fairy tale.

No STORIES WERE SPUN for the six who had learned the barrio's most intimate secrets. In them, lies buried in locked chests beneath the ocean had found escape; the chests cracked open and the lies floated up in bubbles, popping at the surface to set the lies free to fly to the other side of the fluttering curtain in the dead-end market stall. Normally proud demeanors slumped under the fear of aging or failure—only these women saw the breakdowns, when the shell of perfection cracked under the back-breaking guise of pretending, forgetting, pretending, and dismissing. Then there were the hopes, little burning candles offering light at the end of long dark tunnels, tunnels too long to traverse during the course of a lifetime, and yet, that flicker alone was enough to drive them mad and rushing to the stall to ask for something to bring the warmth closer, anything to help them taste those enduring tips of fire licking skin.

These women knew what wives, brothers, mothers, husbands, fathers, compadres, lovers, and children did not know or avoided like some dark and dangerous alley on the clean and busy streets of their daily lives. They'd given herbal pills and avocado oil rubs to the man who needed help with arousal, who could not make love to his wife because another man was always on his mind. They'd unloaded jars of aloe, cucumber, and citrus-based jellies to middle-aged women who couldn't prevent the lines from deepening on their foreheads or on each side of their frowns, regardless of how much money they possessed or how many different butlers drove them from albularyo to albularyo. They'd sold wooden and stone amulets in the shapes of sea turtles, dogs, fish, and birds—the animal forces that granted wisdom, bravery, prosperity, or freedom— whatever was most essential and most lacking in the lives they counseled. And so, when they were there one day and gone the next, no one made a fuss or alerted their families and neighbors as to the curious and sudden disappearance, out of protection for their unleashed secrets, those only the albularyos knew and carried away with them on the mysterious flight that they hoped would be a permanent one.

This silence was just what the albularyos needed to cover their tracks, to disappear as completely as if they had never set foot in a useless mountain crevice called Manlapaz. For years they had banded together like sisters, their sisterhood bound solid by flight—a common need to escape, a common instinct to distance themselves from the source of terror and shame.

When this source came dangerously close once again, reaching them with the quiet of smoke in the shape of a man, deceptively solitary, with a larger network of unscrupulous errand boys at his beckoning, they packed their things without too much haste or carelessness. They had learned to control panic and avoid mess-ups. As women with strong minds and few choices, they had already formulated alternate plans, various routes leading to one destination—peace of mind.

Together, they were too conspicuous—six unmarried girls traveling in a group attracted more attention than they could afford to risk now. In their work as healers and through the course of wandering over the past year, they'd come to know and trust a scattered group of individuals. Dalisay fled to the home of a middle-aged couple who lived right there in Manlapaz. He was a farmer, she a housewife, cooking for the farmhands and doing every imaginable chore around the farm, like feeding the chickens and collecting their eggs, and of course, keeping the interior of the house running like clockwork—the laundry always clean, the dishes always washed, the lampshades always dusted and the floor mats swapped out regularly. The couple had no children.

Dalisay had met the woman in the market—they had each reached for the plumpest, reddest tomato in the pile, and the woman insisted Dalisay take it. After the incident, they recognized each other instantly among the stalls whenever they happened to meet. Throughout the course of their polite but enthusiastic conversations that Dalisay always enjoyed, they inevitably pointed out the day's good buys to each other, like in which stall to find a sparkling aqua scarf they each admired on a passerby or how low to bargain for the eggs sold across the way. She always took the woman's advice on the price of the eggs and later discovered that they in fact came from her husband's farm, and that the woman herself had collected the eggs each morning. (During her stay with the couple, Dalisay ate fresh omelets every day.)

Though her friends had long ago ceased to be an intimate couple, they stayed together willingly, out of a regard and preference for order. If the wife knew that her husband snuck away some nights to lie with another woman out in the fields where he toiled in quite a different manner during the daylight hours, she did not show it. Dalisay was a welcome distraction from the everyday habits the couple held sacred. In taking them away from a disciplined routine to entertain her, they had the pleasure of returning to their chores and the rewards of their hard work with renewed vigor. With pride, they spoiled Dalisay and recharged from her appreciation of the home they'd built with their own sweat. Here, Dalisay found warmth and companionship, and more importantly, a house where she could eat, sleep, and wait, without ever leaving the front door.

Imee stayed with a young man, her junior by a few years. She had met him at some past juncture that she never felt the need to explain. Though he was at a good marrying age and attracted flirtatious smiles from the pretty dalagas wherever he went, he remained single, and she was right in suspecting that he lived for the rare moments she decided to surprise him with a letter, phone call, or unexpected visit. He lived two hours away from Manlapaz by bus. And the prize of winning her in his tiny bachelor's apartment for an unspecified length of time made all the past waiting worthwhile.

Ligaya, Sampaguita, and Alma, the youngest of the six, stayed together, convincing their sisters that if they combined their ages they would be the oldest sister of all. These three chose to room with Nanay, a woman whose name meant "mother," yet who had no children and would never bear a child because she lived most of her life in fear of people, particularly the male sex, with whom she behaved like a reticent teenager whenever she was unfortunate enough to come across them. Ligaya, Sampaguita, and Alma were the exception to the rest of the world. These three she treasured like pure living dolls—the idealized children she would never bear, the marriage she would never consummate, the repressed but inchoate love she had never had the relief to loose from her chest in heaping rainbow-colored waves.

They'd met Nanay two years before, on a boat taxi between islands. Nanay had long and thick salt-and-pepper hair that she wore in a fat bun behind her neck. She wore cropped pants with comfortable rubber shoes and a burgundy shawl draped over a cream-colored, long-sleeved shirt. She was neither adorned nor plain in aspect, and even her face, without a discernible expression, was the kind that fell "in between." In between old and young, pretty and ugly, rich and poor. Sitting on the boat, Nanay had been preoccupied with her own conspicuous existence and its lack of belonging outside her own home, where she was anxious to return as soon as she finished this latest of bi-monthly excursions that she willed herself to take in order to keep from going mad. (As much as she disliked being out, these small outings helped her fend off strange, night-soaked dreams and a terrible loneliness that caused her to chatter to herself too extensively.) Attempts by others to engage her during these outings usually ended up with uncomfortable results, but that day on the boat taxi surrounded by a gaggle of girls was different. Young and moon-faced, with their skin's natural perfume, salty breath, and awkward grace, they initiated something entirely unexpected—a two-way conversation. As Nanay heard herself making jokes and posing observations with the girls, it felt like the most natural thing in the world—to talk and to listen. She did not question a thing in the process. Even though the smallest girl had begun the exchange with nonsense—"You have no handbag," she'd observed. "Did you forget it at home?"—to her own surprise, Nanay had answered. "Money and makeup, the things inside handbags, would weigh me down. I like to float. That's why I'm taking the boat taxi today."

During their stay at her home, Ligaya, Sampaguita, and Alma could have gotten away with all manner of childish manipulations. But they preferred to spend their time chitchatting with Nanay. The words Nanay said made sense—she saw the world for all its absurdities.

Florencita found solace in Keebo's home. Both with shy dispositions, they shared small talk before quietly pursuing their own interests. They often sat together on the back porch, where she read her books while he carved his latest walking stick. Keebo was his parents' eldest son, who looked after his younger brothers and sisters in his childhood home. His father had died in a fishing accident; his mother passed the hours in her bedroom completing crossword puzzles. His siblings were loquacious by nature, forever seeking willing ears, so Florencita and Keebo never lacked for conversation. Florencita had enchanted Keebo from his first glimpse of her at the market stall, where he'd sought ointments for his mother's arthritis. She showed up at his door unexpected, hoping for his kindness and embarrassed at her intrusion. He quickly and humbly offered his welcome.

THE BOY, BAITAN, WAS the first to notice. *The albularyos—they're all gone.* First it had been Tala, absent from one day to the next like a missing rainbow when the earth is dry. He continued his daily routine: scrounging, selling scraps, looking in on his mother, eating whatever he could get his hands on. Finally he decided to visit with the albularyos—without Tala. It was then that he discovered the booth had been wiped clean, nothing but dry wooden slats nailed hastily together. The bottles filled with spices, flowers, and roots were gone, the shelves decorated with carvings, stones, and piles of mismatched bowls dismantled. The curtain separating the front half from the back had been taken down, and without its many adornments or the irreplaceable combination of smells he had grown to love, the stall did not seem bigger, but empty and small, half the size of his own shack. Squatters had already laid claim to the sheltered space within, their soiled blankets strewn across the bare ground, empty soda cans, dirty take-out boxes, newspapers, cigarette butts, mismatched socks, and tattered clothing scattered about. As he looked in on the mess and the hapless people sleeping comfortably in the middle of it, he wondered how long ago the albularyos had fled and felt a shadow fall over him.

"What are you looking for, boy?" The man's face was alarmingly sharp, his cheeks pierced with the edges of bones, his expression hard to decipher.

"Nothing, po." Baitan wasn't sure why he used the term of respect so readily with this stranger. He had little respect for adults he did not know and who had not had a chance to earn it. Something about this stranger made him feel uneasy and unsure. As a boy who spent his days out on the streets, he was usually adept at reading personalities. He could see through a liar posing as an innocent, identify the softie camouflaged beneath harsh words. This man seemed ugly and unpleasant on the outside, but Baitan knew better than to judge by appearances alone. Something always spoke from the inside, hinting at a person's character, but from this emaciated stranger, all Baitan heard was a looming silence.

"I'm looking for someone," the man said after peering into the shack window, turning away, and spitting, as if the image he'd seen had left a bad taste in his mouth. "A young lady— pretty, if you like plain, round faces. Nothing special if you like more defined features, like mine." He laughed and touched his cheek, and Baitan could not tell if he was making fun of himself or prone to self-flattery. "She calls herself Tala." With the last word, the faintest trace of a smirk shone on the stranger's lips.

Baitan's senses sharpened at the mention of his friend's name, and he knew his reaction had betrayed him. "I don't know her," he lied, sensing that it was too late, that the stranger had already deciphered a connection in the flash of his eyes.

"I see. We look nothing alike, I know. But I'm Tala's brother. Lost the scrap with her address on it. Don't know her, huh? I'll be around if you happen to run into her." The man walked away, trailing miles of silence, and Baitan hurried back to his mother's mat.

The next day, he saw the stranger again. This time, he came to Baitan's mat. He held a skewer of grilled, marinated pork in one hand, an oily brown bag in the other. Baitan had only shared a couple of figs with his mother that morning. The grease from the pork made the stranger's lips glossy.

"So we meet again," he said between bites, waving the hand that held the bag as he spoke and swayed like a drunkard. "Did you know that your friend Tala is married to a fancy doctor? Oh, that's right, she's not your friend. I'm surprised I haven't bumped into her yet. I found out she buys groceries at these stalls at least two days a week. Usually, with a monkey of a boy as her sidekick." He paused and scratched his head, freeing one of the fingers from its grip on the bag. "Hah, that's funny, the description of that boy reminds me an awful lot of you! But I guess monkeys grow on trees around here." He gazed around and above him, as if he expected to witness the phenomenon of monkeys jumping out from the sky at any moment. Baitan observed that the sky was a clear, bright blue.

The man took the last bite of his grilled pork and threw the empty skewer into the street. He squatted down to inspect the intricately folded leaves Inday had worked on the previous evening, and Baitan could see each prick of stubble on the man's chin, the pindrop of barbecue sauce on one corner of his thin mouth.

"Did you make these all by yourself?" He licked his fingers before picking up a grass doll, holding its makeshift hands in his fingertips and dangling it from side to side in a silent, help-less dance as he finished chewing.

"I help my mom make them. She's getting us some lunch. She'll be back any second now."

"It's late for lunch. Getting close to dinner now. You must be hungry." He wiped his mouth with the back of his hand. "Here, have this bag of turon. I was saving it for dessert. Go ahead . . . take it. That's right. It's good, huh?" He patted Baitan on the head. "Remember, if you see the girl who calls herself Tala, tell her that her brother is looking for her."

• • •

BUT BAITAN HAD NOT seen Tala in weeks. He knew where she lived, could still envision her yellow house with white curtains, the tree in the front yard bearing starfruits, the brightly dressed neighbor fanning herself on her front stoop, the nutty smell of kare-kare drifting out of someone's open window. He'd walked her home before, as far as the edge of her cul-de-sac, helping her carry a grocery bag most of the way then waiting until she was safely inside before turning back. It may have seemed super-fluous, in broad daylight, to consider Tala unsafe until she was indoors, but something about his friend seemed vulnerable and worthy of protection. This part of Tala seemed just as much of a child to Baitan as he was, and because of that fragility, whether actual or imagined, he could easily forget she had him by more than a decade. When they'd walked through the market, he often pretended that she needed him there, like he was a body-guard, only half her size.

Baitan considered the fact that the albularyos, Tala's sisters, were gone. He could not be sure that their disappearance was related to Tala's recent absence. He had to tell her about the albularyos, in case she did not know. And he had to tell her about the man who said he was her brother.

The next day he walked to Tala's when the sun was still new, when the strange man's face was reduced to a blur in his memory and Baitan could focus on Tala instead. How she could forget herself while talking about Manolo, describing her husband's quiet passion, dedication to his patients, strong but peaceful hands—traits Baitan could not fully grasp or appreciate except for the fact that they made Tala happy. Happy—the word suited Tala precisely and was perhaps the reason she seemed so fragile in Baitan's mind. He had not come across anyone of her carefree nature before. It did not seem to belong in this world, at least, not in his world, where only the tough or numb or criminal could get by and every passing happiness had weight, imbued with the substance of those hardships overcome or temporarily forgotten. She was either naïve or precious. He'd decided on precious.

At her house he dared not knock, so he lingered outside in the hopes she would appear. She did not, but others did. Two old grandmothers who probably stayed home all day, married to their routines, sensing novelty in the wind like the first prick of rain on the skin. From this monotony they observed his presence immediately, finding him through the window, a woman with long silver hair and another with a fat face and dark mole on her chin. The curtain flickered, changing places with their faces. Only one came out to greet him when the front door opened. She and a pear-shaped grandfather wearing a white Fruit of the Loom tee that bulged at the waistline.

"Hoy, you there," the old man said.

Baitan told him what he'd come for. To let Tala know a man was looking for her, and that he said he was her brother. To tell her that the albularyos were gone.

THE MAN RETURNED TO the mat every day for the next three days, and Baitan discovered he had a name—Charo. Each day Charo brought him a treat in a greasy paper bag. Inday disliked Charo from the get-go, told him to take his bags and stuff them with his bullshit someplace else. She warned her son against such strangers, certain from their walk and talk alone they were up to no good. But Baitan's stomach grumbled all day no matter how well he'd eaten, and the grease on the bags appealed to him with its promise of something deep fried and delicious, so he sought Charo out to ask for his snack. In addition to the food, Charo offered the boy beer and cigarettes. He tried a puff each time, but it always made him gag. He drank the beer until he hiccuped. He preferred the food, but appreciated being treated like a man.

Charo informed Baitan that he'd seen Tala and had had dinner with her family. He reported that his sister had asked after him and sent him a message that she was feeling ill from pregnancy, but would see him in the marketplace soon. With this news, Baitan's suspicions toward Charo subsided somewhat. He listened more readily to Charo's stories of the big city with its buzzing port, where opportunity was abundant and available for the reaching. Charo had been impressed by Baitan's run of the market, but told him there was still far more to learn. The streets of the city were like a video game, he coaxed, and he could teach Baitan not only how to play, but to win. He described the air-conditioned malls and the fountains bursting throughout the outdoor shopping centers, ten times the size of the Manlapaz market. He described the exotic cuisine from all over the world, sizzling on heaping plates for the price of a dime. The crowds on the sidewalks were so thick they held up traffic for hours at street crossings. He would see street performers from the circuses of China and the alleyways of India beside the seaport, alongside American jugglers and Brazilian stilt walkers. He would have a maze of rooftops to jump across, his own pedicab to shuffle him to every part of the city. He offered to bring Baitan along, take him in as a boarder and employ him as an errand boy for his thriving business, and with the money he earned from tips alone, his mother would have enough to own a proper stall and have breakfast, lunch, and dinner twice. Baitan wavered—she would not be happy, not with him so far away. Then Charo told him about the candy, and Baitan's ears perked up like antennae. A big stuffed bag of toffees, jellybeans, caramels, imported chocolates, and pastillas waited for him in the car, globs of sweetness ready to appease him en route to the other side of the mountain.

15. Shadows, Ghosts

THEY CAME DOWN FROM the mountain, sleepless and haunted, the thirst for vengeance following them from dreams, tempered by memories of a previous life. With darkness as their accomplice, they traveled undetected by the sleeping villagers, save those who dared to linger after hours, only to forget their bravery at the first trace of unnatural scurrying in the grass—of night creatures waiting to steal their last breath for immortal wrongdoing.

Weeks after the city of tents had been dismantled and the parts returned to backyard sheds and empty closets, when the dust had settled over new paths made by recent wagons loading and unloading supplies and overheated kalabaw dragging their giant hooves, these same ghosts brought pickaxes and dynamite. They surveyed the mountain, diligently testing the strength of the rock face before lighting their explosives. The blast sounded in the night like a second earthquake, disrupting dreams and sending nocturnal creatures scurrying from their hiding places. It disintegrated the landslide to bits, finishing the work that the villagers had started and the government had ignored. By the time the military arrived with a bulldozer, enough space had already been cleared for passage by that monstrous machine, and the officials from the capital would snap photos alongside the absence of rubble and publicize them in black and white, taking credit for another mission accomplished on behalf of the people.

In the wilderness of the peaks, in the company of mosquitoes, wild pigs, and unbendable wills, they slept in felled trees, hollow with rot. They cleared miles of brambles with machetes and moved from mountain face to mountain face to avoid detection. Had they not been ghosts, frequent starvation, boredom, and unchanging hardship would have broken them. For now, the mountain was their camouflage in a silent, ongoing search for blood that left no one safe from indiscriminate eruptions of violence. They left Manlapaz in peace, though even Manlapaz, like other barrios of similar size and obscurity, could encounter fires, gunshots, death—repercussions of the vengeance against those who despised the ghosts and whom they, in turn, detested.

After the landslide had been cleared, they returned, night after night, leaving the security of dense leaves and untamed ground to walk the village with unusual frequency. They circled the mansion by the barrio square, where the photographers lunched and the military men boasted of their unmitigated sway over the simple residents of this good-for-nothing town. Contracts were signed (with endless amendments and clauses that rendered them useless) and money exchanged. The idea was for Manlapaz to receive a face-lift, just as they'd publicized in the papers: contractors hired, potholes resurfaced, broken fences repaired, and everyone would be happy. But even as they waved their pens and posed for photos, the officials from the capital knew where all the money would end up. The bureaucrat who lived in the mansion wasted no time drawing plans for expansion. A second wing would be built for a hot tub on marble flooring, with an adjoining banquet room boasting floor-to-ceiling gothic windows overlooking a secluded courtyard. As the weeks passed, signage throughout Manlapaz remained torn, and crooked streetlights continued to blink irregularly as they had done since a magnitude of 6.9 had rocked them. Plans for the hot tub moved forward; municipal construction came to a standstill.

The ghosts listened in on the short-lived government meetings that quickly became garish parties, watched through the harsh morning light as the bulldozers and chauffeur-driven cars with tinted windows made their way down the mountain once more. Then they surveyed the remodeling site as they had the face of the mountain, assessing the strength and solidity of the existing structure, counting residents, visitors, automobiles, bullets, sticks of dynamite. They itched to ignite their explosives and watch it all burn.

But they kept the fire burning within, storing up their hatred for another war, another time. Manlapaz sheltered a people with faith and reverence, who had suffered enough at the discretion of unseen forces, only to come together to fix the resulting messes on their own. For them, government promises held little sway compared to the helping hands of brothers and sisters, the comfort of a good meal, and the very real presence of mystery. This mystery had no connection to more formal habits of religion. It drove them to act in a manner that outsiders would have considered irrational. By daylight, they revered the same fascinating and immortal beings, neither gods nor demons, that they feared by night.

They uttered greetings like "Excuse me, sir" to the openings in anthills, avoided long stretches of dark, spoke to the swaying in the treetops. They hiked into the forest to tell the diwata their stories, sat on felled logs beside invisible companions, recounting memories of the dead. They left heaping plates of food in carefully designated locations to win favor or seek forgiveness. The ghosts, making their way to and from their furtive errands, hid in the underbrush and listened patiently, even when the monologues lasted for close to an hour. Then they sought the food, having memorized every drop-off spot. Warm or cold, they licked the plates clean of every crumb and dripping. The villagers, after returning for their tableware, went home appeased by the significance of empty plates, and every bite swallowed reminded the ghosts to surrender them to their peace.

EACH GIRL CLEARLY REMEMBERED the day she had arrived—the memories were different but the feeling had been the same for all six—like dying, without the freedom of death. They shared one room in Charo's shoe factory, where they lived and worked accepting johns, and when they had a few hours' peace to draw the curtains that hung between their beds to write in notebooks, listen to music, paint their toenails, and do the things that young girls do, they recognized the shadows in each other's eyes, the same ones that ate into their flesh from the inside.

When the seventh girl arrived, her eyes clear, the youngest girls fawned over her and the older ones waited bitterly for her eyes to become flat and dull, then flicker once more, with the dominion of the shadows they all shared. But this girl, of legal age and still a virgin, was being saved for a bigger payday. It took weeks for Charo to find the right overseas buyer, and from there, to get all his red tape cleared. In those weeks, her vision remained clear. She convinced the others to see once more with the eyes of the living, and if they could not, to imagine.

Her escape plan worked. It was as simple as stealing a key, waiting for the factory workers to clear out, the attendants to leave, and the pimps to pass out from drunkenness, heavy with the influence of the drugs, presents from the johns, that the girls had slipped in their drinks. They brought nothing but the clothes they wore and the money they'd hidden. Perhaps they succeeded because they bore no illusions to slow them down. Each girl accepted the shadows that bonded them as permanent fixtures. Rather than fleeing from the shadows, they dug deeper in, deep enough to get lost in the smoke and peer through to other side. The seventh, unlike the rest but equally beloved, had yet to reveal her own demons.

16. The Debt

THEIR WALK FROM RIVER to house was not the same as the one they had taken from house to river. There were three of them now, and the return with this new person at their side seemed to occur on a different day, in a different lifetime. Manolo's first impression of Charo as a ghost had stuck, causing all the same premonitions he had gotten as a child whenever he played with malice. The feeling of their last game stayed with him and Tala both, the chill and the cold of pretending under a dark sky, the desire for home and for the warmth of their bodies huddled together for a tender night's sleep. But on this walk, they did not feel the comfort of walking toward a warm bed. No one spoke. Charo smoked like a factory pipe, one Marlboro after the other inhaled into ash as Manolo savored his one. None of the darkness gathered between leaves, beneath cars, or peeking from behind the shadows demanded notice. All of it took shape in the bags of Charo's eyes, the weight of visions he'd once glimpsed, and the secrets they held about Tala's past. But his eyes and his walk were sleepy from drink, and his sway beneath its influence weakened him.

In that quiet countryside nook, the Lualhatis' house was

the only one lit at the hour of their return. Iolana and Andres woke to the sound of their voices, particularly the alluring new cadences of a visiting guest. Regardless of the time, Iolana could not resist bringing the kitchen to life for the occasion, frying thin slices of marinated beef, serving it with steamed rice and a salad of chopped tomatoes, onion, and pickled egg for the guest. She insisted that Tala make a sweetened beverage from grated cantaloupe, and if it weren't for Andres's gentle scolding, she would have had the energy to bake bibinka from scratch to go with the coffee she had brewing.

But Charo showed little appreciation for the efforts taken on his behalf, speaking little if at all, looking up primarily to watch Tala with no emotions showing on his face. He was forlorn and quiet, but not shy, shadowy, but always at the forefront of their attention. He did not inspire fear, but suspicion, suspicion that verged on the brink of anger. His appetite was bottomless, competing with the depths of night. Andres was the only one who joined him to eat, his saliva dripping instantly from the roof of his mouth at the first smell of food. But Charo took four bites for every one of his, and if Andres had had the room for seconds, Charo left him none. He wiped his mouth continually with the back of his hand in a sloppy manner, though his reticence kept him from being sloppy with words.

They assembled around the kitchen table with mixed expectations, a family brought together after midnight, improvising the steps of their reunion. Charo seemed more like a stranger than Tala's brother. For Iolana, he was a source of endless fascination, even when that fascination came from a sense of disgust at something less refined than she. She coughed repeatedly at the smoke that filled her house from the man's cigarettes, dangling at the edge of his plate right next to his food.

For Andres, he was something of the inevitable, like corns on the bottom of a well-traveled foot, someone from Tala's past who was bound to show up, for a girl that pretty had to have ugly relatives somewhere along the line to compensate. Charo was not necessarily ugly, though, just hidden, like a person without a face, with a face underneath a face you could not read. He peered at Charo's gloomy attire, unshaven mustache and beard, and the long stringy hair that did not quite disguise such naked eyes. Eyes that could be spent or waiting. Andres did not attempt to solve this riddle. He basked in the perfect cup of coffee instead, thinking regretfully of the bibinka he'd stopped his wife from baking. Andres suggested that Charo drink a strong cup before leaving to wake himself up for the journey back to his lodgings.

After entertaining themselves back into fatigue, Iolana and Andres returned to their room, bringing the remains of their lukewarm coffee and saving their questions for the morning. Manolo and Tala did not wait long for the answers to their own questions.

"I've come to collect my due," Charo said, bluntly stating the point of his visit. He pushed muddy shoes against the table edge, leaning back on the rear legs of his chair. He picked at the food between his teeth then resumed with his latest cigarette.

"What nerve you have coming into this house and eating at this table, then insinuating we owe you something!" Manolo's spit flew in three directions as he spoke, as he struggled to maintain a civil demeanor. His heart was beating three times its normal rate; he could feel the flow of blood fill his head, hear it gushing in his ears.

"Money?" Tala asked more gently. "You came here for money?" Money she could live without. A soul she could not. Money could take the place of a soul.

"Just what you owe, Sis," he said, addressing Tala and leaning even farther back on two of the chair's four legs. He'd barely flinched at Manolo's outburst. "We had a business deal, or have you forgotten? It was already signed, by you and me both. I accepted the foreigner's offer. He arranged for your visa, he sent your plane ticket. Imagine my embarrassment when you fled."

"What is this nonsense?" Manolo stood up in his chair. "Who are you to come here like this? What thick skin you have!"

"How much money do I owe?" she asked.

She looked at Manolo apologetically as she said the words, and his eyes returned a question, one of the many he had asked since the word *Charo* entered his vocabulary. Instead of springing on Charo liked he'd looked ready to do, he sank back into his chair like a tired leaf.

Charo asked for enough money to cover what he'd lost from the deal (because of her)—plus more cash to cover three more like it. Then he changed his mind, showing what he called his "charitable side," because Tala was, after all, his sister. He would only need the money he'd lost repaying the foreigner, whose pride kept him from accepting any of the other girls and their glossy pictures that couldn't seem to compete with Tala's. He asked for the money in installments, whatever Tala or the fancy doctor could spare. He had faith, he said, in their ability to commit, and he'd be sure his crew checked up on them all the time, now that he knew where the happy family lived.

"But finding you, Sis, is the biggest reward. After all, we're family. I'll deal with the others differently. That reminds me, there's another reason why I'm here, why I found you now after all these years. Ma is dead. Yes, dead, she finally called it quits. But don't worry too much, Sis. She was never really alive to begin with, was she?"

17. Wakefulness

THEY FOUGHT WITHOUT POLITENESS behind the privacy of their bedroom door. At the height of his anger, Manolo wished he was the type of man who could strike a woman across the face. But he was not, and she knew this. She aggravated him all the more with the look in her eyes—a wild, flashing dare that hoped for the chance to be struck and strike back. It made him feel colder inside.

"Is he even your brother, or is he just your pimp?"

He watched the expression on her face change and knew she had found something in him to hate, that at that moment her hatred for him was complete, tapping into something begun long ago, before their time, tracing back to them full circle. If she had the resolve to sustain it, she could wrap that length of hatred around her heart until it engulfed their whole world—slowly, like a painful emptying, until there was nothing left. How many times and to how many couples had this already happened, and all because of that moment when everything changed? When one became capable of despising the other.

In spite of her unhappiness, evident in the jutting of her lips, stooped posture, and inflamed nostrils, Tala was more controlled, almost too much so.

"Why are you acting like this is all new to you?" she asked him with too much stillness. "You told them so yourself."

"Told who, Tala? Told what? I obviously know nothing. What are you going to tell me next? That your name isn't Tala? That everything has been pretend to you, from the very beginning?"

As she built her momentum it was clear she was fighting to keep from losing it. That the words she'd been holding back threatened to come out all at once, and then nothing would be clear. He listened to her say that he'd spoken the truth many times before—to their neighbors, family, and friends. And where did he think such words could come from? Those words that labeled her a runaway, escaping an arranged overseas marriage with no return policy—and with that simple trick they closed their mouths just like that, ashamed to dig for more unless he volunteered the information. Afraid to think of the daughters whom they, too, had forsaken to Tagarro Bay, sold to families as maids and babysitters, torn from primary school to become shop girls earning the family's rice or the male sibling's education? Wasn't that just as bad? Wasn't that what he had wanted them to feel?

No.

But the words had come from somewhere—the truth, the reality of her, a runaway, a poor nobody whose own blood would offer her as trade. He had known it all along, and why, she asked, did he pretend to forget, putting the burden of truth on her shoulders alone? When did she stop being her, enough for him to stop believing her story, her truth? She was no longer apologetic—sorry became bitter, angry at her truth, at her shame, at his denial.

No, Tala, no!

She had told him herself on the night they met at the river, when she'd been soiled from head to toe after spending five nights running, hiding on the back of moving farm wagons, filled with shit, cutting her skin (that he later disinfected) on barbed wire to sleep in chicken pens, tearing her feet (that he later wrapped in a warm washcloth) on hard ground until she'd found solace in the river, hidden from the rest of the world. Her story, her sad awful story, not of the brother but the doomed bride, the marriage that had never taken place, and what about the marriage that did, wasn't she his now? Wasn't it all too easy to sweep the uncomfortable away and hide it out of sight? Wasn't that the reason they had both settled with silence, the never knowing or asking, and why she'd never gotten into the details about the contract or the brother who forced her to sign it? Didn't he forget what he'd heard, was he going to keep forgetting all the hearing and the knowing, running away from what she'd been running away from? Was he going to keep hiding it away in some shameful hole and pretend? That she was some angel? Some innocent?

He shook his head *no* all the while, *no, no, no,* holding his face in his hands.

She stood, pacing, sometimes halting in her steps to face him where he sat at the edge of the bed. Her tone was at its lowest, the edges of her voice sharp. He was forgetting, she accused, he was hiding.

It was after one a.m. Outside, nocturnal hunters screeched in the night, claiming their fill. When he knew that she had had her say, he got up and walked out without a word, closing the bedroom door behind him almost soundlessly.

He would sleep on the sofa that night. Rather, he would lie awake through most of the night until fatigue made wakefulness unbearable, even for his restless mind.

This was the first time they'd slept apart since marrying. He did not bother to grab a blanket or a pillow. The darkness that engulfed him would have to suffice. The sofa was lumpy and too soft. He tossed from side to side, agitated. He thought of her lying awake just steps away, pained and possibly crying. Or, perhaps, she had already fallen asleep, fatigued from their walk from the river, the impromptu dinner with Charo, and then, this. He remembered that she was six months pregnant and felt a tinge of guilt. He remembered one other period of time when he'd slept on the couch, imagining how Tala might be faring steps away behind his bedroom door. It had been a torturous span of nights—torturous and ecstatic. It had been just before their marriage.

Their courtship had lasted a mere two weeks. Even more scandalous was their living together, from the time of that first impossible walk, away from river and field to the sharp lines of windows, lampposts, and fences, when step by merciful step she did not disappear. And every night from the living room sofa he'd marveled at the thought of her sleeping beneath the same roof, across the hall on his bed, her body pressed against the spaces where his had been. He'd waken hourly from fitful sleeps, checking the clock, imagining the heat of her just seventeen steps away, counting minutes until morning when he'd see her face again. At breakfast, she lit up the kitchen with fresh energy, her gentle, lovely voice and manner permeating through them all like warm cocoa, and he learned what it felt like to be full, really full, from his belly to his heart. His parents chatted with their young guest, politely at first, then more and more cheerfully as they let down their guard. It delighted him to see how comfortable she felt in their company, how easily she invited them to relax in hers.

With people there were always layers, and it could take years or hours to peel them away, to get to the real person underneath. It happened with his patients all the time—the reticence when they sat on his examination table, baring their skin and the aches that throbbed beneath it. With their nakedness exposed on that stiff bed, they rarely spoke frankly, at first. He helped them along with disarming touches—approving nods as he checked the ears and the eyes and the mouth, harmless presses on the stomach, encouraging pats of a stethoscope upon their backs, all while they rambled about bygone days (*I was fit as a fieldhand in my youth, all muscle on these arms and no fat*) or favorite recipes (*leche flan did me in, Doctor, a dozen egg yolks per pie, and I can't stay away!*) or quirky pets (*GiGi can sense it when my heart rate goes up, she sings in her cage to keep me calm*). Then just before he asked them to retie their shoes and button up their blouses, they clung to the edge of the examination table and remembered their pain with sudden urgency, describing its every prick, entreating him with their eyes for a sign that their maladies could be cured, that they could return to their recipes and pets and memories without the sticky film of worry nagging beneath the skin. Tala, he learned, was always the person underneath, speaking her mind so bluntly it was funny. He discovered a woman so free of pretense that the love inside him grew beyond what he'd imagined it could. Between messy bites of her omelet, she teased about whose shoes left the worst stench in the hallway, and Manolo met his father's eyes across the table, the same hope buzzing between them—that she would not be a temporary visitor.

During the day, he'd taken time off work to walk with her, pointing out the homes from which chickens strutted off on their happy meanderings, greeting the children who waved or stared, avoiding eye contact with the neighborhood gossips who peered at them from their windows with their dishrags in hand like weapons against the world's dust and grime and scandal. She did not pass the children by with a smile and wave, but chased them with growls and raised claws. He laughed as they fled from her with glee, returning with all the more enthusiasm as they followed her hopefully for half a mile down the road. He showed her the bus route and the stops where it dropped off mail. He brought her to the plaza lined with vendors, introducing her to his favorite fishmonger, butcher, and baker. Nanang Aglibut sent them away with three pounds of fresh tilapia, on the house, Yan-Yan gave them a markdown price on the day's oxtail, and Rommel said hello with a crooked smile, then returned to his flour. They fed pigeons by the fountain and stopped at panciterias to lunch on nest egg soup. As they ate, they talked about his school days, when his father worked for the railroad company and his mother made and sold palm wine to the entire province. Tala avoided the subject of her family, not by looking away or drifting into nostalgic silence, but by staring at him blankly and telling him simply that she wasn't ready to talk. Instead, they had an entire conversation about all the injuries she'd suffered—a sprained ankle, strep throat, purple hands from cold water, and he told her how he would have treated each case—with ice and elevation, antibiotics, warmth and circulation. They didn't discuss the future, how long she would stay at Manolo's or where she would go if she decided to leave. A week passed. Another came.

One evening, she locked herself in his mother's room, and for hours, the two women's shrieks and laughter erupted from behind the closed door. He didn't see her again until dinner, when she came to the table wearing a new yellow dress, embroidered along the edges, with matching gold jewelry upon her wrists, earlobes, and neck, and her hair in a single braid. Their eyes met often during that meal when he hardly swallowed a bite, unspoken word after unspoken word dancing between them. That night, he tossed and twisted on the sofa cushions, straining for any sound of her in the bedroom, dangling upon the faintest wisps of sleep, and when he woke for what seemed like the fiftieth time, hours before sunrise, it was not the clock he saw but the outline of her face in the dark as she knelt beside him. Like the first step into a dream, he drifted into the maddening touch of her lips on his, gentle at first, then freer, and he stopped the fire quickly, begging her to wait. She rubbed a fingertip across his lips. They married the next day.

The priest wouldn't hear of such a union taking place in his church—between an untested couple living in sin. Where was their foundation, without years of friendship and earnest courting to build upon? Without her family's approval? With no history of attendance in his church by either party? By then Manolo's story had spread like soft butter across a loaf of bread and the neighbors ate up every crumb, gathering in living rooms, storefronts, and porches to gossip about the reclusive doctor, who had found himself a penniless and beautiful runaway. Could she be trusted? Could he? Could a marriage based on lust and convenience?

The babaylan had asked no questions. Candle upon candle lit every surface in her hut, sealed from the eyes of the sun, and the flickering light changed constantly, at times radiant, like joy itself, at times a wavy blur that suspended the room in keeping with the flames' strange dance. They stood in a circle on the wedding day, a gathering of souls submerged in the fire glow, all of them accommodated by that one endless room, the shadows they made trailing across one another's faces—Tala, Manolo, Iolana, Andres, Luchie; Little Roland, his wife, and their three children's families; Camcam, Lourdes, and their families.

The babaylan stood in the center, all bones and hair, in an ordinary housewife's dress patterned with purple and white flowers. Her bloodline was said to reach as far back as the first tribe to have peopled the islands. They watched her for any signs of movement—a blink or a twitch or a sigh—as she stood like an ancient tree, knotted eyes closed and wearied arms outstretched. Her fingertips woke to life first, stroking the air's vibrations. Then her voice filled the room, a low murmur that grew to a loud murmur and then to a chant—words they did not understand but felt, its rising and falling matching the rhythm of the candles, and her words and their melody reached into and through them, knowing their worst pain and deepest hopes, weaving a thread between them, through time and bone and everything that was. She chanted, and at once they knew it was a song of the mountains, belonging to the land, it was a sound like wind, whipping through skin, becoming hurricane then blessed relief then hurricane again. She was the song and she belonged to the land, as did they, as did all who came before them, as did Datu's hand wrapped tightly around his grandmother's, as did Iolana's dreams of winged men, as did Luchie's unremembered childhood, as did the palm trees' music outside the one window, brushing up against the glass as the wind and the voice reached new heights. She followed her fingertips' vibrations, turning within their circle like the center of a compass, listening to the wind between their heartbeats, stumbling toward the east, toward Camcam's rapid and fearful pulse, and swaying westward toward Manolo's slow, exultant breaths. When she landed, her eyelids opened like the pages of a book, looking inward to read itself, thirsty and expectant for knowledge. She swayed hesitantly before Tala, staring into the bride's face, and for a moment the flames stopped dancing on their wicks; the thread binding the circle seemed to snap. The babaylan's look changed from intoxication to confusion to something like pain, and her body seemed to harden, no longer a fluid thing as she froze into a tree that was no longer ancient but brittle; her bones looked so stiff that Luchie feared she'd died on the spot, and Datu complained that she'd turned into stone. Tala let out a high-pitched wail, lolling it with her tongue to play, and the flames wiggled their tips once more. Iolana gasped at the girl's insolence; Lourdes burst into giggles; Manolo raised an eyebrow and smiled. The babaylan's eyes widened, the girl's voice like sap for a dry tree, tickling her nerves, unwinding her once more; she threw her head upward in a howl that was laughter.

Then she lavished the bride with attention, rubbing Tala's head with balms, stroking her forehead moist and slicking the surface of her hair. She began to dance, and they saw the chant and its recollections vibrating through her wiry arms and body. The children danced with her. She waved a bamboo scroll etched with writings around Tala and Manolo. She placed necklace after necklace, heavy with amulets, into the children's hands, which they passed, one to the other, the last one placing the necklaces over Tala or Manolo's head.

After the ceremony, they spent the rest of the afternoon feasting in the enclosure beside the babaylan's hut, sharing the bounty of two freshly slaughtered chickens and a whole pig that had been roasting slowly over an open fire through the course of the morning and early afternoon. They ate fish stews, mountains of rice, vegetables steamed and seasoned, a medley of noodles flavored with achuete and ground pork skin, with shrimp, egg, and green onions mixed in. They drank basi and tapuey, celebrating with the gods of rice and sugarcane. Little Roland played the gongs, and all stood to dance, celebrating hand in hand into the night, Tala's hand never far from Manolo's, and he'd never in his life been happier.

Just as he had on their wedding day, he wanted her now. As his wife, his child's mother, his lover, his mate, his beloved. He wanted all of her, even the woman at the river, who had flown, but never away from him, he'd begged in silence, never away from him. If he wanted to claim this life, he knew he could not hide any longer, not even now, when Tala, too, was hiding. And that was the worst of his pain. Knowing that she, too, was hiding, losing her way from the uninhabitable place that was hers alone. How had it happened? And, now, Charo. He would not let Charo win.

Manolo got up from the sofa. All the lights in the house were off, but he found his way easily between the outlines of walls to where Tala was lying sideways in bed with her back to the door. He slipped beneath the covers, pressing his body against hers and wrapping his arm across her inflated belly. She tensed at first, then relaxed, breathing slow and even. Tala was still awake.

18. Shapeshifting

IT STARTED WITH A rumble, then the car was alive. In the passenger seat, Baitan imagined a safari, the car a great big eagle, its giant wings quaking across the distances of their little provincial town. He'd never seen the barrio from this angle, like he was a stranger looking in. The people and the fields glittered like something from a fairy tale, with emerald mountains guarding the periphery. No matter how used to those friendly green giants he'd become, he'd felt comforted when he looked up and saw them there where they'd always been, knowing that no hunger, sickness, or storm would ever be big enough to take them down.

As they drove farther away, he couldn't tell whether the mountains shrunk or grew larger—they somehow disappeared altogether. From behind the wheel, Charo said that they were on top of the mountain, above the world, and soon, they would sink back beneath it, leaving that mountain far behind. This knowledge of leaving the mountains filled Baitan with homesickness, but his pockets were full of candy, and the glittering view outside looked just as sweet.

Baitan had grown up curious of other children grouped in

uniforms with straight white collars, the girls in pleated skirts, the boys in ironed navy slacks. He did not go to any school, though he would've liked to. His teacher was the reprimanding store owner who chased him across the square, beating him on the shoulders and head with the straight end of a broom. Or the one who watched him steal and later hinted at the big houses and all their precious loot. His classroom was a maze of stalls; he knew which hallways to avoid, how to rotate the vendors he stole from like subjects on a schedule. There was a routine to follow, and the daily onslaught of change, good or bad, that he learned from most.

On every street, there were the very poor and the very rich, and he knew which side he walked on. He did not attempt to cross that boundary. He accepted his role, believing that the gamble happened when you were born, and everyone owned as much as chance allowed. Some people were just luckier.

Until that day, Baitan had never been inside a private car. The closest thing he'd gotten was a ride on a jeepney stuffed with passengers and painted on the outside with a colorful forest scene. Now he chewed contentedly on his fifth caramel. Teeth sticking, he did not think of the material things that had eluded him all his life as he sat upright in the seat, leaning with his arm against the upholstered door.

He knew nothing of makes and models and never imagined owning something as shiny or expensive as the vehicle he sat in. He was a thoughtful child, captivated by the way things worked. But he took the mechanics of a car for granted, like the biology of a human body, its every cell working in conjunction with every organ, never sleeping, even while the one who owned it slept.

The novelty was not in the car's lines or texture, but the quick flashes of scenery, the journey across a landscape he had only known inches at a time. He chewed the view with his eyes, swallowing it whole, never wanting to forget its flavors. Even the buses he'd taken with his mama screeched regularly to a halt like complaining old-timers with aching joints. Here the faces he recognized from the market, from the bus, from his daily meanderings, appeared and just as quickly disappeared in a blur of motion. Before stepping into the car he was among those faces on the same plane; now, he was in a parallel universe. One that traveled through space, and quickly. The scattered houses, the green fields and sprawl had never been this wide, this big while he was on foot. He began to discern a sequential order to things, absent of boundaries, house beside house beside hill beside river beside tree beside kalabaw, all in a line that never ended and never looked the same. He knew that witnessing this line was a privilege. He was conscious of looking farther along the line than he had ever seen, and all within a half hour's time. This feeling, one of mobility, aroused in him something glowing and hopeful that he did not recognize as potential. It was the same calling that had tempted him to get into the car with Charo. The possibility that life could be different, better.

At the same time, his heart felt heavy leaving those mountains, the only friends he'd known aside from Tala, and the fairy-tale barrio, one he'd never known was a fairy tale until then, starved nights, chase-downs from the vendors, and all.

The scenery flew by, too quickly, he realized. He felt sick to his stomach and asked Charo to please slow down. Then he closed his eyes and placed his head down against the door as waves of dizziness hit him. His "godfather" lit a cigarette and told him it served him right for eating too much candy. Godfather—it was all a game. He knew how to play along, how to play this lowly hustler who thought he held all the strings. Outside the car, the world glowed, and he knew it was there, could feel it was there with so many pathways to explore, but from inside the car he started to feel as if the sunshine and motion were beginning to close in on him. He thought of his mother and regretted the worry he was causing her. Since the beginning of the journey, he had not stopped thinking of her. She'd stayed in his thoughts like a tree he leaned against, always there, supporting the arch of his back.

He'd hesitated leaving the barrio, wanting to talk to his mother first, but Charo had said business was pressing and they had to ditch this backwater ASAP. "Do you want your life to pass you by in these dead-end streets? Do you want to be a worthless thief forever? Do you want to be hungry all the time while everyone else around you gets fat?"

Now he regretted leaving so abruptly. He'd have to call the sari sari store at the first pay phone, find someone to relay the message to his mother.

Charo had said he would take him off his mother's hands, helping her by helping him, teaching him how to make a future for them both. Did he have a godfather? He would be one, the godfather who gave him everything, who was even better than an actual father. Baitan recognized the falsehood — from complete stranger to father was an overzealous leap. But this Charo had something to offer, and the offers weren't pouring in for a drop-out kid, so he'd taken the candy and hopped into the car. The rooftops and the new maze of streets, the pedicabs and exotic foods — all of this beckoned him like a carnival's colorful illusions.

Charo did not slow down, and the car sped through the high and winding roads just as quickly as before. Baitan clutched at his abdomen.

"Stupid kid, you ate too much candy." Charo handed him a cigarette then turned his face toward the tip to light it with his own.

By now, Baitan could inhale the smoke without coughing, but the candy turned in his belly. Candy and cigarettes, Charo said, would be his thing. He would sell them from a tray strapped to his neck, making a nice profit, and he could even keep a quarter of the tips, but the more important job would be to deliver messages to and from the factory. These would mostly come from the mouths of rich, horny businessmen or worthless thieves, and he'd quickly learn how to stay one step ahead of their predictable, perverted thoughts, unless he wanted to indulge them and make an even bigger payday, but that was something they could talk about later.

He began to think of Tala and how she'd bought every little thing in his basket. He would replace that basket with another, still hawking petty trifles. Was this really moving up in the world? Charo began to whistle, and Baitan realized how much he disliked the sound and especially, its source.

He could not stop the car or make a jump for it. He would have to watch the landscape change and change along with it. He would make money, lots of it, and he knew more than Charo could teach about how to earn tips—which pitying faces to approach, how hungry to appear. He would keep quiet and learn what he needed to, learn what to hate and what never to trust again, and all along he would be in camouflage, disguised in the brush as part of the scene, and when the wilderness left a clearing or the smallest opening of light, he would fly, back to Tala, back to the friendly green giants, back to his mother, back home.

19. A Dream

TALA HAD GROWN ROUNDER by the day, to a point of fullness that seemed impossible. Her body, so transformed, pacified Manolo, as if he somehow shared the womb and all its promises for protection with their sleeping child. He welcomed every stretch mark and centimeter that stretched her skin.

"This is no place for a pregnant woman," she complained, her waddle more exaggerated than before as she swatted the groping arms of trees and crossed overgrown roots jutting up from the soggy ground. "And I don't have the energy for our pretend games. Let's turn around and window-gaze with Luchie while your mom makes us a snack."

"Okay—no more pretending for the pregnant, hungry lady, and we'll head back soon," he said, crunching beside her across a melody of leaves, twigs, and pebbles. "When the baby comes, we won't have time to come back here, where we first met." He held her by the waist, guiding her to a clearing where they could take in the fresh, earthy fragrance of the river and find comfort in the trees' embrace.

Tala, days away from her twentieth birthday, was different from the woman he'd encountered just two years before. He remembered how slender she had been, how she'd swallowed him whole with those eyes. She had sat and waded, waded and watched, and all alone under the stars she'd been exposed and unprotected, with a future so uncertain it pained him. Her arms were plumper now, her face fuller, and her hair shorter, but the biggest change of all was her ownership, of herself and the life in her womb she'd be responsible for. This Tala knew her rightful place under the sun, no matter how endlessly it raged, and alongside this river, even if it were long enough to wrap its legs around the planet, procreating with the earth itself. She would no longer cower beside it; she would dip her toes in and let it cool her.

She possessed the same watchfulness, a stare that could burn through flesh, straight into the fragile, pulpy mess of your heart. The same gift for tenderness he knew she reserved for a chosen few whom she would never neglect in deeds, words, or choices. The same haughtiness, as only someone who has traveled a long and savage distance can possess, knowing they have the will and wherewithal to do so again should the need arise. Only now, maturity had caught up with her—domesticity, sex, duty, and the confidence that comes with certainty. All of these things helped shape and tame the wildness and searching he had found in her and loved and still reached for beneath the bed covers and in the uninhabitable roving of her eyes.

And this was why he brought her here, now, again, for this uninhabitable place he could never hope to reach or curl into or cry for. This mystery and the depths we choose to dive in order to find it, claim it, live it—the life we could breeze through like visitors, or the life we could sweat for and fight to keep and quiver against, truly waking with every ravenous taste bud and sweaty pore.

She had taken off her shoes. She sat in front of the river, with one leg bent beneath her and the other extended as she eased a foot through the water in a languorous glide. She propped her weight against one arm, her other hand resting on her over-sized belly. The birds called from high in the treetops, the water gurgled, and the clicking of insects and impossibly fast wings buzzed around them. She looked so peaceful, resting her head to one side. He walked toward her.

"I saw you here, you know. Before we met. I saw you here and watched you with the other women—your sisters, right?"

She turned to face him, searching his face, his eyes.

"I know what you can do. I saw everything, saw you fly away each night."

She smiled weakly and returned to gliding her foot slowly through the water. "I told you, Manolo. I don't feel like playing pretend games. Not today."

"But I saw you. I know it's true." His voice rose up quickly, his breathing quickened. He kneeled down close to face her, to turn her toward him. She touched his cheek.

"I remember," she said. "How we met here. You had fallen asleep by the riverbank. For hours, I looked for my necklace in the water and watched you while you slept. Then I forgot about my necklace and waited for you to wake up. I sat close to you, memorizing your mouth while it was still and watching the movement underneath your eyelids, like fish darting under-water. I was fascinated by that and imagined that your eyes were searching through the land of dreams. What could this man be dreaming of? This man I did not know, but whose dreams I longed for with the intimacy of a lover. My longing surprised me—its sudden arrival, its brashness. When you woke up, you spoke to me. You told me what you'd seen. You'd seen my face, my sisters' faces . . . many sisters' faces . . . you told me about my wings, my flying. You told me how you never wanted to wake up. And then you told me, somehow, I had become real, following you into life. But it was all just a dream, Manolo, a dream."

20. She Leaves, Returns

ON THE OUTSKIRTS OF the farm houses, where the back-bending pain of working the land could be numbed with drink, where the wives grew tipsy enough to smoke with their husbands, and where the familiar faces of the fields, shops, and nearby offices met over karaoke, bad gin, fritter plates, and gossip, the smug-faced thugs appeared nightly.

They'd arrived like louder, stockier versions of their predecessor: three men in leather jackets and shiny shoes who chain-smoked and asked too many questions. Unlike Charo, who'd slipped through like an eel that left the faintest trace of a ripple, they did not distance themselves from their surroundings. They claimed their right to the countryside's bounty and reputation for hospitality—smacking the vendors' backs while sprinkling their countertops with ash, complimenting the women's figures with booming voices, gliding their fingertips along the shiny edges of knives as they boasted of the fights they'd won, splashing around town with no regard to who noticed or how often. They announced themselves as compadres of Tala's brother, as if this association qualified them into Manlapaz's extended family. They asked for freebies, directions to loose women, refills on tequila shots; they received curt responses and no invitations.

Two of the men were obviously running the show; the third was the fun-seeking tagalong, someone to break the ice and keep things amicable between his more serious companions. They stayed at a boardinghouse near the entrance to the bar where they drank nightly. Sometimes, they brought women from the surrounding barrios to drink and carouse with in dark corners. The locals began to talk, warning their daughters, sisters, and wives that these low-lifes were recruiting women, sweet young faces they could corrupt into returning with them to the underbelly of Tagarro Bay. This was not far from the truth. It soon became apparent that the men pursued a specific roster of ladies. With the same loud voices and carefree manner, they pinpointed ages, heights, a dimple on one cheek for this girl, a sassy attitude on that girl. The most vigilant observers in the bar described every conversation with them like an interview—far from careless or casual, as they depicted themselves to be. From behind cold, calculating eyes and refilled glasses, these men fished for clues, hungry for a lead.

The shadows Charo had left behind became a regular topic of conversation between Iolana, Camcam, and Lourdes on the Lualhatis' back porch as they played cards, traded vegetables from their respective gardens, or shared tsismis over hot coffee and steaming pork buns. Manolo, overhearing the women and filled in on more of the same from his patients, considered the newcomers—the places they frequented while avoiding his house or any involvement in his family's affairs. Rather than deeming them a threat, he considered them irrelevant, inferior. Tala, who had little to say on the subject, must have felt the same.

Around this time, she developed a string of new habits, which Manolo pondered in detail on the night she failed to come home by dinner. Uneasy at the sight of his wife's empty chair, a first in nearly two years of marriage, Manolo had not been able to eat a bite of Iolana's beef steak with caramelized onions. He usually went overboard with three servings of this dish, but that night he stared at his plate, seeing nothing but grease sweating from the meat, the rice, the onions.

Worried about their daughter-in-law's whereabouts, his parents couldn't help referring to the bar at the edge of their neighborhood and its frequent, unsavory clientele. Manolo's worries had other roots, but to appease them and to leave no possibility unchecked, he walked to that smoky room after dinner, finding, as he'd expected, no trace of her. Two of the pathetic thugs in question occupied the barstools, their faces haggard and their lips wrapped around cigarettes. The third was passed out at a table like a schoolboy, his head resting against his arms.

Night fell without Tala's return, and Manolo relegated himself to the room they shared, wrestling with his thoughts and his solitude. *The flower-picking was just the beginning,* he thought, lining the clues to a mystery together, convinced that her absence was not unavoidable, but part of a greater scheme that she had ingrained herself in willingly.

In the past week or so, Tala would leave before breakfast, keeping to the brown fence, following its path to the edge of their cul-de-sac, where she lingered at the wild bunches growing in clumps beside the old maid's house. On some mornings, Andres accompanied her on these domestic rituals, chatting contentedly about the hard work of his railroad days or of the heartsick months when he'd courted Iolana, or nodding his already-pomaded head about one of the fictional characters Tala loved to discuss—her fear and rapture of Bronte's Rochester, her anguished sympathy for Hardy's Tess. Other mornings, she'd go out alone, putting Manolo's sweatshirt on over her nightdress and slipping out the front door without brushing her teeth.

At eight months pregnant, she'd begun to let certain particulars in her hygiene slip. She had never been one to spend hours in front of a mirror and typically wore little makeup. The smocks she'd recently sewn for her vastly expanding size were hastily pieced together with scraps of leftover cloth. She preferred to spend her money on fabric for the baby or on knickknacks, complete in and of themselves, like hand-painted teacups she could cradle in her hands, sweet-smelling soaps, or leather-bound journals she would never write in.

As Iolana prodded at the eggs that sizzled in the frying pan and Andres rummaged around for a can opener, as Manolo crumpled the *Manlapaz Bulletin* to straighten the words on the column he was reading, Tala would pad into the kitchen barefoot with a fresh bouquet to grace the table. Kidnapped from their roots and still wet with dew, the flowers posed with defiant beauty. Upon completing the task and reminded of her vanity, Tala excused herself to comb her hair, freshen her mouth, and slip on a pair of padded house slippers that she loved to wear indoors. In her absence, Manolo would peek at the flowers from behind his paper, a twinge of guilt assaulting him. He'd recently made a comment, half in jest, about the empty vases accumulating dust, and soon afterward, the morning bouquets had reappeared like clockwork. He told himself that when Tala returned to the table, he would remember to express his appreciation for the vibrant colors and shapely petals, responding to her efforts with a break from his reading to brush his fingers against the bouquet, lingering for a moment on the curl of the stem, the prickle of leaves, or the flowers' soft velvet.

On the morning of her absence, he'd only had time to butter a slice of toast, let alone concern himself with table decor. A patient who complained that her dentures prevented her from feeling her food when she chewed had once again gotten a fish bone stuck in her throat. As the smell of coffee brewing filled the house and the ceiling fans spun a soft whir, already in motion against the day's pending heat, Manolo had passed the front window and was not surprised to find his wife outside, facing the short, brown fence at the end of the cul-de-sac, an assemblage of blossoms already in her grasp. What he didn't expect was to see Tala talking, though neither Father nor another soul breathed in her vicinity. He could not hear her from behind the window or from such a distance, but he could see that her mouth gesticulated as though engaged in conversation, with stops and starts and there, a barely perceptible shake of the head.

For the rest of the morning, Manolo had not been able to discard the feeling that something was off. When he returned home for lunch, Father was out front with the gardening shears in his hand, and Manolo hoped he hadn't gone to extremes with the trimming. Once, Father had attempted to create animal shapes out of all their shrubbery, as he had seen on the pages of a fancy architectural magazine, but after all his mistakes and efforts to repair them with a few extra snips, the greenery had practically been reduced to twigs. It had taken over a year for it all to grow back.

"Have you seen the three girls playing in the old maid's yard?" Father had asked as Manolo drew closer.

"What girls?"

"They try to keep their voices down, I think, because of the old maid. I imagine she must be uptight, unaccustomed to people. She's used to being alone, in complete control, and along come three girls with minds of their own. Two of them on the cusp of womanhood—very pretty. Very pretty and no doubt, with minds of their own."

Manolo had been summoned to examine the old maid once, a year or so before meeting Tala. During that visit he'd confirmed she was twenty years his senior, as he'd guessed from the few times he'd seen her, an unrepentant hermit, determined to pass the remainder of her days as far away from human contact as possible. She was obviously a woman of the indoors; her yard looked almost dilapidated, with overgrown weeds and a medley of chipped or rusting items strung about—old potting containers with dying plants here, several unwashed cat food bowls there. But inside, the house was clean, comfortable, pleasant. The sunlight filtered in evenly through light bamboo shades. Solid blocks of neutral colors kept one from being overwhelmed, while the flash of a turquoise mug or a carefully placed orange rug pleased the gaze. There were no photographs or memories on the wall to make one wonder about her past or secrets. The wooden kitchen table had an aged quality, like something from an enchanted cave. He'd reacted to the space with a physical sensation—of wanting to sink into one of her silky-soft armchairs and spend the afternoon napping.

He'd expected her biological age to be at least ten years higher than her chronological age, for those in scarce contact with others generally tended to be weaker in the body, stronger in the mind. Upon closer examination, he was surprised to find her youthful—her arms and legs fleshy, in an appealing sort of way. She was plump but not sagging, her skin still tight and unwrinkled, so that if one were to look at her arms and legs, her breasts and bare belly, without seeing the more aged quality around her eyes and mouth, one might guess she was still in her thirties. She had a flushness about her as someone who's just finished exercising or making love, and her hair was loose and tangled beneath her reclined pose, a far cry from the tight bun that she typically wore outside the house. Like a living blanket, it was incredibly long—she must have refrained from cutting those white-streaked tresses just as she ignored the baby blue eyes, celandines, cornflowers, and dog violets that erupted in hordes in and around her yard, unrestrained by the brown fence meant to establish order and division. She wore a panty but no bra beneath her housedress and showed no signs of modesty when pulling up her smock, revealing brown, virgin nipples around which he pressed the cold, steel ear. This was far from the uptight old maid he'd always imagined she would be up close, and he told himself it was this contradiction, rather than her level of appeal, that caused a hint of eroticism to pass through his breath and fingers when he examined her.

She complained of fever, chills, muscle aches. The aches and trembling made her fear for her health, she said, eyes wide and hands crossed on her chest, once again covered by her dress's thin fabric. She told him she had done something completely out of character, leaving the house and walking for miles in the middle of the night, swimming with mermaids in a remote watering hole, and because her system had never been conditioned for that type of excursion, she feared that she'd contracted some horrible virus from the water or soil, or even from those nonhuman and potentially viperous beings with whom she had mingled. She had walked barefoot, swum nude, and nearly drowned. She had returned home alone in the dark, wet and in a daze, and it was a miracle she hadn't been swallowed by a vampire swooping down to feast on her blood. After checking her vital signs he reassured her she showed no indications of bacterial infection and prescribed two painkillers every four hours until the aches subsided. Her immune system had been more vulnerable due to the exercise she wasn't in the habit of taking, he explained. As a remedy and to keep her ever youthful, he recommended more regular excursions out of doors, in reasonable increments.

"Just stay away from the mermaids and the vampires," he said, smiling.

Though he teased, he'd been impressed by her vivid imagination. At the same time, he felt a wave of pity for the woman, isolated from the world and left to the workings of the mind for entertainment. But the old maid must have grown tired of her fantasies and latched upon him as a vehicle of escape, or rather, a means of reentry into the actual world. She uncrossed her hands to clutch one of his, removing from his grasp the stethoscope he was in the process of repacking and leading him into the opening of her housedress, between wonderful, fleshy thighs and the soaked-through fabric where they met. He did not move and barely managed to breathe. Soft at first, then urgently, she pressed his hand, releasing a moan and moving her hips against the pressure of his fingers, still directed by her own. Caught unsuspecting, with one element of surprise building upon another, he'd been aroused instantly. Manolo took a deep breath and shivered involuntarily. He hadn't been intimate with a woman since Dalaga. He could easily have lost himself kissing this woman's supple flesh, starting with her neck, then caressing the length of her skin, the ample thighs, smooth belly, and ripe breasts, squeezing them tight between his fingers, tasting their salt with his tongue. But he had called on her as a doctor and professional, a code he would not violate, so wiping the sweat from his brow, he pulled reluctantly away and stood to go. He left abruptly.

The following nightfall, he'd returned, without the medicine bag. When she opened the door, he touched her hand eagerly, fondling her fingers for an instant before she pulled back, a hiss on her lips.

"Doctor, you should be ashamed of yourself."

Her long hair was pulled back in its familiar bun, and her lips had shriveled in size, pulled in by wrinkles that lined the rim of her mouth. She seemed decades older.

"After all, I'm old enough to be your mother."

But the old maid had taken his advice. He noticed that she left her house regularly from that day forward, hair pulled tight and conservatively dressed for an outing, returning sometime in the evenings. Where she went, no one knew. She did not call upon his medical services again, and he no longer associated her with the vigorous woman he'd glimpsed—the anomaly who could have been her true person behind closed doors, though he doubted this given the old maid she steadfastly embodied to the outside world.

"I don't know what children you could be talking about, Father," Manolo had responded. "As far as I know, the woman who lives in that house is called 'old maid' for a reason. Plus, I haven't seen anyone coming to visit her in the last thirty years."

"When you are a child and your elders point and huff and yell, all you can do is laugh at their seriousness," Andres replied, without addressing his son's confusion. "The harder you try to be quiet, the louder you burp or hiccup or snort with laughter fighting to get out through your teeth. The more they shush, the more you have to say in messier whispers, the clumsier you play and send the house colliding in pieces around you. I could see it in the girls' faces the first time I spotted them through the overgrown shrubs, when they pointed at me and escaped in three directions."

After lunch, Manolo asked Tala if she knew anything about the girls Father mentioned. She narrowed her eyes to convey her suspicion.

"There are no such girls," she said. "I pick flowers next to that house every morning. I've seen and heard nothing but insects and the silence of neglect. Father is charming us once again with fantasies of youth."

But when he approached Mother with the same inquiry, she wasted no time contradicting Tala and defending Andres. "Female voices carry. The younger the voice, the longer the trajectory. I tend to my garden every afternoon. The wind sent their voices in my direction, and I followed the sound to the old maid's house. They had cornered a cat and were coaxing it from its hiding place," his mother had said.

Puzzled, Manolo had returned to work for his last two appointments. He had not seen his wife since.

After searching for Tala for hours that evening, through the neighborhood, in the bar, and along the outskirts of their barrio and the empty square, tempering his desperation all the while, Manolo had passed the old maid's house. Restless and forlorn, he'd peered into her dilapidated yard, listening for the voices of children and hearing nothing, wondering what deceitful ghosts had visited upon the lonely woman. He'd considered knocking, but the thought of doing so felt painfully awkward. He couldn't imagine repeating the far-fetched reasons that would explain such a drop-by.

Manolo sat up in his room thinking many things and avoiding thinking of others. He knew the local authorities well and his parents had already filled them in on the details.

Tala also had a new arrangement with Luchie, who continues to do all the shopping, except for the eggs. After a bad egg had made her sick, his wife had insisted on hand-selecting them herself, consulting directly with the woman who picked the eggs, in order to protect the baby. This required a special trip to the market about once a week. She did not go on any particular day, nor did she tell anyone when she left to do so. When she returned, she'd simply proceed to whip up an omelet, as if that were the only explanation necessary for her sudden departures. Tala's recent interest in the mail had been the subject of jokes between the two of them, but now, it was another clue, a possible explanation for her absence, like the flowers and the eggs.

She'd made it a game to check the mailbox before Andres did. Andres, who subscribed to half a dozen magazines, normally took pleasure in the small journeys to the mailbox to collect his reading supply. But lately he'd woken from his hammock with a shiny magazine on his belly, and not the one he'd fallen asleep reading. The new issue would have been procured by Tala, who timed the mail's arrival each day, showing up at the line of mailboxes along the main road just as the postman pulled away with emptier sacks in tow.

Was it possible she had gone to these pains to communicate with someone, plotting . . . what? He dizzied himself with every possibility. It had been Luchie's day off. After lunch, his parents had stepped out to the next town. When they returned and Tala was not at home, they'd assumed she was out shopping or collecting the mail.

Manolo nodded off once or twice, for about half an hour. When the morning sun lit his room the next day, he blinked in his bed alone, deprived of sleep, half of him believing Tala might be gone for good. She was back by breakfast, with a fresh bouquet and a profusely apologetic Inday.

The explanation came out in a jumble, sincere, full of urgency. She had stumbled upon Inday the day before, when she'd craved an omelet and was out buying eggs. Inday had been inconsolable, a hurricane rushing madly through the stalls, pulling clothes off racks and goods off shelves, close to attacking the other vendors when they could not produce her son. Inday interjected—it was true, she said, only Tala had been able to calm her and guide her home. *The slimeball took him*, Inday had babbled in the fever of night, repeating almost deliriously, *he took him*, and Tala explained that she could see the face that haunted the bamboo weaver's nightmares, had felt somehow responsible for the mess he'd created as she'd comforted the stricken mother through the depths of a long and sleepless night that had separated her from home.

21. The Mourning Lover

Manolo knew that she'd promised Inday, and herself, that she'd confront Charo about Baitan—it was the least she could do. She could not even wait to check into a hotel before leading Manolo to a bar called the Hideaway—a front for Charo's dirty business. They walked through the gurgling belly of the city she knew by heart to find it, the dense air tainted by dumpsters along one bend, by exhaust from a running motor on another. Horns honked around them, a thumping disco song escaped from a nightclub, voices of every pitch ascended and faded, and one could only guess at the errands curious wanderers pursued in their determined strides through empty streets that cut into the shadows. It was dark, but they couldn't imagine the setting around them dressed in anything but the deep pitch of night. Tala concluded that daylight must not exist—not here.

Their destination was so inconspicuous they almost missed it altogether. When they entered the little hut-like structure, a large man on a small stool nodded at them to come in. The lighting was dim and the hanging bulbs emitted a buzz. There was just a handful of painted wooden tables in the joint, spaced far apart on a hardwood floor, with bare walls around them, the worn paint unable to disguise all the dents. A jukebox stood silent in one corner. Seated at the bar, the man held a newspaper with one hand, helping himself to a plate of food with the other. On a far table, a couple sat isolated from the rest of the world, conspiring in whispers. Their faces nearly touched, so at first glance Manolo thought he saw one head with two bodies. Manolo noticed the remaining patron last of all, even though he'd been sitting at a center table with his legs crossed, a toothpick in his mouth. The toothpick swirled from side to side, a prop to engage the tongue, and he imagined this man who did not speak kept a bundle of toothpicks at the ready in his pocket, never going through a day without one twirling in his mouth. Facing the door, this man stared them down without apology, eyes sweeping over both their faces. He wasn't a patron.

She told him they were looking for a little boy named Baitan. And she asked to see Charo, her brother. The toothpick man seemed to expect them. Without a word, he led them from entryway to entryway, through bizarre outdoor foyers and little courtyards that connected a series of buildings. After a few turns, Manolo looked over his shoulder, unsure how they'd find their way back if they were forced to try. But Tala walked determinedly on, unruffled and confident. They found themselves in a modest office, papers cluttered on a desk, a chair tucked behind it. Manolo did not notice another door until they walked through it to a warehouse, packed floor to ceiling with cardboard boxes. The boxes were arranged in rows, with narrow hallways of space between them to navigate through. Their guide wound them along the passages, and at the end of one Manolo noticed an open box filled with smaller ones. Shoeboxes. They were in a small factory. Around them, the people were sorting, piling, sewing, snapping, clasping, and boxing. White-haired grandmothers and young children barely old enough to pour their own cereal. Dull and sluggish; half-asleep, half-alive.

Their arms and legs moved, but their faces did not, aside from the mechanical blinking of the eyes. The sound was eerie, too, so much bustling and bumping around and a machine's steady hum as the sneakers went down the line for emblems and packaging. The children never chattered.

Sneakers, and most of them counterfeit. Would she be able to recognize the difference—between the real and the fake?

They kept on walking, down a hallway, through a door.

"Oops. Wrong door," the toothpick man announced.

They moved farther along a smoky hallway, where they were asked to wait, catching a glimpse of the room the toothpick man had entered. Four men gambled around a table, two others stood watching, and a third sat on an upturned crate against the wall.

The toothpick man emerged with tidings on Baitan. He was not at the factory. He was out in the field with Charo— on-the-job training, learning the ropes and the lay of the land.

"No idea when they'll be back. Don't worry, he's in your brother's hands."

The next day, when they arrived at the cemetery, Manolo did not follow behind Tala, who ambled off on a leaf-strewn path without a word, making her way across the cobblestones. Since the Hideaway she'd been locked in her own thoughts, and it was just as well; his heart felt equally heavy.

He watched her crisscross aimlessly among the gravestones, without direction through a cemetery where the toothpick man had said Charo's mother was buried in an unmarked grave. Around them, a dreary stretch of ground, a waste of beauty in a patch of city untouched by commerce and cars and the busy grind of it all. It was a place of death, but he did not feel death, the dead beneath them long gone—he felt awake. He mourned all the time wasted on worries and lies, secrets and doubts.

At the perimeter of the graveyard, Manolo waited against a spot on the brick wall. Iron bars protruded vertically from the top edge of the bricks, separating the dead from the living. He itched for a smoke and reached for a stick, lighting it deftly and breathing in its contents. Cigarette in hand, he assessed the scene in front of him with some degree of calm.

He no longer saw Tala and directed his attention to a mourner who had entered the cemetery at some fissure in the haze of time. The man was about seventy, and something in his carriage was seeped in familiarity. Manolo placed him in his mind; at some crumbling city church, this old man would be the worshipper who attended faithfully at the same hour, always wearing his Sunday best, as he had today. He would be one of the few people in the pews praying in earnest, leaving quietly and unnoticed. He had a full bouquet of red carnations in his hand, which he placed at the base of an indiscreet gravestone on the western end of the cemetery. His clothes were neat but not fancy, his shoes shined, and his gray hair trimmed and combed. Manolo felt certain that he came to the cemetery every week, and that each week, the faces around him were new—another set of anonymous mourners being summoned by the long reach of the departed. In this unwelcoming expanse he would appear through the rusty gates, regularly and out of nowhere as others came and went. He alone would be faithful and punctual for the dead.

The man sat now beside the resting place of the one he had lost, unmoving then looking to the trees in the distance, the outline of skyscrapers beyond them, and the sky that encompassed it all, finding, Manolo was certain, traces of his lost love everywhere. He was sure that he'd be sitting there still, looking after the gravestone, remembering and honoring the one in his heart, long after he and Tala went on their way. Manolo wondered how long the mourning lover stayed.

But he soon left the old man to his personal sanctity. Tala had returned.

"I found you." She placed her long, slim fingers upon his,

leaning her head against the bricks and closing her eyes, the smile fading into repose.

The sun was still high and the weather was hot and stuffy. Manolo did not wear his jacket, but carried it with him foolishly, forgetting that even nights in the city were hot, unlike those in the mountains. He slipped his free hand into the folds of his coat till he felt the hard edges of the box he'd quickly stashed there. He well remembered lying like an insect in the dark, his antennae connected to whatever was inside of it. Funny thing is, he had never opened it. It had been enough to know that the box involved him, too, that he wouldn't be left in the cold. He'd always been more interested in her, the way she maneuvered around him with her secrets and surprises.

He thought back on their visit with the albularyo. She was not the young woman in an unflattering pantsuit and yellow bandanna, who had handed Tala the box on the day he followed her. The older woman with the wild hair had looked right into him, seeing the box in his eyes. He could feel it. And she had wanted it for herself. Since that day, Manolo had never quite felt safe around the trinket.

Tala still had her eyes closed. He listened to the sound of maya birds chirping, watched them hopping around on the nearby branches of a tree. Now and again he glanced over at Tala's face, not knowing if she was listening, dreaming, mourning, or thinking.

He loosened his hand from hers and reached for the box. It fell with a heavy weight, and he nearly dropped it. The commotion roused her, and as she looked at him and the box, he felt the weight fly. All the while that he'd carried it in his jacket, the sensation of carrying the box had never shifted in such a manner.

"Surprise," he said, withholding his own surprise at the way the box had suddenly come to life.

"What's this?"

"Show me what's inside. Tell me what you see, Tala. Describe everything." He studied her face. She did not seem to recognize the box. Tala opened it and seemed disappointed.

"Nothing. It's empty."

The lid was up, but he could not see past it to the interior. Instead, he looked at the texture of the box in Tala's hand, the grainy, dead wood against her soft, living skin. How frivolous it would be to look too closely at the hands, close enough to get lost in the endless network of lines that crisscrossed every millimeter of skin, close enough to lose sight of the hand itself.

"Tala, there's something I want to tell you."

"That you forgot the surprise at home?"

"Do you remember the night we met?"

"Please, Manolo, not the dream. Not again."

"No, not that. Do you remember what I told you about my compadre, Palong?"

"He was the one who drowned. You'd just found out."

"Years before I met you I had been engaged to another woman. She was Palong's sister. She left me on the morning of the day before we were to marry."

Tala looked surprised, then thoughtful. She gazed into the distance, as though envisioning his past somewhere there, the other woman a speck on the horizon. The box felt like a shell in his hand, weightless and thin.

"Why are you telling me this now?" she asked.

"Every time I saw a patient, I saw pity in their eyes. Here's the man who was abandoned on his wedding day, they all seemed to be thinking. Here's the neighborhood cuckold. I didn't want to dig her up again. I don't even know why I thought of her now. I just remembered. And I thought you should know."

He considered placing a feather in the box, a feather from her wings. After giving this to her he'd take her to the wings themselves. The idea cheered him, then felt futile.

"So you've surprised me with a memory. A gift of knowledge about your past. How many more secrets are in that red box?" she asked. She held her hands on her hips, elbows up, as though she were scolding him. The city beyond them dilated in the heat and the graveyard stretched barren. Life could not thrive in such desolate places. Tala walked ahead, absorbed in thought.

When she was a good distance away, Manolo found a rock with sharp edges and began to dig, as quickly as his two hands would allow. The hole was about a foot deep when Manolo felt satisfied. He wedged the box in and replenished the hole with earth, then patted it down so that it was smooth. Then it looked too smooth, and he rumpled the surface with the stone so that it resembled the surrounding landscape. He scratched an X on the face of the bricks alongside him and placed the stone atop the burial ground.

Just as he finished, a thought crossed Manolo's mind, and he looked quickly to where the old man had been not too long before. The mourning lover was gone.

A week later, Tala gave birth. He never imagined that she, too, would go, before their baby would be old enough to walk, and in spite of his struggle to keep her from the moment he'd laid eyes on her, he would do nothing to stop her.

Part III

22. The Hour of Daydreams

IN THE SUMMER OF my fifth year, I discovered Grandmother Iolana's special power: she could make the entire barrio sleep, in the middle of the day.

I could never understand why she forced me to take naps every afternoon without fail, marching me into shadows while the world was bathed in light. It was unjustified punishment, reserved for me alone and for no other reason than to make me suffer. When the unwelcome hour came, I did my best to hide, avoiding the awful feeling of lying still and quiet in Grandmother's bed while my whole body yearned to jump up and down and I could barely suppress one thought after another from escaping me in the form of a run-on sentence, the flail of an arm—anything to remind myself of the sound of my voice or the sensation of motion.

She summoned me with her serious voice, typically reserved for grown-up talk or the inevitable reprimand after I'd done something bad. Hearing that tone and my name called in short, clipped syllables, I knew my hopes of escaping her were lost.

Before she could wave her slipper in the air and threaten me with its sting, I resurfaced from behind a long curtain or shaggy hedge, following Grandmother to her bedroom, where the bare, white walls closed in dreadfully and the strangely pleasing smell of Vicks VapoRub invigorated the stillness hanging in every molecule of dust. I could not smell but saw the dust, a fine powder of ancient things, now crumbled and forgotten, accumulating on stacks of old magazines piled against the wall, lids of jewelry boxes overflowing with bead and shell, the curvy base of a lamp on the wooden nightstand. Grandmother positioned herself lengthwise beside me on the bed, stroking my broad forehead, still hot from hours of baking beneath the sun, and sweeping aside the long, fine strands, damp from play, she sang a lullaby:

> *Antok na, anak*
> *Tulog ka*
> *Sayo lang, anak*
> *Ang lahat*
> *Araw, hangin,*
> *Bulaklak*
> *Sayo lang, anak*
> *Ang lahat*

At first, I rebelled against this ritual, surely a thing for grandmothers, not to be imposed on children. I squirmed on the mattress and interrupted her song with questions, and if this did not faze her determined melody, kicked her repeatedly in the shins, so that Grandmother would stop her song abruptly, retrieve a slipper from the foot of the bed, sting me with two hard slaps on each palm, and return to her singing. Not long after succumbing to Grandmother with feigned sleep, I discovered her secret. Wakefulness never left me as her husky tone and stern expression gradually calmed, followed by the droop of wrinkled lids and the faint odor of stale coffee drifting from her open, lightly snoring mouth. *Antok na, anak. Tulog ka* . . . She had opened the land of daydreams.

Her arm, now doubled in weight, was like a felled log on my chest. Wriggling from beneath it, I tiptoed from her room to find the neighborhood under the spell of her lullaby. Over the fence lines on opposite sides, the hollow shells of hammocks had grown full with the slump of bodies in repose and out front, rocking chairs and small talk had been abandoned for cool sheets on neatly made beds. Even the neighbor's terrier with its rough, speckled coat had fallen asleep at its post, its whiskers twitching and four paws pointing at the sky. Only the chickens remained on vigil, craning and releasing their necks like mechanical toys scraping mindlessly against the gravel.

I felt alone just long enough to listen. A million hidden sounds filled the loneliness—insect wings and ripe fruit falling, the ancient creak of trees and cats scratching their own itchy backs. In their stillness, the most ordinary objects shone with dreamlike clarity—a pattern of rust on the wheelbarrow advancing just so, empty plates and half-full saucers from merienda leaving traces of a moment, never to be relived. Silence became noise, then music, and all of it mine.

Open lanes between sparkling trees invited running. Dirt invited digging, rocks throwing, and fences climbing. After flipping every brick and stone to see what bugs recoiled underneath, I explored my neighbors' gardens, kicking empty buckets and chasing silly roosters so that their wattles jiggled. Little by little, the faces of other children emerged from behind bushes or the tops of trees. Immune from Grandmother's spell, we played hide and seek or ran together in twos and threes, wreaking havoc quietly, at first, so as not to awaken our elders. But the enchantment ran deep, and the sounds of our laughter became part of its rhythm, even for the old men in their hammocks, who must have heard our laughter in their dreams.

When hunger called I beelined for home and raided the kitchen for anything sweet—the pastillas first, next the dried mangoes or the flaky biscuits in the tin, and if there were none, I would open a can of condensed milk and pour it over bread, which we always had—fluffy bags of round loaves for Grandmother's sardines, Papa's eggs, or Grandfather's jam. Around this time, a neighbor's screen would slam open then shut and a dog would begin its incessant bark, and I knew that Grandmother's spell was breaking. With a single sweep of my arm across the counter, I wiped the crumbs clean then crept back to bed with my soon-to-waken grandmother, already clearing her throat from the phlegm that had accumulated in the past hour.

I must have gotten away with this three or four times before Grandfather Andres caught up with my tricks. One afternoon, after the same routine—Grandmother's sleepy spell, walking out to an arrested world, playing among my solitary props and newfound accomplices, and returning to raid the cupboards— he appeared. His kindly face, at that hour, stung like an invasion, one that promised unwelcome repercussions. I willed myself to hold back the tears that would betray my disappointment.

By this time the sticky milk had run down the sides of the can and found its way onto my hands, clothes, and hair. Standing on a chair in front of an open drawer, from which I'd removed and scattered every utensil, I had left a trail of dirt and mud across the kitchen floor. I gazed at Grandfather's small, accusing eyes, trying to figure him out and coming to one con-clusion: being married to Grandmother, he must have been immune to the sleepy spell.

Instead of getting angry, Grandfather dragged the chair that I was standing on to the sink, where he washed my hands gently and ran warm water over the tips of my hair before combing it through with his fingers. Then he sat me down at the kitchen table. He served me a bowl of fluffy rice, sliced fresh, ripe mangoes on top, and spread the sweetener generously. Every bite fulfilled my craving and refueled my joy. As I ate, Grandfather rinsed then replaced the utensils in the drawer and swept up the debris on the floor—*so that Grandmother wouldn't know a thing*, he said. From then on, he and I were inseparable during the hour of daydreams. Grandfather's stories freed me from emptiness without roots, threatening because it existed for its own sake. While my grandmother's lullaby made the barrio sleep, my grandfather's words made dreams awaken.

He began with the story of my birth. My mother had just pulled her needle up from the last stitch of my first gown when her waters broke. After I was born, Grandfather said what could only be described as magic took possession of our barrio. After months of dry weather that had left the fields sagging and the farmers scratching their heads with worry, it rained a melody that lovers danced to while families sat together on their porches, thankful for a respite from the heat and bearing witness to nature's beauty. Grandfather said the rain was the first sign—that the angels themselves were celebrating in the heavens.

The downpour continued for six days and nights without end, constant and rhythmic. On the sixth night, fish replaced raindrops. They pounded onto rooftops and slapped against windows. When a layer of fish covered the streets, replacing cobblestones with scales, the villagers came out one by one, wearing nightclothes and slippers, drawn by their collective intuition, woken by a mysterious thumping that had pervaded their dreams. Soon everyone was out in the dark, starlit hours of morning with pails of ice at the ready. The rains cleared, magnifying the sound of the stars and the magnificence of night. Grandfather told me that a famous constellation, the Lost Sisters, was named that very evening.

The next twelve hours were like a holiday in our barrio. No one went to work; instead, our neighbors stayed home cooking fish every way possible—fried, steamed, baked, salted, and simmered. Those who did not man stoves played music from their porches while the children played kickball in the streets. Every house was open to visitors, who swapped dishes and compliments and gave generously of their pantries when a few eggs, extra chilies, or a sack of flour were needed. Grandfather and Grandmother visited each neighbor to boast about their new granddaughter, so beautiful I broke their hearts, and everyone dropped by to offer their respects to Papa and my mother, who never released me from her bosom.

I did not question Grandfather's version of events till I was much older and Grandfather had already passed to the next world. After purchasing a bag of groceries one afternoon, I decided to ask the old shopkeeper if it had ever rained fish in our barrio. A fixture at the sari sari store for decades, the shopkeeper had always proved trustworthy with the lowest prices and the latest news. If fish had once fallen from the Manlapaz sky, he would know. The idea made him chuckle at first, then he scratched his chin and grew thoughtful, recalling an occasion when several acres of tilapia farms lost their harvest to a flood stream that swept past the fields and barrio streets, depositing hundreds of fish before doorsteps and upon the open road, their tails still flapping. It had been raining for days upon end, and I had probably been much too young to remember, he said.

GRANDFATHER WAS THE FIRST to describe the sound of Tala's voice—like the trickle of water. Imagining that sound, I knew I had been born ready to love her. But I also knew that the same willingness to love can be said of all babies and children, while not every mother is deserving.

Up until then, she existed as a series of associations: a smile full of pain, the quiet that settled into the cracks of the house, longing hidden deep in shadows. With Grandfather, I directed my confusion into questions, seeing that there must be an answer and believing I was entitled to it: "Where could she be? Why isn't she here?"

Grandfather did everything he could to avoid explanations that summer, most likely because he had none. I was happy with the bits and pieces, little glimpses into a past that filled me with wonder. Tala was not the only thing we whispered about during those bright afternoons before the doubt and bitterness began gnawing a hole into childish innocence. One of his favorite subjects involved the mountain's many phantoms. Grandfather introduced me to the local ghost stories that made every child squeamish.

"We've been called many things," he told me once. "Backward, provincial, superstitious. We are not superstitious—we simply believe what we see. A tree is a tree is a tree. A rock is a rock. I've come to learn that Manlapaz is no ordinary place. It is a way station."

It had been the hour of daydreams. We had walked to the mailbox, and as we idled our way back, the houses had stood like props along the empty road, which crunched underfoot as busy songbirds scrambled about, their trills especially lively. Grandfather shared another story from his vault of words reserved especially for me. They filled up the silence, not the one that blanketed our barrio during the napping hours when everyone disappeared in their rooms, but the one that had followed me everywhere, for as long as I could remember.

"What is a weigh-station, Grandfather?" I imagined the church square covered with scales like the ones used for weighing fish and produce at the marketplace. Only these scales would be big enough to weigh people, animals, furniture, piles of brick, or sacks and sacks of money—whatever might need weighing at a weigh-station. The scales would cover the square on weekends with their platforms, ladders, and cranes used for lifting heavy objects onto them. People from all over would come on weighing days, blocking the entrance to the church and filling the square with strange inventions and wondrous contraptions.

"A way station is a place to rest and refuel before making your way to the place you intended to go." He must have seen the disappointed look on my face, because he added, "Though it is a temporary stop, it is carefully chosen and of utmost importance for the weary traveler."

Papa sometimes loaded me into the car to visit nearby orchards, where we'd pick our own fruits, bringing home boxes full to share with the neighbors. Or he took me along on a house call or two before driving us into the city, where we watched a movie in a theater or rode the carousel in the shopping mall. Grandfather and Grandmother did not drive, so every now and then, when Papa was not home to do the chauffeuring, they sat me between them on the bus to visit relatives or fill up our shopping bags in the market near the coast, where seafood, spices, and the shell earrings Grandmother liked to wear were easier to haggle for. In all of these instances, we did the leaving, and it never occurred to me that people who lived elsewhere got into buses and cars, making it a point to come to Manlapaz — the carefully chosen and important way station.

"Where do all the travelers eat and sleep?" I asked.

"These are no ordinary travelers. They feed on hopes and dreams; they feast on fear. They sleep during the day and wander the empty streets at night. Some of them are always hidden beneath disguises; others cannot mask their true forms and must conceal themselves beneath the ground, in the trunks of trees, or behind the clouds. Between the hours of midnight and three a.m., they are fully visible and wander about in the open. But anyone foolish enough to be out during those hours will be at their mercy. These travelers can be vicious, immeasurably strong, and dangerous. They are capable of imposing twisted enchantments and cruel, unthinkable punishments.

"They can also be beautiful and good. Even with the ugly ones, there is no reason to worry, as long as you follow the rules: Stay away from suspicious strangers. Seal your curtains well before midnight. Treat your guests like royalty, for you never know what forms they truly assume and with what powers. As for why they come here, it's no mystery why they favor our mountains, like ladders between heaven and earth, our river like a highway through the land, and of course, our many remote hiding places and polite and accepting ways. Many of these travelers stay on indefinitely. You may tremble with revulsion and say these unwanted guests don't belong here, that Manlapaz is ours. But in truth, they've been passing through for centuries, well before our earliest ancestors dipped a toe in the river or planted a seed in the fertile valley. In a way, you may even say that we are the guests."

I learned much more about the unusual citizens with whom we shared Manlapaz. Grandfather himself had seen a duwende every day from the bedroom window of his childhood home, always sitting in the same spot on the fence at the same hour, and much later, he had seen a friend go through the second half of his life under a duwende's spiteful spell. It infuriated him that anyone would consider him gullible, untruthful, or even infectiously bored for believing in such phantoms. He became convinced that the phenomenon witnessed in our mountains could not be isolated. In search for proof, he subscribed to a rolodex of magazines, determined to learn the landscape of faraway places, the accounts of other witnesses who'd confronted monsters, fairies, witches, and sprites. He read himself to sleep every afternoon, and hundreds of articles later, his beliefs were confirmed. There could be no doubt these way stations were scattered across the globe, from here in the Philippines to the North Pole. The travelers that frequented them had many names, but their habits and rituals were consistent and indisputable.

At the end of that summer, Grandfather died, but not before he passed on one last story, the one I had been waiting all summer to hear. By then, I already believed Tala was one of those temporary guests who'd landed in Manlapaz en route to vast and mysterious places beyond our comprehension. She never quite belonged or intended to stay, and she held in her being a magnificent power whose calling she could no longer resist.

Grandfather's words confirmed what I knew in my heart to be true, but I didn't realize then that this knowledge had been planted there by Grandfather himself after months of careless disillusionment.

He had probably been in considerable pain, suffering in silence through another cavity that he believed would pass, when in reality the infection would do no such thing, not dying, but spreading all the way to his brain. We no longer did any walking for candy or treats, to run errands to the mailbox, or to dangle our feet side by side along the edge of the river. As he leaned against the ceiba tree in our backyard, his eyes had been transfixed, transported to visions of that afternoon long ago, when everything had changed.

"We were resting here—against this same tree. I had just finished rocking you to sleep in my arms when the air around us came to life, a soft hiss, swirling with pain. Instinctively I held you closer, and then she appeared. There . . . at the edge of the patio, floating just a foot or so above the ground. Tala's young features were the same but on her face glared the frightening, unrecognizable expression of a beast. Her wings were imposing and brilliant, stretched to their full width, billowy with feathers but capable of knocking a man out with one swipe. I trembled, not at her transformation and obvious power, but because I knew just by looking at her that something was terribly wrong.

"All those years, she had hidden her true nature, from her

own husband, from her own child, and most likely, herself. It was the only explanation I could think of for the rage and confusion that heaved from her chest and directed her stare toward me like the point of a blade. I found no trace of the loving daughter-in-law whom I had grown to cherish. And I suspected her grief was for that very reason—she had lost herself.

"But there was no time to feel pity or fear. Her presence had woken you from your rest, and your whimpering broke her contemplation and redoubled her anguish. The veins on her once-slender neck rippled as she cried out, and the memory of that wail still sends a wave of revulsion down my spine. Then her wings sprang to motion, their pulsing sending leaves, nests, and debris adrift and swirling. She was upon you in an instant, snatching you with those claws, but just as she began to fly away, something terrible flooded over me. I would have died fighting for you. I grabbed her arms, now muscular and unwomanly, fending me off like a worthless tick. I tore into her feathers, screaming in retaliation but inaudible in the heavy gale. Each time Tala began to lift off, I rushed for her legs, and she flapped harder, releasing herself from my pathetic hold, her long hair stretching far into the wind. Just when I thought all hope was lost, you came to me. You wriggled free and jumped, right into my arms. Tala's wings beat down, deepening the windstorm in their final, heavy strokes as she flew away for good.

"She didn't look back. Afterward, you buried your little face in my armpit, shaken but no longer crying. Afraid to renew your tears with any movement or sound, I held you that way for some time, mute and still, only to realize I was just as terrified for my own safety as for yours."

We sat quietly against the tree for a long while, as still as I imagined we had been in Grandfather's story. The spell of his words washed over me. Though he'd described her as a monster, in my mind she had been a beautiful monster to the end, tragic in her ugliness, and ever more so in her desperate need to flee. How lonely she must have been, I thought, and would have continued pitying her indefinitely if the next incident hadn't occurred, the first in a string of similar incidences that redirected my pity inward.

My former playmates—the ones with whom I'd hidden and rolled in the wildflowers, played pranks on sleeping ya-yas, and failed at my first games of sipa—emerged from their hiding places behind fences or crouched among the weeds. At first I thought they'd come to reclaim me from Grandfather, still to them one of the shortsighted elders who didn't belong in our enchanted world of the napping hours, but for whose company I'd traded all their silly games. Then I saw the rocks in their balled-up fists and the anger that twisted their faces into alarming sneers.

"Freaks!" they yelled.

"Witches!"

"Demon child!"

I managed to duck as they deployed their weapons, but Grandfather wasn't quite as fast. As soon as they saw the blood on his forehead, they scattered. Alerted by a neighbor, Papa rushed home to tend to Grandfather's wound. After cleaning off the blood, Papa told my grandmother that Grandfather would need a few stitches, but the cut to the head wasn't what bothered him. In the days that followed, Grandfather's condition deteriorated rapidly. Papa had found and removed the rotten teeth, decomposed to practically nothing, but the tests showed that Grandfather's blood was poisoned, and Papa's best medicine was no match for the infection.

Two weeks after Grandfather's funeral, I started school. My former playmates passed me carefully folded notes in class and tagged me during recess so I would chase them, unlocking their circle to let me in once more. I could have come back to being one of them, but I chose the opposite direction, leaving the notes unread, their gleefully fleeing backs unchased. Whatever guilt they suffered over Grandfather's death quickly evaporated when they felt the chill of my cold shoulder. They banded together against me, recruiting the other children to their side, and I became known as the demon child with a witch for a mother.

Papa knew nothing of my troubles at school. Perhaps he was too distracted by my changed appearance in the neat, two-piece uniform and hair done in braids, for he gazed upon me as if I were a rare and exquisite doll. For the first week, he walked the mile and a half to and from school alongside me, smiling with pleasure and pride, oblivious to the fact that none of the other kids ever greeted me "hello" or "good-bye," and many of them huddled into whispers when we passed them.

On the first day of the second week, when I was to begin walking alone, his biggest concern was that I'd get lost, so he insisted I repeat the directions several times before setting off. But finding my way was the least of my problems. I walked briskly that day to avoid an encounter with the caravan of neighborhood kids, but found myself colliding straight into them.

"Don't have your daddy to protect you this morning, witch baby?" they taunted.

I was outnumbered but fast, racing to the protection of the school grounds before another of their words could bite me.

On the route home, having avoided all signs of them, I began to relax my breathing. That's when they ambushed me from all sides. Someone pushed me and I crumpled easily, more from surprise than weakness. They laughed and my eyes stung.

"Where are your magic powers now?"

"Show us your fangs!"

"Why don't you fly away?"

They searched the ground for debris (dirt, leaves, spoiled

fruit) and threw it at my face, which I'd covered with both hands. They departed with a final threat:

"We'll get you tomorrow!"

The ambushes continued all week, each time at a different spot along my route home. Had I known any detours, I would gladly have taken them, but Papa had shown me only one route to and from school, and as much as I dreaded the taunting, coupled by a smattering of leaves or dirt thrown my way, I was more afraid of losing my way and worrying Papa. Each night at dinner he asked how my day at school had been, that same look of pleasure and pride lifting the corners of his eyes.

"How are you enjoying your classes?" he would ask.

"I'm ahead in reading." I had learned my letters early on, for Grandfather had shown me the alphabet and simple word recognition in his magazines. "Teacher says I'm smart enough to be a doctor like you."

And the corners of Papa's eyes would rise even higher.

Before long, the name calling and dirt throwing escalated. I don't remember which kid hit me, for I'd been covering my face with my hands when the stick flew. Arriving home with a swollen lip, I had no choice but to tell Papa everything.

Though he did not say much, he absorbed every word.

The next day, I was crestfallen when Papa told me to run along to school without offering to walk me. I set off, and the morning came and went without incident. The school day unfolded in a haze, my stomach twisting into knots during the last few hours before the final bell. My lip had healed overnight for the most part, but I couldn't stop biting on the tiny nub that remained of my wound.

They waited in the cluster of trees where they had surrounded me on the first day, but before they could hurl their first insult, a woman approached and redirected their attention completely. Her white hair fell to her knees, framing a face that had been swallowed up by wrinkles. But her eyes revealed her power, beady and intense, taking us all in. She looked a hundred years old. I willed my body to run away or scream, but I could not move or speak or unpeel my eyes from the sight of her. Equally paralyzed, each of my classmates turned varying shades of white. She scowled and raised both hands in a pouncing gesture, and we instantly unfroze, our hearts in our throats as we ran for our lives.

"Curse your wicked little hearts with worms if you bother Malaya again!" she threatened before they had fled too far to hear.

At the sound of my name I flinched and considered looking back, but instead I ran harder. I would not let myself be deceived by an evil ghost.

When she showed up at home, I was alarmed, but remembered Grandfather saying ghosts rarely attack you in your own home. Papa introduced her to me as Babaylan Jasmin, a direct descendant of the first tribe to have peopled our islands. She knew many, many secrets that were guarded within our mountains. And she had married my parents. I was all curiosity once I'd gotten over my fear of her. I wanted to know all about the first tribe and the ghosts of the world that Grandfather had spoken of. I did not expect to hear the things she told me about my mother, the powers that billowed within her, unbeckoned, overshadowed by the forces of love.

"So you see, Malaya. You can't blame the children completely. The stories are true in the sense that she was not a creature of this world."

True or untrue, I did not care. The babaylan lost her charm at the mention of my mother, and from that point on I realized that none of the ghosts were real, like the old woman sitting crumpled before me, powerless and finite.

And like my mother, who had the might to haunt me only because of the stories, passed on to make believers out of the innocent, to replace our sadness with awe. I would no longer be tricked. I would no longer be one of them.

23. Many Colors

I CAME TO APPRECIATE Grandmother Iolana, her backbone and strength, and how what I'd once considered harsh or unforgiving was necessary for living a practical, decent life. In time, taunting from my classmates became a distant memory—they left me to my peace, and with this I found pleasure rather than pain in loneliness. While those at school rarely mentioned my mother or forgot about her completely, she remained lodged within me like a hard rock with sharp edges. As the years passed, the rock did not dissolve, but grew more compact and heavy.

Outrageous stories lost their allure; fairy tales were not enchanting, but dark and deceptive. On the occasions we gathered with Grandfather Roland and my "cousins," Grandfather Roland's grandchildren, for a day of feasting, I relocated to a solitary corner when talk grew sentimental or when fantasies of the supernatural sprung from their merry mouths.

Under Grandmother's wing, I learned how to supplement our meals with roots and vegetables I'd nursed in our backyard. By the time I was ten, I could cook our dinners from scratch, from the radishes I pulled from the ground, sliced, and boiled until their color became translucent to the tamarind I dried and powdered to flavor the broth.

Not wishing to deprive me of the energy and company of other children, Papa sent me to my cousins' house on weekends. There, I caught up on the latest dance moves and adolescent gossip and developed a sense of what it must feel like to be a regular girl. I came to love my cousin Jorella, who was five years my senior, for her boundless energy and natural compassion. Back at home, though, the sense of isolation from the world grew more pronounced, and I spent more and more time in the classroom gazing out the windows. Just as my classmates had long given up on me, my teachers began to do the same, saving the effort of constantly redirecting me to leave me to my musings.

At twelve, my hips and waist began to change, and my monthly bleeding started, but my mind outpaced the body's slow evolution. I was desperate to understand the meaning of things, my identity and circumstances. In quiet frustration, I often fell asleep with my cheeks streaked in tears.

As if she could sense my longing, Grandmother's demeanor toward me shifted ever so slightly. She wasn't necessarily warmer, but less technical and more reflective in her words. I learned to believe in magic when I least expected to and in the most satisfying way, because the lesson came from the woman I knew to be stern and upright and unfrivolous to a fault. She unearthed the little girl I had buried, who'd snuck away every afternoon to the land of daydreams.

As we sat in the garden or bent down to our chores, Grandmother told me more about her history, her youthful fantasies of castles and faraway lands. Like every other girl, she had been convinced she was different and would someday be singled out from her more common peers to live an exceptional life. But her father was a butcher, and immediately after high school, she was obligated to work in his shop for the least glamorous and most degrading work a girl could imagine. She had recently begun a new and unhealthy habit — romanticizing her lowliness as a means of accepting her fate — when Andres appeared. The first time she saw him, he was dressed in a freshly pressed suit and tie, with a rose tucked into the pocket. In the recesses of her mind, she had long ago envisioned what the handsome and elegant man she'd marry would look like — Andres embodied her prince in the flesh. His eyes twinkled and his shoes shone. She, on the other hand, had just left the shop, and her dress contained smatterings of chicken livers and pigs' blood. Her hair hung limp with grime, and she was anxious to bathe off the dead animal smell that nested in her pores. When she saw Andres standing there, he looked at her and smiled, handsome and twinkling, and all she could do was run.

From then on, in addition to her apron, she wore gloves all day and a shower cap over her hair. She kept a change of clothes, a hairbrush, flowery soap, and a bottle of perfume in her bag to freshen up for her walk home with Andres. His job on the railroad yard meant he was up before dusk and off work in time to shower and pick her up with a different flower each day, plucked fresh from his neatly ironed pocket.

After they married, she quit her job at the butcher shop, but the dead animal smell continued to plague her. While seeking a way to deodorize her skin, she perfected a method of making rice wine, which she used for cooking and entertaining, in addition to washing her hands. Her guests were so impressed by the wine's clarity and flavor that they ordered bottles of it for their own homes, and for a time, Iolana was busy running this new business, earning regular money that would one day pay for her son's medical school bills.

The early years of marriage passed, and Iolana and Andres were content, except for one thing — they could not conceive a child. She worried that she was barren, so when my father finally arrived she dedicated all her energies to raising him.

Iolana's stories tended to linger around the men in her life— Andres and Papa. When the topic branched and it seemed she might venture into the realm of my mother, interruptions never failed to ensue: a neighbor dropping in, the phone ringing, a teakettle whistling, or the dogs barking. But Iolana's newfound chattiness had made me bolder; I seized the next opportunity to ask her about Tala directly.

"Why did she leave?" I asked as we harvested our sweet potatoes, and she did not pretend ignorance about the subject of my question.

"All this time I spend gardening, tending the vegetables in our little back plot, because nothing compares to the feeling of home, making it comfortable, making it yours, and watching what you've made surround the people you love with peace and joy," Grandmother said. "I've dedicated my life to this little plot and have never felt ashamed to flaunt its bounty, which is much more than vegetables and fruits. It is a faithful husband, dutiful son, and then, a beautiful granddaughter of my own.

"But there are those to whom life deals less fortunate blows," she continued, sweeping the dirt off of a kamote with her fingers before dropping it into the basket, not looking up as she worked. "And I don't consider myself above them. Who am I to judge when so many are born with less from the moment they open their eyes to the world? Your mother was one such individual. But I must say that character is established when such individuals are given choices—to continue upon their wanton paths, or to rise above when such an opportunity presents itself."

"So you know the truth?" I pleaded. "I know the stories of wings and flying away are lies." My heart thumped a faster rhythm, and for a moment I felt overwhelmed by the loss of breath.

"Truth has many colors, at times wondrous, at other times deceptive." Her voice changed, softening even from her reminiscing tone, and Grandmother stopped her work to stare into the foliage of the garden. "Sometimes the colors are not always distinguishable from one another."

"I want to see it in black and white. For once, Grandmother, please."

She turned her gaze to me and switched from a kneeling to sitting position. I took her lead and did the same, knowing this was a sign that gardening had, for the moment, come to an end, and a different yield would be harvested. We had planted ourselves in the soil.

"We'd always known she had a past, one that had nearly swallowed her whole. She kept her distance from it, and we respected her silence in that regard. She and your Papa fell in love the way you're supposed to—without shame, without patience, with their whole selves. I don't remember when the picture began to crumble. Perhaps it was when her past began creeping up on us. She had a so-called brother, and it turned out that for who knows how long, three of her so-called sisters had been living next door to us at the old maid's house. One day, they all disappeared—Tala, the brother, and the sisters. You were still a baby.

"I found your Papa huddled up in his office on the morning she disappeared. His things were scattered everywhere; this could have been his doing or hers. His closet was thrown open and a big hole gaped from one of its interior walls. She had apparently been hiding things there: drugs, weapons, money—who knows? But she had taken it and fled. They suspect she left as a means of protecting you and us, to keep her gang from getting too close. A few days later, a woman's body was found in the river several miles downstream. The authorities said this woman had been surviving in outhouses and barns, in the hollow trunks of trees. She had died in the river's clutch after drifting along its path for days. No one knew or claimed her; her face was bloated and unrecognizable. Many believe it was Tala, for the other three girls had been younger, smaller. Your Papa refused to identify the body."

I sat and blinked, conscious of my eyelids opening and shutting while the rest of me sat motionless. None of it surprised me, as if I had heard it all before, or more likely, it had matched one of the many explanations I'd dreamed up on my own. Still, the finality of this reality filled me with sadness.

"So that's it, then. Thank you, Grandmother. Now I know everything."

Grandmother lifted my chin with her finger and placed a hand on each of my cheeks.

"Truth has many colors. Maybe, most likely, you know nothing."

I questioned her with my eyes.

"One of our neighbors, a quiet housewife who lived two houses that way, pronounced that Tala was not the drowned woman. She affirmed your Grandfather's story about Tala flying away on a pair of wings, said she had been outside hanging laundry when a sudden, intense wind tore her clothespins off the line. She'd chased a damp sheet across the yard, only to witness a giant angel floating over a tree in our yard. According to this woman, the angel spent a good deal of time spinning in circles above the courtyard, holding you in her arms, then kissing you and placing you on the ground before flying away alone. She did refute one aspect of your Grandfather's story, said he had not attempted to fight her off, as he'd claimed, but had hidden behind the trees in sheer fright."

"Which story do you believe, Grandmother?" This time my heart didn't plunge me into sudden chaos. Anticipating an answer I was both frightened and thrilled to learn, my chest heaved slowly, deeply.

"In answer to that, I'll tell you a story of my own, one I'd intended to take to my grave. But you alone may have it, with the condition that you never bring it up in my presence again after this day."

24. Conception

THOSE WHO KNOW ME hold me in the highest esteem, but I am no different from any other woman. I have my secrets. I've committed my share of sins, none of which I'm proud of. Still, if I had them to do over again, I would. I would sin again; I would not change a thing, because some acts are essential to survival. Just as violence can be essential to maintaining the peace, infidelity can seal a marriage into permanence. The logic isn't something I know how to explain. I can only ask that you listen with your heart and what you know deep inside to be true.

As a young girl, I held lofty expectations of my future. These shrank with each passing year, until all I hoped for was to marry a respectable man and escape from the prison of my parents' business. Your grandfather was this man. Beyond that, he taught me love. I quickly learned that he was more than just a vehicle, but my destination. Walking side by side, we embodied beauty and strength, whatever perils might come our way. Your grandfather taught me how to feel at peace.

And so I became a protector of that peace, watchful against potential intruders as I insulated the nest for our days of love. We both knew how to work hard, and our initial years of marriage passed in both material comfort and physical satisfaction. But disappointment was inevitable. We could not have a child.

This is where my story twists. I had thought that your grandfather was the interceptor, the one who'd knocked my comet in an alternate direction, but I still had so much to learn—about life and about myself—before I could begin to put my marriage into perspective.

I could not imagine a life without children. Though that reality had been presenting itself for years, I realized it suddenly, and the impact was that much sharper. I spent that day sitting and staring, unable to lift the weight of my body off the chair. When I finally got up, it was to go to bed, for night had settled and your grandfather had long since turned in, having given up trying to elicit a response from me. The next morning did not shake me from my doldrums. I wandered around listlessly, without motivation to cook, eat, or clean. For days on end, your grandfather came home to an empty dinner table, and even though I did not remember the last time I'd prepared a warm meal, dirty dishes found a way to pile up around the sink. I neglected a dozen orders for my rice wine—this in fact is the time I stopped making it altogether, and your grandfather was obligated to refund my customers who'd prepaid for their supply.

I did not spring to action, even when he resorted to eating dinner at the neighbors', bringing home a covered plate for me. Maybe because he knew or shared the cause of my suffering, he did not question or prod me. Every day, he made some sort of contact, rubbing my feet as I stared into the empty spaces or filling me in on the goings on around the block or within our extended family. During one of these moments, when he rubbed my feet and I stared into the fog, I managed to look at him and see that his eyes were full of pain, sucking in a well of tears, even though his voice was calm and soothing, his body bent into a source of comfort. I could bear my pain, but not his.

The next day the kitchen sparkled and rice porridge waited on the stove when he awoke in the morning. We went back to the way things had always been, never bringing up the anguish of recent days. Your grandfather assumed that the old me had come back, but something inside me had broken from the mold. I was not misplaced in my home or marriage; I was more certain of this than ever. But secretly I sought every remedy to fill the missing piece. I listened to my doctor and consumed more protein. I purchased herbs from the local medicine woman. I came up with my own inventions before, during, and after sex. Nothing worked. Pride in house and home left me embittered, wishing I could go back to the woman who'd once aimed for intangible greatness. But I could think of no role more bountiful than motherhood.

At the time my hair hung long, down my back, past my hips. After staring too long in the mirror one day, I felt the impulse to cut it all off. I walked to the river with black ropes of it in my fist, swinging in the wind. "Give me a child," I implored. "Please find a way to give me a child." I opened my fist and thousands of strands swam and separated, disappearing into the tumbling waters.

He came that very night. No sound awoke me, but I sensed him approaching from the other side of the window. I sat up, intensely aware, afraid because no logic accompanied this certainty. Your grandfather slept deeply beside me, his head reclined, by choice, on our flattest pillow. I looked at him and almost retreated into our sea of blankets. But something dark and irresistible called me. I was impatient to reach the window, to disappear behind the curtain's veil.

At first I could not see anything but darkness. He began as the movement of shadows, a whirling cloud that rose and dove in the spaces between earth and sky. The whirling gradually widened and slowed, anonymous night shadows coalescing into the outline of a man.

He was almost too beautiful to look at, with a depth to the eyes that seemed to contain centuries of pain. This did not soften his expression, but heightened the intensity of his scrutiny, the way he read me, hearing my thoughts, the corners of his lips upturned in a knowing dare. His muscles rippled, exposed at the chest, arms, thighs, hinting at the strength to dominate and carry forth the secret maneuvers women dream that men will know. Only he was more than a man; a creature, demon, or god, with an intensity that made me shudder. Two humps folded into his back bobbed in a beastly fashion as he crept toward me. He held out his hand, half smiling, half sneering, and I leapt.

What followed could have consisted of hours or days. I cannot tell you exactly what happened except for the fact that I lost myself in that strange mirror—a world identical to ours were it not for the reflection shimmering on the other side—the reflection of us. A single strand kept me moored to the fabric of my previous life, and as my lover and I grew in desperation to lose ourselves in pleasure, each day greedier than the last, I longed to sever that strand forever.

I conceived my son in the mind before the body, as if I could see him waiting on the other side of the cosmos. I could see his face, every little feature, fully formed—his perfect lips and inquisitive brow. When I had long abandoned the possibility of returning to your grandfather, it was your grandfather whom I envisioned as I writhed beneath my lover's pumping wings, manifesting my son from a mental image to physical molecules replicating that image atom by atom. When my son called out from the void, demanding to be claimed in a high-pitched register that resembled the language of whales, I responded, a new and forever mother, instinctively wired to that cry, and reaching for him, I found myself leaping out of that world as I had once done toward it, only this time I was alone, falling into an endless reflection.

I awoke with a start, wet from head to toe with perspiration, covered by too many blankets. The room's familiarity returned, object by heavy object, though it had shrunken in size and the air within felt compacted and stuffy. Your grandfather slept peacefully on the bed, undisturbed by my rude return, and for a moment I dreaded that my lover had sprung from a wild invention, a cruel trap of insanity in which I was breathlessly spinning. I closed my eyes to regain some balance, fearing I might faint or scream. It would have been too much to bear, losing the reality of what I'd known with the winged man. I remembered pushing his nakedness into me as he clung on harder, responding to thoughts I never said aloud, understanding my body's every gesture. I wept with longing and willed myself to walk the cliff into permanent delusion. Then I felt the feather tickling my chest, sticking to the sweat on my skin. I picked it up and inspected it ravenously, the soft underside of wings. Knowing was enough. So that your grandfather would never see, I swallowed it.

So you see that even though logic reveals the obvious, I believe what I know to be true, the unlikely and the unproven, because how else could it be that my son, your father, would grow to find and choose a woman with wings, an aberration, though there are hundreds of thousands enough with legs and arms, if not for the fact that he alone could see her, bestowed, no—cursed—with a vision of where he comes from, of what he is, though he does not, and shall not ever know. Not only do I believe the far-fetched stories of your mother's flight, I blame myself for it, for that and so much more.

25. A City Rising

I GATHER THE COURAGE to confront Papa at the river, where he sometimes wanders to at night. Walking the distance across quiet pathways streaked with moonlight, I ponder the darkness and what people fear. It's not so much what they can't see, but what they can't know.

When I get there, his eyes widen. I'm clearly not who he expects. I doubt anyone could be. He tells me to go back to bed. Instead, I sit with him on the long, flat stone. With light tosses, I sprinkle pebbles into the water as he gazes up into the treetops. Neither one of us speaks, and something about the river feels suspended in time. He is part of this mistiness, this waiting, as if all his muscles were connected to the water, the pebbles, and the leaves, roots and veins intertwined, and none of them existed except in memory. I remember the ghost stories, vampires feeding on pregnant women, dwarfs from underground hypnotizing farmers, and as much as I don't believe, there's something of them here, eerie and frightful.

With Papa, it is not make-believe, it is something tangible in his communion with the river. He is the first to speak.

"Your mother did not leave me. I asked her to go."

And finally, Papa told me his story.

• • •

As I DID IN the rest of the house, I kept my professional area neat and tidy. I alphabetized my medical books, left my desk bare except for a mug full of identical pens, promptly filed my patients' records, and organized my instruments by order of use on a rolling tray beside the examination table. I sanitized surfaces, disposed of used examination gloves and tongue depressors, and restocked my own supplies, leaving the women little excuse to go meddling there. Tala had understood the sanctity of this space, believing it had something to do with my being a doctor and the sacred rites I shared with my patients. At my request, she only came in on occasion, to find some lost household item I had left there or to call me in to dinner. Sometimes, when I was out on rounds, she sat in my chair, fiddled with my pens, opened drawers, and lay down on the examination bed. I knew even this about her.

On the night she came to bed after being too long in my office, I knew she had discovered my secret. She shook like a leaf, her eyes infused with silent panic.

"Manolo, what have you done? What have you done?" she asked with every angle of her body, from the slumped shoulders and crumpled hair to the desperate elongation of her neck.

We clung to each other tightly through the night. Her inner suffering manifested into physical illness. As she sweated through alternating fits of fever and chill, I did not encourage her to speak. It was a sorry refuge for my shame; I could not bear to imagine the first word in a conversation I'd skirted for so long. I shushed her like a coward when she murmured senseless words like *Boatman* and *the Land of the Dead*. "Baitan can't go," she whispered, then recited the names Dalisay, Imee, Florencita, Alma, Sampaguita, and Ligaya. She repeated Ligaya most often, interchanging the name with yours, and at times I could not tell if she was saying "Ligaya" or "Malaya." Your mother's anguish invoked you from sleep, and we combined our efforts to pacify your discomfort. She promised me she would never leave us, but only stopped shaking when I insisted she must take her wings and fly. "I'm sorry for what I've done," I managed to finally say. Or perhaps, I had grown so tired that I convinced myself I had said what I'd been willing myself to say for years.

"Fly, Tala. Go. Release me from my crime. Fly."

When I awoke in the morning, cursing myself for having fallen asleep, she was gone.

I went straight to my office, where I sat for hours until my mother found me and salvaged me from the wreckage. I fully believed your mother would return, if not after a day, then a week. When they found the woman's body in the river, I still believed she would return, if not in a month, then two, if not in a year, then in five years.

After she had gone, they knew it would be useless to convince me out of the self-pity. I was like a man who'd thrown myself into the sea, not knowing how to swim, but still refusing to drown. In time I began to smell like I'd in fact emerged from the ocean. My own stink convinced me to take a shower, put on a fresh shirt, comb my hair, and sit at the breakfast table with my parents and with you, Malaya. No one mentioned the empty seat. My parents behaved as if it were just another ordinary day.

At the time, Old Luchie was still alive. You wouldn't remember her—she moved out soon after Tala left, said she couldn't live in a house with so many "bad vibes." After breakfast, I drove to her place. It was easy enough to find, as if Luchie had worn a path into the ground between our house and hers. I asked her what she'd known of Tala, anything she noticed about her at home when I'd been out working. She could think of nothing, she said. More likely, judging from the uncharacteristically motherly look on her face, she felt too much pity for me to say anything and risk incurring any more pain. When I threatened not to leave without some answer, she suddenly remembered the day of her dark misgivings, after a visit to the albularyo. She told me her suspicions after that day, when Tala had somehow become the albularyo, become two women in one. Perhaps Tala had given herself up, she said, sold her soul for love, and whether the angels had saved her or the devil had stolen her, she did not know.

Straight from there I set off for the Hideaway, to question Charo once and for all. Tala couldn't have been his sister. What was she to him? I thought it would take determination, and perhaps days, to find Charo now that I really wanted to. When I got to the spot where the Hideaway had been, I was sure this would be the case. I saw nothing but buildings—flat, dull warehouses flanked by businesses and restaurants I had never cared to notice on my previous trip, when Tala had been by my side. I walked between edifices, looking over fences and climbing a few. The pebbled landscapes stretched far back, the hallways and courtyards were still there, connecting one building to the next. But the hut out front, wedged into incongruity, with its barstools and patrons like escapees from the night—it was simply gone.

By now I could hardly function, and I realized hunger had gotten the best of me. I decided to eat at the nearest restaurant. There, standing beside a fat man with a newspaper, was Charo, scarfing down his chow mein with a pair of chopsticks. I considered rushing straight for his throat, but didn't have the energy or the will.

"Where's the boy," I said more than asked. Much later, I would learn from Inday that Baitan had abandoned the factory after sharing a pedicab with a descendant of Bandalay, who spent an hour detailing her tribe's forced and violent evacuation, followed by the government's possession of their native lands. She invited Baitan to join a guerilla training camp, of which she herself had graduated, and after months of learning how to wield a gun and counteract local corruption, Baitan had linked up with the Bandalayan forces scattered in the Ogtong mountains.

"I know you," Charo said. "I never forget a face. Baitan's not here. He ran off."

"Prove it."

"You don't have to prove a thing to this toothpick!" the fat man, standing up from his stool, said to Charo. "Walking in here like you owe him something!"

"I think it's you who owes me something," Charo said to Manolo. "Baitan robbed me on the day he left. And we both know your wife was in on it."

"My wife. You mean your sister?"

"I have no sister, man. The only sister I have took the first ticket out of this rat maze." I pushed past the two men to the kitchen behind the restaurant and to a small, cramped office behind that. The fat man was too slow on his feet to catch me. I shuffled through papers and hunted through the trash bin, not knowing what I was looking for.

"What do you think you'll find?" Charo asked behind me, gesturing to the fat man to calmly step aside. "Your wife in the kitchen, washing dishes?"

"What happened to the hut, the Hideaway?" I asked, remembering the warehouse, its stacks of shoeboxes, and the wan-looking factory workers at the machines.

"Look, man, I don't know what you're looking for. Baitan's gone. He came here on his own a few weeks ago, begging for work as a delivery boy. He showed me his address on a piece of paper and told me my sister sent him, and a few days later, he was gone. With a day's profit. I think we both know someone's got to be accountable."

"I will be. I'll pay you back everything the boy owes. Just tell me how you knew Tala. She wasn't your sister. So how did you know my wife?"

Charo had been waiting for the mention of money. I gave

him all that had been in my pockets, which was much more than typical that day, since I thought I'd be gone for a while, and he started talking, shoving the wad in his pocket without counting it.

"Don't you remember me, man? She was with you when we met," Charo began.

He gave me pieces, and they connected with my own, so I could see a missing portion of the puzzle that made Tala. It was like watching something being made from thin air, but rather than invention, it was a memory someone else owned. I remember thinking it was a miracle how a possession such as memory could be shared. I watched it rather than heard it.

It had been during one of our first trips. Tala had wanted to explore the islands. We didn't go too far that day, just to Tagarro Bay, to see the great naval ships and the rows of uniformed soldiers who occupied them. I remembered Tala's comments, about all the different kinds of people we saw: those with white skin, those with brown skin, and all the shades in between. There were people from every part of the world there, she'd noted. And people from every background. She'd said everyone has their own story. Then she asked me, if I could be part of someone's story, whose would it be? Yours, I'd said, I'd be part of yours. And she had replied that I was already the main character. Continuing our little game, she said the answers seem obvious. Look at that healthy sailor with a family waiting at home. Look at the fishermen, busy in their trade. Look at the women selling their crafts, bargaining and cajoling every buyer. Look at the crazy preacher poking the sinners with his crucifix. They all had the energy of support, she said, a backbone that came from somewhere, someone. Then she'd pointed to a man, all bones underneath his clothes, baggy-eyed, smoking a cigarette, and watching the scene as if he owned it. She said, I'd be in his story, because he looks rather lonely. His story, she went on, isn't an easy one to be in. But it wouldn't be fair if we all chose the fairy tales.

And when I had gone off to get Tala the food she craved from the seafood vendor, she approached that lonely phantom. Charo told me that he had noticed us all along, the two country bumpkins, believing he had guessed everything there was to know about us before we realized he was there. But he never expected her to ask all those questions. She was one weird girl, he said. He answered her because it was always easy for him to talk when he was drunk. He told her about his mother, and how sick she had always been, the days she brought sailors home when she was well, and about his sister, who'd left them years before, just before she could have married someone who would pay up big, help everyone out. After that, she'd asked him to look at her closely, to remember that she was in fact his sister, their mother's daughter. She gave him an address in Manlapaz. The address matched the one the boy Baitan later brought with him.

Charo told me that Tala seemed to anticipate his replies, nodding as if confirming what she already knew. And she looked so much like her, the sister he had barely looked at for years. Of course, he didn't believe she was his sister and thought she was either crazy or referring to some general human connectedness in saying so. He reminded me that we, too, had met that day. I had tossed him a few coins before leading Tala to a little seating area filled with tourists, where we ate our shellfish platters.

"So you thought you could come to our home and start stalking us, then?"

"I've never been out of Tagarro Bay, man. What are you on?"

"What about your mother?"

"She had a stroke soon after my sister left. She's been dead for years."

After leaving Charo, I walked. As dark set in, the sounds of lovers unwilling to part and of loud groups on joy rides began to fade, then disappeared altogether. I thought of how back at home, Mother had been worried about me going out in the

dark. But I knew the most frightening thing under the stars—
the emptiness in the heart of a man who walks alone.

I passed the abandoned church and entered the graveyard.
In the presence of so many deaths, I felt at home and unafraid.
It was not from bravery. I would not have had the strength to
fight death if it found me then. I walked deeper into the cemetery, where only the moon and stars could guide me. I passed
brick wall after brick wall until I found the one facing the wilderness. It made me shudder to look into the black density of trees
beyond. Skimming my eyes across the surfaces of the bricks I
realized—the X was not visible or it was gone. I gazed around,
calculating the distance between the nearest gravestones and
the wall. Then I got to my knees and began digging with my
bare hands. The upper surface was rough and hard and tough
to penetrate. I felt the ground for a stone, and, finding one, used
it to grind through the surface into the softer earth. Finding
nothing, I took a few steps to the left and dug again. Then I
moved backward and tried. I kept on moving and digging until
I grew tired. I knew it had been along that side. I sat and leaned
against the wall. Tomorrow, I thought, the mourners would see
the holes I had dug and think it the work of a wild animal.

I blinked into the stars, wondering. I did not want to give
up. Then I looked at the surface of the ground in front of me
and saw a bare patch just three feet away. I crawled there and
dug deep with my fingernails. I scratched and pawed the earth
until my knuckle hit a hard obstacle. I'd found it. I pulled the
box free and opened it.

Not recognizing the sound of my own laughter, I thought
I heard howling in the distance. When I'd opened the box, I'd
seen a reflection of myself in the river. From her eyes. Eyes that
loved me hiding in the leaves, eyes that had forsaken the wings
long before I'd hidden them. I saw myself under the moonlight,
searching for a necklace that she told me she'd lost. I saw a city
rising, from the first cobblestone she'd kicked into its perim-

eter to the wild garden of rubbish she had carefully planted in front of the Hideaway. I saw the haunting yet familiar face of a winged man, and my own divinity in the bottomlessness of the box, the eternity that belonged to Tala, and to me. Then. Emptiness that was fullness and then emptiness again. I saw her rushing to the mailbox to hide letters from the albularyo, the one who'd gone missing, then consulting with a woman selling eggs at the market, about a sister who was not a sister, someone who'd been running, like her, for her, and because of her. I saw her pregnant and leaning against a long, brown fence, shushing a little girl who crouched on the other side, entreating her to be good and stay quiet. I saw her kneeling in front of a hole in the wall, remembering everything, the accumulation of her past and of our life together, of those who should not have crossed paths at that juncture, and her wishing she could forsake her wings still. Still! Wishing she had a choice. For the man in the water. For me. Then I saw myself on the same patch of ground. I had just buried the box. I was watching an old man in a suit, mourning a lost love, seeking her everywhere, bringing her red carnations. The man had my face. I was watching myself, then, and now. Except something had changed, the entire horizon shifting slightly to the left, barely perceptible, the contents of the box reshuffling, as I could see, too late, that they could, that we had been the creators all along, not two characters at the mercy of someone else's narration, and she, ever beautiful, ever brave, had always known, but I had learned too late, but now the mourning lover was not alone: beside him the child, unbroken by the fairy tales of others and wildly present in her own, gazed above at the same sky, searching with an even deeper longing, which I'd forsake all of my heartache to appease.

Author Bio

RENEE MACALINO RUTLEDGE WAS born in Manila,
Philippines, and raised in the San Francisco Bay Area from the
age of four. A long-time local journalist, her articles and essays
have appeared in *ColorLines, Filipinas Magazine, Oakland* and
Alameda Magazine, the *San Francisco Bay Guardian, Literary Hub,
Mutha Magazine, Ford City Anthology, Women of Color Anthology,*
and others. *The Hour of Daydreams* is her debut novel. She lives
in Alameda, California, with her husband and two daughters.

Acknowledgments

THANK YOU, CHRIS. YOU know best how many hours this writing took over the course of how many years. I'm grateful to be married to you, the one I have the most interesting conversations with, who is always up for exploring a different path with me.

Maya and Raina, this book is dedicated to you, for renewing my sense of wonder daily. Life couldn't be more full than it has been and continues to be as I live, laugh, and learn with the two of you.

Thank you, Mama and Papa, for placing family above all else and passing that value on. You dance to your own song, and because of this, I learned early on to embrace individuality. I'm so appreciative of your support and active presence in our lives.

Thanks, Laura Stanfill, my publisher and the force behind Forest Avenue Press. I couldn't have found a better match for *The Hour of Daydreams*; your conviction, passion, tireless work, and ingenuity toward publishing this book have been the best gift a debut author could wish for.

Thank you to my kuyas, Noel and JC Macalino, for being the first two people I could trust to read the final draft of this book. I am lucky to have the both of you to count on.

To Bob Kanegis and Liz Mangual, my in-laws, for keeping folktales alive and inspiring me with your tales, and for gifting me with a copy of *Tales from the 7,000 Isles* (retold by Art R. Guillermo and Nimfa M. Rodeheaver), where I first came across the star maiden folktale.

Thank you to Meilan Carter-Gilkey, Fowzia Karimi, Allison Towata, and Muthoni Kiarie, with whom I met regularly over the course of writing this book to read aloud, feast, do nail art, take swimming breaks, ride gondolas, and discuss the many changes in our lives. The energy and connection have been invaluable to many a creative spark.

Thank you to all the professors I worked with at Mills College, particularly my thesis advisors, Yiyun Li and Cristina Garcia, who encouraged me to keep on going and write the story that I believe.

Thank you to Christine Garcia and Melanie Robinson, who read and shared valuable insight on very early drafts.

I'm appreciative, Gigi Little, for your vision and collaboration on the book cover. Your design captured the mood, symbolism, and magic of the story in the perfect way.

Thanks, Tesa Lauigan, for taking the author photo, bringing out the fun, and being up for spontaneity.

Everyone in the '17 Scribes, I lucked out being connected to such a supportive, talented, and fun group of writers. You helped to make the journey to publication unforgettable.

To my Ulysses Press family for your enthusiasm and encouragement. Special thanks to Bryce Willett for going to bat for this book during the Ulysses Press sales conference slot, and to the PGW/Legato Publishers Group reps who took special care with my debut.

Finally, to Maya Myers, my copy editor, I'm grateful for your sharp eye and valuable suggestions that helped to bring the best version of this book to the reading public.

The Hour
of Daydreams

Readers' Guide

Readers' Guide

1. A Filipino folktale of seven star maidens inspired the writing of *The Hour of Daydreams*. What other myths do you come across in the story? How do they influence your reading?

2. What secrets do Tala and Manolo keep from one another? Why? How do these withholdings impact your impression of their love?

3. What does the box represent?

4. There are many variations of truth in this story. What do you feel is real versus imagined regarding: Tala's past, the seven sisters, Luchie's vision in the marketplace, Manolo's memories, Tala and Manolo's meeting, Iolana's memories, other visions or plot points?

5. How do you compare the grandparents' love story with Tala and Manolo's? What does the grandparents' story reveal about marriage and myths?

6. In literature, a doppelganger is a mirror image of a character, who is not known to a character but can be perceived as that character's shadow or evil counterpart. Did you sense a doppelganger in this story?

7. How does Baitan influence the decisions Tala makes? How do you think the story would change without him?

8. Malaya begins and ends the story in her own voice. Why do you think the author chose this framework? How does Malaya's perspective influence your interpretation of her parents' lives?